It was a locket, like the o [...] very handsome man, his h [...] his blue eyes bright and amused, his expression somehow sad and happy simultaneously.

She bent down so close that her face almost touched the glass.

It was so distant now. Almost like a dream.

CHAPTER
1

When the snow began to fall, it fell so densely that it covered the old city like a neat cotton shroud. Every low building, mean little alley, and cramped and crooked house was obscured beneath its blanketing silence.

People hugged themselves to keep warm, wrapping their heavy coats more tightly around them, pulling down their broad-brimmed hats over narrowed, suspicious eyes. The bleak white sky seemed to lower over them, planting a heavy ceiling on their daily lives, depressing and oppressing them.

It was a sky only an English winter could conjure and beneath it a despairing mood of fear was palpable.

An onlooker might sense it, despite the bustle of commerce and the shouted cries of street vendors.

On one corner, beneath the black-and-white-beamed houses, there was cloth and wool for sale, available in heavy bolts of plain, rather drab colour. The ammonia stink of horse manure vied for attention with the sweeter perfume of cloves and lemons, which a little man with one arm was doling out in pewter mugs for a ha'penny.

He shivered beneath his ragged old coat and shot a nervous glance down the narrow, vile-looking street in which he stood. The snow around him had been churned into ruts by the passage of carts and carriages and the footprints of the Londoners who daily passed him by.

At the end of the lane stood an inn, a grim, black-fronted pile, its eaves shoddy and dilapidated, its brickwork crumbling gradually into fine brown dust. A sign, hanging from one old hinge, proclaimed it as the World Turn'd Upside Down and there was a faded picture of just such a catastrophe as imagined some years previously by an artist friend of the owner.

William Kemp, for such was the owner's name, emerged from the doorway of the inn and shot a vicious look at the drink-seller and then a worse one at the snow-heavy sky.

A thick-set man of some forty years, Kemp wore his hair shoulder-length in the fashion of the day. He had a pale, rather dangerous-looking countenance with a mean rat trap of a mouth and wide green eyes. Dressed in a bulky jerkin with hooped sleeves, fawn-coloured breeches, white stockings and buckled shoes, he had a greasy leather apron, splashed and stained with old beer, hanging around his neck.

Despite the snow, the little street hummed with life. Somewhere a dog was barking incessantly, punctuating the rhythmic roll of barrels over cobbles as the tavern's coopers went about their work. Their hammers slammed and knocked, iron on wood, followed by a satisfying hiss as a new red-hot hoop was plunged into a bath of water. They cried out to each other as they worked, cracking filthy jokes or humming tunes in time to the beating of their tools.

The one-armed man sidled up to Kemp and proffered a cup of his winter grog.

'A drink, sir? Would you help me? I have lost my livelihood 'cause of the wars.'

Kemp looked down at him, his brows beetling over his green eyes. 'How much?'

'Ha'penny, master,' said the vendor hopefully. 'To keep out the chill.'

Kemp scowled at him. 'Is there gin in it?'

The man grinned. 'Aye, sir! My little toddy is packed with the juniper!'

Kemp grunted. 'Well then, you scoundrel. You're taking my custom away from me, ain't you? So get along before I rip out your lights!'

The one-armed man tipped his hat and scrambled backward, the drink sloshing onto his shoes.

'Sorry, sir. No offence, sir,' he gabbled, grabbing the pail in which he carried the drink. He abandoned his makeshift brazier and took to his heels, his shoes ringing off the road as he put as much distance as possible between himself and the ominous-looking Kemp.

Kemp kicked the brazier over and watched the hot coals roll away over the snow-covered cobbles, then coughed and felt a ball of phlegm rise in his throat. He spat it out and watched it hit the road, thudding into the snow among the rubbish and the yellow pissholes.

Crippled fool, he thought, remembering the vendor. Thinks he's the only one to have suffered.

He glanced up at the sign above his inn.

The World Turn'd Upside Down

Aye, that it had been.

He brushed the freshly fallen snow from his shoulders and shouted at a young boy who stood at the trap-door entrance to the cellar. 'Come on, lad! Look lively! I don't pay you to dawdle. Look lively there!'

The boy sighed and struggled on, rolling barrels and blowing into his numb hands to warm them.

Kemp turned back to his contemplation of the sky, wiping his hands on his apron and muttering under his breath.

Suddenly, among the plethora of strange smells that whirled through the street, something particularly evil began to assault his senses. It was like the worst kind of rotten vegetable, mixed with a dreadful, sewer-like odour. An image suddenly flashed into his mind of himself as a boy, playing in his father's barn and uncovering the tiny corpse of a rabbit, its hide suppurating with maggots. The stench from it had been nauseating but this...

Kemp turned to see a strange, crook-backed old man crunching cheerfully through the snow drifts towards him. He groaned and placed his broad, splayed fingers across his face in a none-too-subtle effort to avoid the smell coming off the newcomer.

'Good day to thee, Master Kemp,' said the old man, his voice high and cracked with age.

Kemp did no more than grunt in reply and slowly shook his head at the fellow's rough appearance. His tunic and breeches were black but so stained and filthy as to appear almost like a new colour altogether. His collar, ingrained with grime, had not been white for many a year and his holed and wrinkled stockings hung like loose skin around his ankles and ruined shoes.

'Good day, I say!' said the man again.

This time Kemp acknowledged him. 'You may find it so, Master Scrope. For myself I have things pressing on my mind.'

Nathaniel Scrope let out a funny little giggle and smiled, exposing a gallery of loose black teeth. 'See a surgeon, Kemp. They say water and all manner of things can press on the brain.'

Kemp ignored him, his eyes rolling heavenward again. 'This weather, I mean. It'll keep my customers abed, mark my word. And if they're abed they're not drinking and, as a consequence, Master Scrope, I am not a happy man.'

Scrope shrugged. 'Nay, man. A little frost never harmed no one. I'm living proof.'

Kemp let out a short, unpleasant laugh. 'Living proof that a little muck never harmed anyone, that's for sure.'

Scrope looked affronted and ran a liver-spotted hand through his mane of matted hair. 'You know very well, Kemp, that the work I do is vital to this country's wellbeing.'

Kemp suppressed a smile. The nerve of the man!

'Oh, aye, Nat. I was forgetting.' He gave a formal bow. 'Please excuse me.'

Scrope nodded, apparently mollified. A stiff wind blew a wave of snowflakes in their direction and Scrope suddenly stiffened. 'What's this?' he muttered.

Kemp listened. In among the cacophony of street sounds they could make out something else. A regular, drumming beat, flattening the virgin snow and echoing around the squalid lanes of the city.

Both Kemp and Scrope turned swiftly as the sound coalesced into the unmistakable tattoo of horses' hooves.

There was a shout and then a troop of soldiers clattered into view, perhaps thirty in number and dressed in heavy breastplates over thick, buff, skirted leather coats. They had on huge, thigh-length boots over their crimson breeches and each wore a segmented helmet that tapered down his neck, revealing almost nothing of his face.

As they passed, breath streaming like smoke from the mouths of their horses, all work in the little street came to a sudden halt. It was as though the violence in the air had suddenly taken on solid form.

Kemp shuddered and it had nothing to do with the cold.

'God a'mercy,' he whispered as the soldiers disappeared in

a tight pack around the corner. 'What next for this benighted land of ours?'

Nathaniel Scrope wiped a drop of moisture from the tip of his nose and watched the last of the mounted men vanish into the freezing fog, his face as grave as an effigy on a tomb.

Nearby was an alley even narrower and more disreputable than the one where Kemp's inn stood. The buildings that abutted it were black, wet and grimy, the upper window casements on either side so close that they almost touched, forming a dingy archway over a muddy floor strewn with slimy straw and manure.

There were many things a passer-by might expect to find in such a place. A seedy gaming house, perhaps, or a den of thieves. Beggars might cluster in its shadows and dogs find a rough meal of greasy bones in the litter-fouled snowdrifts. But there was one thing no one could rightly expect to find: the rectangular blue shape of a twentieth-century police box was nevertheless there, materialising out of thin air with a strangulated, grating whine.

The light on top of the police box stopped flashing and the unexpected arrival stood there in the diffuse morning light, snowflakes collecting in the recesses of its panelled doors. A sharp wind blew up, almost disguising the fact that this battered blue box was humming with power.

No one passed by to inquire what was amiss and so the TARDIS remained unmolested, its occupants, for the moment at least, undisturbed.

Inside, in defiance of at least the laws of terrestrial physics, was a vast, white chamber, its walls indented with translucent roundels. At its centre stood a six-sided console, the panels of which were covered in a bewildering array of buttons and switches. In the middle of this was a cylindrical glass column which was normally to be found rising and falling when the TARDIS was in flight. Now it was still, as still as the rest of the strange room, save for the constant hum of power.

Suddenly the calm was shattered by the arrival of three young people from the interior of the craft.

The first, a brawny, good-looking boy in kilt and cable-knit sweater, walked straight over to a chair and sat down, brushing his black hair out of his appealing brown eyes.

'Would you no' hang on a moment, Ben,' he complained to his companion. 'I cannae understand you.'

Ben, a skinny, blond young man with the face of a disreputable cherub, threw up his hands in frustration. 'Blimey! You can't understand me, Jamie. You're the one who talks like Bill Shankly.'

Jamie frowned. 'Who?'

The third arrival, a very pretty girl with long, straight, blonde hair and heavily made-up eyes in a Sixties style, gave a little groan. Her name was Polly and, like Ben, she came from a time well in advance of their young Scots friend. He had joined the TARDIS crew after an adventure with the Jacobite rebels of 1745 and was still having some difficulty acclimatising to travelling in time.

'Don't confuse him any more, Ben,' said Polly 'Look...'

She rested her hand on Jamie's shoulder and took a deep breath. 'It's quite simple. England and Scotland signed an agreement, an Act of Union, which made them one country.'

Jamie's face clouded. 'Aye, I know that. I'm not daft.'

Ben grinned. 'Well, mate, by the time me and the Duchess come from, we live in what they call the United Kingdom. And there ain't no Stuart on the throne.'

Jamie cast his eyes to the floor. 'I dinnae believe it,' he groaned. 'And what of the Prince?'

Polly frowned. 'Bonny Prince Charlie? Oh, I think he ended

up abroad. In exile. Got fat and died. Isn't that right, Ben?'

Ben shrugged. 'Search me, love. History was never my strong point.'

Polly turned back to Jamie, who was tugging his hair in a nervous, slightly anxious fashion.

'Anyway,' she said brightly, 'as Ben says, the Scots and the English get along perfectly well by our time.'

'I wouldn't pay too much attention to them, Jamie,' cut in a new voice. 'Your fellow countrymen get a bit restless around the end of the twentieth century, if memory serves.'

The newcomer was a small man with a humorous, slightly mocking expression. There was a deep line on either side of his smiling mouth and his hair hung in a messy black mop over eyes that sparkled blue and green as the sea.

He was dressed in a shabby black frock coat – stitches bursting, pockets full of holes – a grubby shirt and bow tie and a pair of gaudily checked trousers, which bagged at the knee. The whole ensemble terminated in narrow suede boots, which, like everything else the little man wore, had seen better days.

The Doctor walked to the console and fussed over a panel of switches.

'Well, we appear to have landed,' he said in his gently gruff voice.

Ben, however, was more interested in what the Doctor had said about the future of the United Kingdom. He tucked his brightly striped shirt into his drainpipe trousers and advanced on the little man.

'What did you mean, Doctor?' he asked, brow crinkling with worry.

The Doctor looked up. 'Mm? Oh that.' He chuckled and put his finger to his lips. 'Don't ask so many questions, Ben. You don't want me to spoil all your surprises, do you?'

Ben grunted. 'The only thing that'd surprise me is if you ever got us home.'

The Doctor shot him a venomous look and turned back to the console, where he twisted a dial with piqued aggression. Then, like a cloud passing away from the sun, his expression changed and he clapped his hands together happily.

'Well, come along, everybody. We've been cooped up in the TARDIS for far too long. Let's see where we are.'

So saying, he flicked a switch and the double doors opened on to the frosty alley outside. At once, a wave of cold air rushed in to greet them.

Polly shivered, walked across the room, and peered outside. She swiftly withdrew.

'It's freezing!' she cried, but the Doctor ignored her, gazing over her shoulder with delighted curiosity. Outside he could see that the alley opened onto daylight. There was a suggestion of housing with smoke billowing from tall brick chimneypots. And snow. Everywhere. The Doctor loved snow.

'It's certainly bracing,' he admitted. 'I wonder where we are this time?'

The Doctor looked up at the sky, as white and featureless as an upturned china bowl.

He frowned and stuck his tongue into his cheek so that it bulged outward. 'Shan't be a moment,' he said and vanished through the interior door.

Ben and Jamie stepped out together on to the cobbles and began to look around. Ben placed the flat of one hand against the cold, wet stone of the alley walls and then let out a little groan as he realised he had stepped in a pile of horse manure.

Jamie laughed and then turned to Polly, who was still standing in the TARDIS doorway.

'Are you no' coming out?' he said.

The glamorous woman looked down at her short black

minidress and shook her head. 'Are you kidding? Not unless I—'

She stopped abruptly as the Doctor reappeared, carrying four thick woollen cloaks over both his arms. He handed them to his companions and pulled the last one around his own shoulders, tying it under his chin with a rather sloppy bow.

'Doctor,' laughed Polly. 'You think of everything.'

'Yes. Don't I?'

With a flourish of his cloak, the Doctor stepped out. Polly immediately followed, closing the TARDIS door behind her with a soft click.

The snow was falling heavily now, speckling the air in flakes the size of autumn leaves.

The troop of soldiers had drawn up under a massive stone archway, its brickwork mottled like a chessboard with two small wooden doors inset, one either side. It was one of the old city gateways and abutted a small square ringed with rather grand houses.

Stamping and whinnying with cold, the troopers' mounts moved restlessly beneath the arch, jostling the men together so that their armour clashed. One soldier's powder horn was crushed against the leg of his companion and the contents, black and sparkling like coal dust, sprinkled onto the snow below. He cursed and then silenced himself as his commander turned his horse about to address them.

Thomas Pride shifted in his saddle and lifted his visor from his face, revealing an honest but rather severe face with milky-grey eyes like shallow frost on a pool of water. He let his gaze range over his men and then nodded to himself.

'Very well,' he said at last. 'We are almost there. Are you all clear as to what must be done?'

A low murmur came from the men, almost drowned out by the jostling of their horses.

Pride raised himself up in his saddle and bellowed at them. 'I said are you all clear?'

His rasping voice rang with authority and this time a great shout of assent came from the troopers.

Pride took a deep breath, feeling the frosty air sting his throat.

'For God and the Army!' he yelled.

The soldiers cheered. Pride smiled, watching as the settling snowflakes bled the colour from the men's uniforms.

He jabbed his spurs into the flanks of his horse and the beast turned slowly about. Then, crossing himself, he lowered his voice to a grave whisper.

'Then let us get on with this business.'

The TARDIS crew padded through the rapidly drifting snow, their footsteps muffled, their shoes collecting great lumps of the stuff like extra soles.

The alley had broadened onto a much bigger street, crowded with people, all hurrying to find shelter from the weather. Only a few stray beggars, huddled in corners, seemed forced to remain outside.

The Doctor was already some way ahead of his companions, his quick gaze taking in the details of the buildings around them.

'Clearly Earth again,' he said with a small sigh, stooping to examine horseshoe prints in the snow.

'And the middle of winter,' moaned Polly, pulling her cloak tightly around her.

Jamie laughed. 'Och, lassie, this is nothing. One time me and the Laird were stuck out on the moor for nigh on three days—'

'Look!'

Ben's voice cut across Jamie's reminiscence and everyone turned to see the young man pointing over their heads towards a familiar black silhouette.

The Doctor scurried to Ben's side. 'What is it?'

He peered at the shape on the skyline and then nodded.

Ben's face was wreathed in smiles. 'It's the Tower, innit, Doctor?'

The Doctor frowned. 'It would appear to be.'

Ben almost punched the air. 'The bloomin' Tower. I don't believe it. We're home!'

Polly grinned and looked longingly over at the familiar bulk of the Tower of London. It was a landmark she had only ever visited as a child, a thing for tourists that was glimpsed occasionally out of the window of a train. But now it seemed to be a perfect symbol of all that she missed about her own time. Safe. Dependable. London!

'Oh, Ben,' she cried. 'Do you really think so?'

Ben folded his arms and assumed his most stoic expression. 'It's got to be, innit, Duchess?'

The Doctor shook his head and wet snowflakes tumbled on to his cloak. 'Now wait a minute, Ben. You're forgetting that the TARDIS transports us through time as well as space. Look around you.' He swept his arm around in a circle. 'Do you see any other familiar things?'

Ben looked about quickly, impatiently, anxious to be right.

Polly looked too. There was something wrong. She knew it. Everything was too old. There wasn't a sign of modern life. Her shoulders sank and she moved forward on her own.

Ben shrugged. 'No, I can't say as I do. But that doesn't matter. I mean, what's a few years here and there?'

The Doctor looked unexpectedly grave. 'Oh, quite a bit, I should say.'

Jamie stamped his feet on the ground and hugged himself, wishing he was wearing rather more than a kilt beneath his cloak. 'What year is this then, Doctor?'

The Doctor let his fingers trail over the rotting brickwork of the nearest wall. 'Well, judging by these buildings I should say—'

Horses' hooves thundered on the ground and the air was suddenly full of clamour as a troop of soldiers stormed through the street.

Jamie leapt forward and grabbed Polly by both her arms. He almost fell backward, dragging her with him and flattening them both against the wall. She had missed being crushed by a matter of moments.

The Doctor and Ben took their cue and threw themselves into the nearest doorway as the horsemen passed by, blurred into one great silver and buff shape by the speed of their motion.

When the last of them had gone, the Doctor stepped forward, his face beaming, his eyes sparkling. He clapped his hands together in childlike delight.

'Oh, I say!' he cried. 'Roundheads!'

She had a face like an angel, Thomas said, and he should know. Why? she asked. Because he loved her. Loved her above all things. Above any girl he had ever known. Loved her and planned to marry her. He had said so every time they met, including the day a week or so back, when she had dropped the neat little watch he had given her as a present. The beautiful silver thing had slipped from her hand and fallen clean through a sheet of ice into a puddle.

Now the watch had been returned to her and, in the privacy of her room above the inn, Frances, daughter of William Kemp, read and reread the accompanying letter.

Mistress,

The artificer having never before met with a drowned watch, like an ignorant physician has been so long about the cure that he hath made me very unquiet that your commands should be so long deferred. However, I have sent the watch at last and envy the felicity of it, that it should be so near your side, and so often enjoy your eye, and be consulted by you how your time shall pass while you employ your hand in your excellent works.

But have a care of it, for I put such a spell into it that every beating of the balance will tell you 'tis the pulse of my heart, which labours as much to serve you and more truly than the watch; for the watch, I believe, will sometimes lie, and sometimes perhaps be idle and unwilling to go, having received so much injury by being drenched in that icy bath that I despair it should ever be a true servant to you more. But as for me (unless you drown me too in my tears) you may be confident I shall never cease to be,

Your most affectionate, humble servant,

Thom. Culpeper

She thought it the most wonderful thing she had ever read and clasped the crisp white paper to her breast, her heart full of joy.

The door to her bedroom opened and her father stood there, his pale face sullen, his mouth turned down in a permanent look of disapproval.

Frances managed to hide the letter beneath the bedclothes before he could notice it and turned her face to him, her delicate features fixed into a sweet smile.

'Why do you mooch about here, girl?' rumbled Kemp. 'Your mother would not object to help in the kitchens, I'll warrant.'

Frances got to her feet and adjusted the little white cap that crowned her golden hair. 'Yes, Father.'

Kemp grunted and she squeezed past him through the door. He stayed a moment, looking around the plainly furnished room with its framed embroidered mottoes and heavy furniture.

Then, sniffing dismissively, he shuffled back into the corridor and made his way downstairs into the inn.

The troopers had come to a final halt outside a huge, ornate building that resembled a Gothic cathedral. Its two towers were crowded with stone niches in which statues of saints had been placed. Some were missing a head or a limb or even missing altogether but the overall effect, combined with the massive central window between the towers, was as impressive as befitted Parliament House.

Colonel Pride swung his legs from the saddle and dismounted, immediately barking orders for his men to remain on horseback but to arrange themselves into ranks before the arched entry to the Commons.

As the troopers moved to obey, their swords and armour clanking like ancient machinery, Pride took up position by the left-hand side of the arch, directly below a statue of St Stephen.

He glanced up at the stoic face of the martyr and sighed. What it was to have such faith.

A soft crumping in the snow hailed the arrival of a newcomer and Pride steadied himself as a tall, prematurely grey haired man with sharp blue eyes and an intelligent, if weary, face sauntered into view. He nodded to the colonel and then looked up at the statue.

'Stone me, eh?'

Pride frowned. 'My Lord?'

Lord Grey of Groby managed a thin smile. 'St Stephen. A pun, Colonel.'

Pride nodded. 'You will forgive me if I do not share your levity, sir.'

Grey suddenly felt very foolish and shivered despite the thick layers of bulky clothing he wore. He took off his hat and narrowed his eyes as he looked at the assembled troopers.

'A grim day for it, eh?'

Pride looked straight ahead, his mouth set into a thin, determined line.

'If the sun were to shine as summer, this day would be grim enough, My Lord.'

His shaky voice betrayed his emotion and he cleared his throat rapidly in an effort to hide it. 'Never did I think to find myself in such a position.'

He fixed Grey with his milky eyes. 'Do you have the list?'

Grey nodded and passed him two sheets of rolled parchment. Pride scanned the names that had been carefully inscribed on them. Snowflakes fell and began to seep into the paper, blurring the names until they seemed written in black blood.

Sighing, Grey wrung his gloved hands. 'To face down a tyrant king is one thing,' he lamented. 'But now to vilify the very men who helped in his defeat…' He trailed off miserably.

Pride rolled up the parchment and tapped Grey on the shoulder. 'We must be resolute, My Lord. This discredited Parliament must go. It must be purged. Else all our labours, all our… sacrifices, have been in vain.'

Grey's head snapped up as three men approached. One was very plainly dressed, wearing a black jerkin, breeches and stockings beneath a brown cloak; the others were rather more splendidly attired, their long, curly hair falling on to lacy collars, the sleeves of their richly coloured coats slashed to

20

reveal the shirts beneath. Both wore large hats with gorgeous, ostrich-feather plumes projecting from the brim, although the heavy snow had rather dampened the effect.

'Look sharp, Colonel,' announced Grey curtly. 'Here comes the first of 'em.'

One of the men, stroking his chestnut-coloured beard with one hand and holding his other hand on his hip, approached, his jaw dropping open as he caught sight of the soldiers, three ranks deep.

Pride held up his hand before the astonished man's face. 'By your leave, sir, return to your home. You shall not pass today.'

The man turned to his colleagues as if seeking confirmation that he had heard right. 'Do you know to whom you speak, sir?' he managed at last. 'We are Parliament's elected representatives. On whose authority do you deny us access?'

Pride pulled himself up to his full, imposing height. 'In the name of God and the Army, sir. You have forfeited your right to represent the people of England.'

'Forfeited our right!' spluttered the newcomer. 'This is an outrage!'

Grey stepped forward out of the shadow of St Stephen. 'No doubt,' he muttered in a quiet, dangerous whisper. 'But you will do as the colonel says.'

The second of the men cocked an eyebrow. 'Grey? Is that you? 'Sblood! What goes on here?'

Grey's noble face twisted into a sneer: 'Would you insult us with your feigned ignorance?' he spat. 'We have waged a war against Charles Stuart, King of England. A war that has cost us dear. Yet now you would make a dishonourable peace with this wicked man. How can you claim to represent the people?'

With a snarl, he grabbed the parchment from Pride's hand, found the members' names, and scored them out with a thick piece of charcoal. Then he turned back, his blue eyes glittering with rage. 'Get ye gone!'

The Doctor managed to find an orange-seller sheltering under the entrance to the World Turn'd Upside Down and bought four rather splendid specimens from her. After some time spent fiddling with the extraordinary amount of junk inside his capacious pockets, he finally found a fat leather purse of coins which appeared to be of the correct period. The orange-seller thanked him and tapped the brim of her snow-covered hat before scuttling away.

The Doctor tossed an orange to each of his companions in turn and dug his thumb into the thick peel of his own.

'It's a bit complicated, I'll admit,' he said, squeezing the soft flesh of the fruit and jamming a segment into his mouth. 'Didn't you study this period of your history at school? I seem to remember Susan was very keen on it.'

Jamie looked up from contemplating his orange. 'Who's Susan?'

But the Doctor did not seem to have heard him.

Ben bit into his orange and juice sprayed out all over his hands and cloak. He shook his hand dry and spoke between gulps. 'I was just saying to the Duchess, Doctor,. history's not my strong point. I always get the kings and queens mixed up. There's so many of 'em. All those wives Henry Five had.'

The Doctor sighed. 'Eight.'

'Was it as many as that?' said Ben in genuine surprise.

The Doctor shook his head. 'No, no. Henry the Eighth, not the Fifth, Ben. And it was six wives.'

'Divorced, beheaded, died,' cried Polly brightly.

'Divorced, beheaded, survived,' concluded the Doctor with a grin.

Jamie gave them both a puzzled look and the Doctor sighed,

turning to face Polly as though she were his last chance. 'What about you, Polly?'

Polly shrugged and brushed her blonde fringe from her eyes. 'Well, I seem to remember the King fell out with Parliament, didn't he? He thought he could do pretty much anything he wanted because his power came directly from God.'

The Doctor nodded. 'That's it. Divine Right, they called it.'

Ben gave a rueful smile. 'Have you got a rhyme for that, too?'

Polly poked out her tongue at him and then continued with a giggle. 'Anyway, there was a civil war and the Roundheads cut King Charles's head off.'

'Blimey!' cried Ben.

Polly finished her orange and wiped her hands on her cloak. 'It always made me rather sad,' she said. 'Poor old Charles.'

The Doctor cleared his throat. 'Yes, quite.' He stuffed the orange peel into his trouser pocket and turned to Jamie. 'And what about you, my lad?'

The Highlander pulled a face and looked away. 'Oh, I'm like Ben,' he said. 'I never fashed myself much about history.'

The Doctor looked appalled. 'But this only happened a hundred years before your time, Jamie. You should be giving us the history lesson.'

Jamie's face clouded. 'Aye, well. I was a piper, wasn't I? I never had much time to look at school books.'

The Doctor gave a little smile and winked at Ben and Polly. 'Well,' he said at last, 'I've an idea. As we might spend some time here perhaps we should be a little better prepared.'

'How'd you mean?' asked Ben.

The Doctor twiddled his thumbs and looked up at the sky. 'The fact is, I'm not quite the fount of all wisdom which you think me.'

'Oh aye?' said Jamie with a chuckle.

'No,' continued the Doctor. 'I think a little refresher course in the customs, manners, and politics of this time wouldn't go amiss.'

Polly pulled a face. 'That's not like you, Doctor. We normally just go blundering into things.'

'Eh?' snapped the Doctor testily.

'What she means,' said Ben placatingly, 'is that we don't normally prepare for these things. Isn't that half the fun?'

The Doctor smiled. 'Of course. Of course it is. But this was a very dangerous time. We must be careful.' His expression grew suddenly grave, emphasising the deep lines on his face. 'Loyalties are in a state of constant flux. This conflict tore apart friends and families and it wasn't unusual for fathers and sons to fight on opposite sides.'

Polly's mouth turned down. 'A civil war in every sense.'

'Exactly. So we don't want to upset anyone or get ourselves into trouble needlessly because we're ignorant of what's going on. I'll pop back to the TARDIS. There's bound to be just the sort of thing we need in the library.'

Jamie nodded. 'All right, Doctor. We'll wait here.'

The Doctor headed back the way they had come, his cloak flapping behind him. 'Shan't be a tick. Don't talk to any strangers.'

The three of them watched him disappear into the dark alley.

'I hope it's got lots of pictures,' said Jamie with a groan.

William Kemp stamped his feet on a rough twig mat as he entered the rear of the inn. Snow fell from his shoes and onto the stone floor like powder. He gave the kitchen the benefit of his scowl, ignoring the pleasant atmosphere of busy cooking which permeated the room.

Huge copper pots were affixed to the walls, hanging above cheeses, meats, and preserves of all kinds. Dried, salted fish were stacked in a pile on top of three or four long wooden tables, their surfaces blotched and cracked with wear.

Kemp closed the door behind him, shivered, and made straight for the large fire blazing in the kitchen hearth. Before it stood the firedogs, great iron constructions on which spits turned incessantly, dripping hot fat into a row of black tins.

Just in front of these, about to thrust a tray of oat clap bread into the brick oven, stood Kemp's wife, Sarah.

Despite her daughter's looks, she was as plain as her own dress, a simple, red affair with a full-sleeved white blouse and apron. Her thick auburn hair was tucked up under a lacy cap. She turned as her husband entered and gave him one of her ready smiles. Which he ignored.

Sarah could remember a time when William had considered her beautiful, had been unable to keep himself from embracing her, even as she cooked. She imagined what it would feel like to have him come up behind her now and nuzzle, laughing at her neck, calling her his 'little goose' the way he used to.

Her face was flushed and strands of her hair kept falling into her eyes as she bent down to open the oven.

'I heard there were soldiers,' she said quietly.

Kemp said nothing and seated himself at the kitchen table. He grabbed a hunk of bread and began to chew noisily on it, glancing around at the cluttered parameters of the small, warm room.

Sarah Kemp stood back from the oven and closed the big iron door. She decided to try another tack with her husband. 'Many in?'

Kemp swigged some water from a pewter cup and scowled. 'That girl not back yet?' he said gruffly, ignoring his wife's question.

Sarah brushed the hair from her eyes and began kneading a lump of dough which sat on a marble slab before her. 'No. Not yet.'

'Can't see what could keep her,' growled Kemp. 'An errand's an errand. She should be making better time now she's grown, not worse.'

Sarah Kemp bit her lip. She knew that the truth was bound to come out sooner or later. But, oh Lord, let it be later. She couldn't bear to see her little Frances upset. And with William in this kind of mood, anything might happen. Of course, he was perpetually in this mood, nowadays, since... since...

She moved quickly as hot tears sprang into her eyes.

Kemp did not notice. 'I ask you,' he said, holding his big hands palms upward, 'how long can it take to bring back a sack of flour?'

Sarah sank her hands into the dough and worked on. 'Expect she got to talking with someone. You know what girls are like.'

'Aye,' said Kemp. 'I do. When there's work to be done and not time to waste in idle gossip—'

He broke off as the door opened and Frances came inside. She looked first at her mother and smiled broadly, then, as she noticed her father, her expression changed. She took off her cloak and laid it over a chair by the fire, where it began to steam in the heat.

She smoothed back the hair from her delicate, rather otherworldly face and sat down opposite her father. He banged his fist on the table, setting the cheese rocking on its plate.

'Where's the flour?' asked Kemp, his sour expression unchanging.

'In the outhouse, of course,' said Frances quietly.

'And where, might I ask, have you been all this time?'

Sarah Kemp looked across the table and caught Frances's eye. She shook her head imperceptibly and Frances nodded her understanding.

'All this time?' she said with feigned indifference. 'Why, I've not been more than half an hour, Father. And I needs must be careful in this weather. I'm sure you wouldn't want your flour spilled all over the highway.'

She flashed him her sweetest smile and Kemp grunted. He swigged more water and stuffed the remainder of the bread into his coat pocket, then got up, the chair legs scraping on the floor.

'I've got word that we're to expect guests, Sarah,' he said, looking his wife directly in the eyes.

'Guests?'

'Aye. So you'll see the upstairs is made up good and proper, won't you?' He crossed the kitchen and, without looking back, threw open the inner door and went into the tavern.

Sarah and Frances exchanged glances.

'Guests?' said Frances at last. 'What kind of guests?'

In the queasy yellow light of a lamp, the man cut a noble figure. His face was long and intelligent, his complexion, like his hair and beard, so dark as to have once earned him the nickname Black Tom. But the raven hair was streaked with grey now and, though he gave the outward appearance of a man very much at peace with himself, Sir Thomas Fairfax, Commander-in-Chief of Parliament's New Model Army, was nothing of the kind.

He was pacing up and down a modestly sized apartment, its small, mullioned windows letting in scant amounts of the feeble light of that freezing morning.

He had ordered his secretary, a young man of only twenty years, to light the lamp in order to lift some of the gloom

Fairfax was feeling. But, if anything, the tallowy illumination only depressed his spirits further, throwing dense shadows over the furniture and the heavy, panelled walls.

The secretary scribbled away furiously on a large sheet of parchment, the nib of his quill scratching and squeaking over the smooth surface.

'It is an outrage,' dictated Fairfax, his coal-black eyes blazing. 'No, an illegal outrage. And I strongly urge that General Cromwell be remonstrated with for sanctioning this action against the lawfully elected Parliament of this nation. Signed, Fairfax, Commander-in-Chief.'

He paused, his head sinking onto his breast, and then waved a hand to dismiss the secretary.

The young man got up, clasping the still-wet parchment to his chest. 'I will have this delivered with all due dispatch, My Lord.'

Fairfax nodded, his attention already drifting elsewhere. There was still so much to be done. The Army had not been properly paid for months. The King was imprisoned, awaiting trial. But what kind of trial could it be if the legally elected Parliament had not voted it through? If Cromwell had to get his way only by this outrageous purge of all those who did not see eye to eye with him?

After a while, Fairfax realised that the secretary was still there, hovering in the doorway.

'What is it?' asked Fairfax, frowning.

The secretary cleared his throat, fiddled with the border of his wide collar, and looked down at the faded embroidery of the carpet.

'I was just wondering, My Lord...'

'Well?'

The secretary cleared his throat. 'I was wondering... what kind of a remonstrance Parliament might be expected to pass when two-thirds of its members are being thrown out of office.'

For a moment, the secretary thought the noble Lord might explode with fury, but, gradually, the fiery light in his eyes faded and he gave a harsh laugh. 'Aye, fair point, lad. I know what General Cromwell will say.'

'My Lord?'

'He is still in the North, you know. But he won't object to what has been done. It leaves the way clear for his followers to vote through the King's trial.'

The secretary inclined his head to one side. 'Then this letter…?'

'Is useless. I know,' concluded Fairfax mournfully. 'But I will have it known that I object most strongly to this course of action. History will not say that Thomas Fairfax conspired to murder his King.'

The secretary gave a neat bow and exited.

Fairfax slumped down onto a cushioned chair and stared at the flickering flame of the lamp. 'Where are you, Oliver?' he whispered to himself. 'Where are you?

The TARDIS seemed warm after the freezing atmosphere of the London morning and the Doctor threw off his cloak as he walked briskly through the console room. He thought briefly of extracting the relevant data from the ship's index files, but he had never liked computers and there was something homely and comforting about a book that the clinical printouts could never match.

He went through the interior door and marched straight past the cluster of rooms that made up the main TARDIS living quarters. Pausing at a junction, he stopped to get his bearings and held a finger up to his mouth.

'Library, library,' he muttered to himself. 'That would be

this way, wouldn't it? Yes. Past the pavilion, left, right, left again, tertiary console room dead ahead.'

He smiled and rubbed his hands, pleased that his knowledge of the TARDIS's twisted geography had not let him down, and set off, whistling happily.

In ten minutes he was hopelessly lost.

CHAPTER
2

A fierce wind had whipped up the snow into a blinding curtain enveloping Parliament and muffling the sounds of activity within its precincts.

Pride and Grey still stood before the ranks of troopers, eyes narrowed to slits, their shoulders thick with wet snowflakes. Three more men, three smudged black figures against the whiteness, were in the process of being turned away.

Pride sighed angrily, his breath smoking from his mouth. 'If you do not retire in peace, sirs, I shall be forced to arrest you.'

The latest victim of the purge snorted in derision, his fat cheeks wobbling. 'I've never heard anything so outrageous in all my life. Arrest me?'

'Well, if you insist,' said Pride, signalling to one of the soldiers, who rapidly dismounted and marched over to his colonel.

'Sir?'

Pride nodded towards the three MPs. 'These gentlemen are to be confined until further notice.'

The soldier nodded and shoved the leading member in the small of the back. Still protesting, the three men were bundled away.

Grey looked down at the list, now thick with black lines where the members' names had been excised. 'Almost a hundred and sixty, Colonel.'

Pride nodded in satisfaction. 'And the remainder will vote through the King's trial or I'm Prince Rupert.'

Grey smiled grimly, his mouth forming a thin line like a knife wound. 'Then our work today is almost done.'

Pride gave a low chuckle. 'If you fear your blood's turning to ice, My Lord, then off you go to your fireplace. I'll stay as long as it takes.'

Grey shook his head. 'Nay, you'll not shift me, Thomas Pride. Let's continue.'

He pulled himself up to his full height as another knot of unfortunates approached.

The Doctor slid down the roundelled corridor wall and gave a little whimper of frustration. Really, it was absolutely intolerable for him to lose his way inside his own TARDIS.

He had been walking round and round in circles, sometimes catching sight of a familiar chair or a bust of some long-dead emperor. But there was no way to tell if he was making any kind of progress. He half suspected the TARDIS was toying with him, getting a little revenge for all the hard work he made her do.

'Wretched thing,' he snapped, kicking against the wall with his boot.

There was a strange, low sound, almost like a groan, and the Doctor looked up in surprise.

Then, with a soft click, a door opened in the wall where he had never noticed one before. It was a perfectly reasonable door, rectangular, soundly constructed and ordinary. But the room it opened onto was quite another thing altogether.

The Doctor scrambled to his feet and stepped gingerly

forward, pushing the door back to its full extent. 'Well I never,' he said, a smile creeping slowly over his face.

The room was small, cluttered, and rather airless. It was musty and cobwebbed with a smell like old books and damp clothes combined. And, in contrast to the warm luminescence of everywhere else in the TARDIS, it was completely dark.

A funnel of light from the corridor beyond showed up some things the Doctor recognised at once. Alphabet building blocks were scattered over the floor, which was itself covered by a thick Turkish rug. Clockwork cars, tin soldiers, and slightly sinister Victorian dolls, their fat cheeks and blank eyes grimy with dust, were strewn about the place. In the centre of it all, jerking back and forth, back and forth as though someone's hand had only just set it in motion, was a rocking horse.

The Doctor walked slowly and carefully through the litter of toys and placed his palm on the cracked varnish of the rocking horse's head. It stopped suddenly.

'What are you trying to show me, old girl?' asked the Doctor to the air.

He looked about and caught sight of a hurricane lamp which was standing, rather incongruously, on top of a box of bricks.

Picking it up, the Doctor slid open the glass front and examined the wick. The lamp stank of paraffin and he rapidly lit a match, illuminating the little room with a soft, pleasant glow.

As he did so, another door opened in the far wall, smaller this time, as though it wasn't meant for a man to walk through at all.

He looked puzzled. 'Curiouser and curiouser, said the Doctor,' he mumbled.

He walked on to the door, popped his head through, and

realised, with a start, that he was looking out onto the corridor that led directly to the main console room.

He let out a little laugh and patted the wall affectionately. 'Oh, bless you,' he said happily.

Then, as he squeezed himself through the narrow door, his eyes alighted on something lying on the rug right beneath his feet.

The Doctor frowned, then stooped to pick it up. It was a book, solid and heavy, covered in a smooth paper dust jacket and decorated with a pleasantly idealised colour painting dating from some time in the 1920s.

He pressed it to his chest and shook his head in bewilderment. The TARDIS never ceased to surprise him.

As soon as he had stepped out into the corridor, the little door behind him seemed to vanish.

The Doctor blew out the flame in the hurricane lamp and made his way through to the console room, picking up his cloak and swinging it over his shoulders. He drummed his fingers over the book's surface as he opened the doors and stepped back into the cold alleyway.

It wasn't exactly what he'd been after, he had to admit, but, in its own particular way, the TARDIS had found what he was looking for and given it to him.

At least Jamie would be pleased, thought the Doctor, plunging *Every Boy's Book of the English Civil Wars* deep into his pocket.

The attic room was a low, dark place which William Kemp normally kept empty. It was used occasionally to put up a guest if the inn was unexpectedly full, in which case a shaky old bed and mattress would be disinterred for the purpose.

Today, though, Kemp stooped beneath its rafters, pouring ale into a heavy jug which sat upon a table which he had spent most of the previous afternoon trying to manoeuvre inside.

Half a dozen men were sitting around it, champing anxiously on clay pipes and, as a consequence, wreathed in a fug of tobacco.

A few moments before, they had been arguing fiercely, but now Kemp's arrival had stilled their voices. He finished his work and the man at the top of the table, an imposing, silver-bearded figure, nodded to him.

'Will there be anything else, sir?' Kemp asked, hoping to be privy to the conversation.

Silver Beard shook his head. 'Nay, Will. We will call if anything is required.'

Kemp bowed disappointedly and withdrew, looking quickly at the other figures before closing the little wooden door after him.

When they were sure Kemp's footsteps had faded, the group began at once to speak again in tones of barely concealed fury. The silver-bearded man, Sir John Copper, held up his hands in a conciliatory gesture.

'Peace, peace, gentlemen, I pray you.'

By his side sat Christopher Whyte, a handsome, cocky young fellow of thirty-three with long, flowing chestnut hair and brilliant-blue eyes. His face, fixed in a sardonic half-smile, managed to look interested and indifferent simultaneously.

Sitting just across the table was the sweating, flushed form of Benedict Moor and it was he who chose to speak now, lowering his voice in deference to Copper's gesture.

'Turned out!' he croaked. 'Turned out of the Commons! And by Thomas Pride. God save us, he was a drayman before the wars.'

Whyte shook his head, his long hair brushing over the velvet collar of his coat. 'If the Commons required us all to be of noble birth, Ben, then it would hardly live up to its name.'

Moor scowled at him. 'You know what I mean, lad.'

Copper turned to Whyte and patted his hand amusedly. 'Yes, you do, Chris. And do not play merry with Master Moor's feelings.'

Moor banged his fist on the table, making the ale in the jug slosh about. 'By what authority would they try their King? Have they taken leave of their senses?'

Sir John Copper stroked his beard and looked down at the table, his almond-shaped eyes unreadable.

'You know what they would say, Ben,' he said, his voice measured and calm. 'Fairfax and Cromwell have got it into their heads to depose their monarch and that's all there is to it.'

Moor sank back into his seat, his gaunt features pooling into shadow. "Sfoot. I never thought it would come to this. I fought Charles, aye, fought him because he thought to rule this land without recourse to us, his Parliament. I cheered when we beat him because I thought... I thought...'

Christopher Whyte poured himself a mug of ale and contemplated its foamy weight in his hand. 'You thought the Army would be content with that. A chastened King. But you underestimated their ambition, sir. The Army chiefs are set to be more the despot than ever Charles was.'

He drained the glass in one draught and wiped his clean-shaven face with the back of his hand.

Copper looked sideways at Whyte and gave a small smile, his gimlet eyes crinkling at the corners. Then he turned back to Moor.

'You were away from the House the other day, Ben. You know Fairfax has given orders to move him?'

Moor looked up. 'His Majesty? Aye. To Hurst Castle, is it not?'

Copper nodded. 'On the Solent.'

Moor gnawed at his knuckle and looked around the room at the other men. The weather and the winter made the place depressingly dark.

'My friends,' he murmured earnestly. 'What are we to do?'

Whyte and Copper exchanged glances, then the older man spoke, his voice still calm but betraying a measure of contained excitement.

'Never fear, Ben. There are ways and means. The Queen awaits His Majesty in France. Let us see if there is not some way they can be reunited.'

He smiled broadly, as did Whyte, leaving Moor and the others frowning in puzzlement.

'Now then,' said the Doctor cheerily. 'What say we have a little look around?'

He had returned to find his companions just as he had left them, which was something of a relief as they often tended to go astray

It had stopped snowing at last and the sky had brightened considerably, lending the street a sparkling, virginal charm.

The Doctor looked around, breathed deeply of the crisp air, and sucked absently on his finger. 'Jamie and I will head towards the river, I think.'

'Oh,' said Polly. 'Shouldn't we stay together?'

The Doctor waved his hand airily. 'Oh, it should be all right if you're sensible. Anyway, Ben, wouldn't you like some shore leave?'

Ben shrugged. 'Suppose so.'

'Well then,' continued the Doctor, 'that's settled.'

Polly wasn't so sure. 'What about all that stuff about getting acclimatised?'

The Doctor cleared his throat and pulled his cloak more tightly about him, as though he feared discovery of the children's book in his pocket.

'Yes, well. I didn't have a lot of luck there, as I've explained. I'm sure we'll get along all right. Just watch your tongues and be circumspect.'

'Eh?' said Jamie.

The Doctor patted him on the shoulder. 'Yes, you come with me, Jamie.'

Polly held up her hand. 'Hang on, Doctor. We don't even know what year it is. We could be slap bang in the middle of the Civil Wars.'

'I don't like the sound of that,' lamented Ben.

'Och,' said Jamie, his Jacobite mettle showing. 'Where's your pluck, man? And you a sailor, too.'

Never one to resist a little baiting, Ben set his face determinedly. 'All right. We will. Come on, Duchess.'

The Doctor clapped his hands together and gave a quick glance up and down the street. 'We'll meet you back at the TARDIS at sunset. All right? Come along, Jamie.'

Jamie turned to him. 'Where're we going?'

'Come along,' said the Doctor firmly, tugging at his sleeve.

Now the snow had ceased, the street was beginning to crowd again with carts and people, hurrying through.

'What was all that about?' said Ben with some asperity. '"I think it'd do us all good to spend some time on our own."'

Polly laughed. 'I don't know. Perhaps our constantly harping on about getting back to 1966 is getting on his nerves a bit.'

Ben rubbed his chin. 'Yeah but he's not on his own, is he? He's got Jamie.'

Polly smiled. 'Mm. Haven't you noticed he prefers having someone around who doesn't ask too many awkward questions?'

Ben ruffled his blond hair. 'I hope we haven't hurt his

feelings. I mean, not everyone gets the chance to go back in time, do they?'

'You're dead right, sailor,' said Polly. 'Come on. Let's get on with it.'

They began to thread their way through the snowbound London streets, gazing about in a mixture of awe and amusement, peering into every shadowed corner.

The streets, now teeming with people, were extraordinarily narrow. Houses with twisted, distorted beams leaned across towards each other like freakish trees struggling to reach the sun. Twice, the travellers had to step aside as the contents of a chamber pot were unceremoniously dumped out of an upstairs window onto the white drifts below.

Ben had once told Polly that he could handle Daleks and Cybermen and all the futuristic horrors that went with them, but what really sent his senses reeling was seeing their own history replayed before their eyes.

Polly's face was beaming as she watched a little girl with ginger curls jump out into the snow and begin to fling it into the air. She let out a peal of giggles and threw a hastily assembled snowball in Ben's direction.

'You know,' said Polly, 'I was just thinking. When I was at school I used to love reading about the Cavaliers. I remember pictures of them. All frills and velvet and lace. Not like that misery guts Cromwell and his pals.'

'Oh, yeah?' said Ben, absently throwing a snowball back at the little girl.

Polly warmed to her theme. 'Oh, he was a terrible killjoy. You know, he even banned Christmas?'

Ben looked rueful. 'Yeah. Well, if his family were anything like mine that was probably a very good idea.'

Richard Godley hated the gulls. He hated their swooping,

irritating presence. Hated their harsh, shrill cry. Hated the way they seemed to single out his richest and most attractive coats to defecate upon.

He shot them a poisonous glance as he hurried towards the wharf, keeping his face well covered beneath a thick scarf.

Godley clattered down a flight of rickety spiral steps, their wooden surface slick with snow and wet weed, and threaded his way through the timber yard to the ship.

She lay in her berth, rocking gently in the swell, a monster of a man o' war, four decks deep with rigging so vast and complicated that it resembled a spider's web. Her sails were folded now and her ensigns fluttered gently in the biting wind.

Godley walked cautiously on to the gangplank, the tails of his blue velvet coat wafting behind him. He glanced about quickly, almost nervously, aware of the jauntiness with which he would once have done this thing.

But it was all different now. Even he had to admit that.

Ignoring the shouts of the coopers and merchants who were slinging sacks of provisions on board, he strode across the deck towards the huge, elaborately carved stern, where he knew the captain's cabin to be located.

As it was, the captain saved him the trip, emerging from his room and blinking in the bleak white light of day.

'Ah!' he cried. 'You are here!'

His voice was clipped and heavily accented. Godley marched up to him, still looking shiftily over his shoulder.

'Captain Stanislaus,' he murmured with a small bow. 'When do we sail?'

Stanislaus let out a small, musical giggle. 'You must not be so afraid, my friend. There is nothing to fear. We sail upon the next tide.'

'And when is that?'

Stanislaus sighed and shrugged. He was an uncommonly

tall man with a shock of raven-black hair. His features were strong and faintly swarthy, with black brows and beard, deep-brown eyes and a huge, charming smile. He was dressed in a big, three-quarter-length red coat, its lapels bristling with silver buttons, and a broad black hat was jammed on to his head.

'Some time this evening,' he said to Godley. 'Alas, we are a little short-handed so I have men out looking for… er… volunteers.'

Godley laughed. 'More desertions, my dear Captain? Really, you will be getting yourself a reputation.'

Stanislaus's smile froze on his lips. 'I have a reputation, sir,' he said coldly. 'And no man ever deserts my ship. Not alive, anyway.'

Godley pulled down the scarf from his face. He was a dashing, handsome young man with huge brown eyes and a thin, aquiline nose. His dimpled chin showed a suggestion of beard.

'Have a care, sir,' he warned Stanislaus in a whisper. 'This is no pleasure cruise. And no pirate's endeavour. You will obey my orders. And mine alone. Is that clear?'

Stanislaus smiled his shark's smile and then, without a word, turned on his heel and went back to his cabin.

A freezing fog was rolling over the banks of the Thames, lending its muddy, derelict embankment an air of unexpected romance.

The Doctor and Jamie emerged from out of the haze like spectres and, while Jamie shivered, the Doctor seemed inspired, gesturing expansively towards the unseen river.

'Such a majestic old thing, the Thames, don't you think, Jamie?'

Jamie threw a cursory glance towards the river. 'Aye.'

41

The Doctor sniffed and pulled a face. 'Of course, it pongs a bit. Always has.'

He turned to his companion but Jamie didn't seem to be listening. In fact, his face had assumed a rather solemn expression.

'Are you all right, Jamie?' asked the Doctor concernedly.

Jamie gave a little smile. 'Aye, aye.' Then he looked down at the snowy ground. 'Well, I suppose so.'

The Doctor put his hand on Jamie's arm. 'What's the matter?'

Jamie shook his head and avoided the Doctor's gaze. 'I'm not sure, Doctor. I'm just finding all this is making me a wee bit… giddy.'

'All what?' asked the Doctor, frowning.

Jamie shrugged, his boyish features crumpling into a hurt expression. 'You know. Travelling through time. It takes some getting used to, you know.'

'Of course,' soothed the Doctor. 'Of course it does. And you mustn't worry if you feel a little disorientated.' He crossed his hands over his chest. 'There's a thing people call "culture shock". That's what you get if you're exposed to a foreign way of life totally different from your own.'

Jamie nodded.

'Well,' continued the Doctor, 'for us in the TARDIS, culture shock is more than that. We don't just visit different countries, we visit different planets, alien places that would make the most… the most boundless imagination reel.'

Jamie shrugged. 'Aye. It's not that, though, really. It's just that sometimes Ben and Polly make me feel a bit daft. Like they've been at it for ages.'

The Doctor smiled. 'Oh, so that's it. I thought as much. That's why I suggested we all split up. Sometimes people's little jokes can cut very deep, can't they?'

Jamie nodded silently.

The Doctor looked up thoughtfully. 'Mm. Well, they have been "at it" a little longer than you, Jamie. But not much. And things were very different when they first travelled with me, I can tell you.'

Jamie seemed cheered by this. 'Really?'

The Doctor chuckled. 'Oh, yes. Polly was just as unsure as you are. And Ben was such a headstrong fellow. Insisted I take him back to his ship because he'd be late. I kept telling him he was two hundred years early!'

Jamie laughed, his dark eyes twinkling.

'And it was all new to me once, you know,' said the Doctor, looking out over the fog-shrouded Thames. 'But that was a very, very long time ago.'

The Doctor's reverie was interrupted by a sudden burst of incoherent shouting and the unmistakable sound of a scuffle close by. Jamie whirled round.

'What's that?'

He and the Doctor ran through the snowdrifts towards a knot of young men who were clustered together like spectators at a cockfight. Dressed in the plain tunics and aprons of apprentices, they appeared to have a grievance against something in their midst and, at first, the Doctor thought it might be a dog, or even a bear.

As he came closer he realised with horror that the youths were attacking an old man. They were taunting and kicking at his crouched form and he was gamely lashing out with gnarled old fists.

Without a second thought, the Doctor waded in, bellowing like a beast. His cloak ballooning impressively behind him. With Jamie bringing up the rear, the young men began to scatter.

Jamie grabbed at the ankle of one of them and pulled him

to the ground, then landed a punch on his jaw. With a yell, the youth slid away through the snow and scrambled to his feet, holding his jaw and looking more than a little afraid. This was enough for the gang and they took to their heels, leaving the old man in a heap on the ground.

'Away with you, you cowards!' cried Jamie.

The Doctor helped the old man to his feet and made a valiant effort to dust him down. But the copious stains that covered his clothes seemed to date from some considerable time before the fight.

'Are you all right?' said the Doctor.

The man looked at his rescuers and nodded his filthy head.

'I am. Thanks to you.'

The Doctor sniffed and wrinkled his nose as a wave of the old man's none-too-pleasant aroma washed over him. Fixing a cheery smile on to his face, the Doctor did his best to ignore the smell.

'What… what was all that about?'

The man pulled up his wretched stockings and scowled in the direction of the retreating ruffians.

'Royalist scum!' he spat. 'They set about me like a pack of wolves. You see…' He gave a conspiratorial wink and beckoned the Doctor and Jamie closer, something that neither was very keen to do.

'You see,' he continued, 'I caught them singing songs in praise of the King and I told them what I thought of them.'

'Oh,' said the Doctor. 'And then they told you what they thought of you, I imagine?'

'Aye, sir, they did. With their ruddy Royalist fists, they did.' He shrugged his shoulders, straightened up and held out a calloused and mud-caked hand. 'But thank you both again, sirs, for your help. I am Nathaniel Scrope.'

The Doctor cleared his throat and gingerly shook Scrope's

hand. Jamie did the same but turned away, fighting the instinct to gag.

'I'm the Doctor,' announced the Doctor. 'This is Jamie.'

Jamie flashed his eyes at the Doctor in dumb appeal. 'Och, Doctor,' he hissed under his breath. 'He reeks!'

The Doctor elbowed him in the ribs and turned to Scrope, smiling sweetly. 'Tell me, Mr Scrope, what precisely did you object to about those men?'

Scrope sniffed. 'What I say. Isn't it obvious? They would have the King released and pardoned! As though the last seven years of slaughter had been but a dream!'

The Doctor nodded slowly. 'I see.'

Jamie looked at the Doctor and frowned, aware that he was missing something. Holding a hand across his nose in what he hoped was a subtle gesture, he turned to their smelly new friend.

'Aye, well, I reckon you could do with a little something to calm your nerves, eh, Mr Scrope?'

Scrope grinned. 'I wouldn't say no, my young friend, but it will be my pleasure to treat you to a plate of oysters and some ale a little later on. Just now, you see, I have important matters of state to attend to.'

Jamie looked puzzled. 'Eh?'

The Doctor smiled. 'Well, well, we shan't keep you.'

Scrope turned to go. 'Will you meet me here at seven, gentlemen? I know a local hostelry which will make us very welcome. Now I must away! Good day to you both and thanks once again.'

He shuffled away, in a cloud of stale vapour.

Jamie let out a long breath. 'Och,' he spluttered, 'where's the fellow been keeping himself? He stinks like a cow's carcass.'

The Doctor chuckled. 'He's certainly pungent. But very entertaining.' He laughed to himself again and then came to a decision. 'You know what, Jamie? I think we'll meet up with Ben and Polly and then take up Mr Scrope on his kind offer.'

'Aye, I would nae say no to a little food and ale.'

The Doctor scratched his mop of black hair. 'He helped us get our dates right, too, did you notice?'

Jamie nodded. 'Aye.' Then he looked down at his feet and frowned. 'Well...'

The Doctor opened his cloak and retrieved *Every Boy's Book of the English Civil Wars* from the pocket of his frock coat.

He scanned its pages quickly and then carried on blithely. 'Yes. Here we are. Now our friend said they'd been fighting for seven years. That means the Civil Wars must be over and they're about to put the King on trial. It must be some time in... 1648. December I should say.'

'But they'll no have sprigs of holly out, eh, Doctor?' said Jamie brightly. 'I remember that much at least. Those Puritans weren't so keen on Christmas.'

The Doctor toyed with the tassel of his cloak and stuffed the book back into his pocket. 'Oh, they've not banned it yet, Jamie. And it never did go away. Not properly. A lot of that is just propaganda.' He looked up and smiled. 'Come on. Let's see if we can find any wassailers!'

'Any what?' said Jamie.

But the Doctor had gone.

Parliament House was joined to a series of newer buildings which had been erected earlier in the century. Their black beams and white plaster contrasted sharply with the old stone of the main section but seemed nonetheless charming to Ben and Polly, who were skulking in a doorway close by.

Their wanderings had brought them to the square and they had stopped at the sight of the soldiers who had so nearly run them down.

Ben shivered inside his cloak and peered at the activity in fascinated bemusement.

"Ere, what d'you reckon's going on, Pol?' he said at last.

Polly shrugged, feeling the cold numbing her nose and hands. 'Search me. This is Parliament, though, isn't it?'

Ben frowned. 'Is it? Looks different.'

'Well, that's because the one we know hasn't been built yet,' chided Polly impatiently. 'This one was burnt down.'

Ben grinned and gave a low whistle. 'You must've been a right swot at school, Duchess.'

Polly grinned and then returned her attention to the soldiers. She seemed deeply interested.

Another great shiver convulsed through Ben and he pulled his cloak tightly around him like the wings of a sleeping bat.

'It's taters out here,' he complained.

'Pardon?'

'Taters. Taters' mould. Cold,' he explained.

'Oh,' said Polly without much interest.

Ben felt a shiver run through his jaw and tried to laugh. 'I can't believe it. My teeth are chattering. I thought that only happened in stories.' He turned to Polly and put his head on her shoulder like a tired boy. 'Can't we go somewhere warmer to look at the local colour, Mummy?'

Polly tutted at him. 'Where's your sense of adventure?'

Ben gave a wry grin. 'I think it's dropped off.'

She continued to peer ahead, her eyes and nose running with the cold. 'I wonder what they're up to. Looks like the soldiers won't let those other men inside.'

Ben hugged at his cloak again and this time heard a faint jingle. He looked down. 'Hello?' Putting his hand inside the cloak, he produced the little leather purse which the Doctor had used earlier. Ben smiled. 'The crafty beggar. He's set us up nicely for the day, hasn't he?' He spilled out a selection of

47

silver coins from the purse. 'It's like getting pocket money on a school trip.'

Polly examined some of the coins. 'Lucky for us they're the right period. I wonder how the Doctor does it.'

'Probably a happy accident, Pol,' said Ben with a shrug. 'Like the rest of the Doctor's life.' He weighed up the satisfyingly bulging purse in his hand. 'So. What d'you say to a pie and a tot of rum?'

Polly pulled a face. 'I wouldn't say no to a pie but you're on your own with the booze.'

'Well, you can't blame me, love,' laughed Ben. 'I'm a sailor. And they still had rum rations in these days!'

Polly turned back towards Parliament, her numbed features fixed in a frown. 'I wish I knew what was going on here.'

Ben pulled at her sleeve. 'Well, maybe we'd find out more if we actually mixed with some people. Come on, Pol. I'm perishing.'

He ushered Polly away from the strange scene and the biting wind which was surging through the narrow precincts of Parliament.

Unseen by either of them, a skinny man with a face like an old saddle, slipped out of a doorway and watched them pass. His eyes remained fixed on Ben and, nodding to himself, he began to follow.

The Thames took many twists and turns along its course. Some, like the wharf where Captain Stanislaus's vessel lay moored, were fast-flowing and full of traffic; others, like the broad bend where the Doctor and Jamie found themselves, were much more sluggish. In such temperatures as that December of 1648 produced, the old river was wont to freeze and, to the Doctor's undisguised delight, a fair was being held on its solid, white surface.

'Are you sure it's safe, Doctor?' queried Jamie, setting one foot gingerly off the snow-covered bank.

The Doctor had no such qualms and launched himself onto the frozen river, jumping up and down to show how thick and deep the ice went. 'See? Solid as a rock. Londoners were used to it at this time. Something of a mini Ice Age, I think. Now come along, we're missing all the fun.'

From one bank of the river to the other, a motley collection of stalls and tents had been erected. Some were rather plain, like simple market stalls which had simply migrated to the river; others, gaily patterned and bearing flags, betrayed their theatrical origins.

There were people everywhere, bustling and chattering and laughing. Children wheeled great iron hoops across the ice and some were daring each other to slide, scrambling and falling on their backsides, only to get up, giggling, and do it all again.

Men, huddled in knots, played dice or skittles, balls of one kind or another in permanent motion over the frozen surface of the river. Everywhere, there was food and drink, steaming in great copper pans, ladled into tumblers, a smell of rich spice and gin. Ginger, cloves, nutmeg; Jamie found himself grinning from ear to ear as he and the Doctor made their way through the crowds.

Suddenly there was a shout and laughter. A little fellow in ludicrous breeches that were three times too big for him ran across their path, hooting and whinnying like a mad beast. He carried a stick with some kind of bladder attached to the end and proceeded to beat himself over the head with it. Everyone laughed and turned to watch.

The Doctor pulled Jamie to one side. 'Mummers,' he whispered.

Jamie frowned. 'Is that bad?'

The Doctor laughed. 'Not at all. Well, I suppose it depends on your sense of humour.'

The little jester threw up his arms. He was wearing a costume of pale green, embroidered with ribbons, scarves, and laces. He wore gold earrings and there were other rings attached to his clothes as well as scores of bells on his legs so that he jangled whenever he moved.

'Pray silence!' he called. 'For the Lord of Misrule!'

Another man emerged from a tent, wearing a paper crown and fluttering coloured handkerchiefs in both hands. Behind him came a man on a hobbyhorse, a drummer, a piper, and several figures who looked very like Robin Hood and his Merry Men.

'What's it all about?' asked Jamie in some bewilderment.

The Doctor stuck out his lip in mock seriousness. 'Being silly, I think. These poor people have been through an awful lot lately. They're letting their hair down. And,' he said, slipping away into the throng, 'I think we should join them.'

Jamie followed after him, passing straight through the mummers' pageant. The Doctor was already at a stall, buying what looked like a fruitcake. He tore it in half and gave the larger portion to Jamie, grinning and stuffing his share into his mouth.

'Now eat that up and we'll find ourselves something to drink.'

Jamie suddenly felt thrilled with excitement, like Christmas when he was a boy. The wintry afternoon was already darkening and, now the snow had gone, the sky was a rich, midnight blue, speckled with stars.

Somewhere a man's rich baritone was singing 'Adam Lies Y'Bounden', a carol Jamie could remember his mother singing as he sat at her side by the hearth at home.

Goodwill seemed to pour out of these people as though,

50

as the Doctor had said, they were throwing off the miseries of the recent conflict.

Jamie saw jugglers, a performing monkey on a striped pedestal, and something that looked very like a primitive Punch and Judy show with Italian marionettes executing a strange, wild dance.

He caught up with the Doctor at another stall and this time he was handed a cup of steaming liquor. The Doctor sipped his drink and gave a little burp.

'Oh, I say,' he murmured. 'It's rather potent, isn't it?'

Jamie was cold and took a deep draught of the stuff. He felt immediately warmed and not a little woozy, turning to see a great burly man who seemed to be swallowing hot coals.

'Look at that!' he cried excitedly.

The Doctor turned and clapped his hands appreciatively as the man placed a coal on his tongue and then a raw oyster upon that. His assistant then placed bellows in the man's mouth and pumped air into him until tiny flames and sparks whooshed from between his lips.

The crowd were astonished and delighted and then the fire-eater opened his mouth and spat the oyster neatly into his hand.

'He's cooked it!' said the Doctor, clapping again. 'Bravo!'

Jamie shook his head. 'Aye. But I wouldn't want to eat it.'

The Doctor smiled and then they were off again, laughing and talking at the tops of their voices.

In the warmth of the World Turn'd Upside Down, the atmosphere was very different. The chill of the weather seemed to have crept like a living thing into the interior of Kemp's inn, settling over the groups of long-faced customers, most of whom were staring either into their tankards or into space. Their voices were lowered to a steady mumble, like the drone of sleepy bees.

The place itself was rather cheerfully designed, a reddish-brown colour that was made almost amber by the multitude of beer stains that covered the walls. The ceiling was supported by thick oak pillars which branched out into beams. Stools and tables were scattered haphazardly about and candles, set in great, wax-covered pots, were everywhere.

William Kemp stood behind the small wooden bar, indistinguishable from any landlord in any age, his mean face settled on his hand, staring ahead.

Ben drained a tumbler of rum and looked about warily. He and Polly were sitting in a little nook by the blazing hearth and the flickering flames lent their faces a warm, orange glow.

'Blimey, Pol,' said Ben under his breath. 'I'm glad this place isn't my local. I've never seen such a miserable lot.'

Polly gazed around the cramped, dark room and sighed. 'Don't forget they've been fighting a war, Ben. The Doctor said loyalties were divided. It must've been hard on all of them.' She frowned and looked down. 'I never really thought about it like that before.'

Ben shrugged and lined up his next tot of rum. 'Well, it's still a bit of a muddle to me. Cavaliers and Roundheads.' His face brightened and cracked into a wide grin. "Ere!' he cried. 'If we're lucky we might see them cut old King Charlie's head off!'

The inn went suddenly and devastatingly quiet. Like little lamps springing into life, several pairs of eyes suddenly widened and scrutinised them closely.

Kemp straightened up and stared directly at them, his eyes narrowing. He seemed to think deeply for a moment and then, with a glance back at Ben and Polly, he disappeared into the back of the inn.

'Ben!' hissed Polly between clenched teeth.

The young sailor pulled a face. 'Why do I suddenly feel like

I'm in a western?' he said mournfully.

Polly grasped his hand under the table. 'You clot! Keep your voice down. We don't know what year it is, remember? We could be years off the King's execution. And you might be speaking treason.'

Ben slid the tumbler of rum away from himself. 'Sorry, love. It's the booze. Always gets me a bit lively.'

Polly gave him her most reassuring smile. 'Yes, well go easy. We have to get back to the TARDIS soon to meet the others. And I'm not carrying you back half cut.'

Ben gave a throaty chuckle and winked. 'Not half as cut as the King, eh, Duchess?' he whispered.

Polly laughed in spite of herself and returned her attention to the flagon of ale on the table before her. Neither noticed Kemp and the slim figure of Christopher Whyte as they entered the room.

Kemp pointed towards Ben and Polly. 'There. That's them.'

Whyte examined the newcomers. 'They're not regulars of yours?'

Kemp shook his head. 'Never seen 'em before.'

Shrugging, Whyte turned to go back up the stairs to the room above the inn. 'Well, it may be nothing. I shall consult with Sir John.' He gave Kemp a small, tight smile. 'You did well to bring this to our attention, Kemp. Thank you.'

Kemp gave an obsequious little bow and made his way back to the bar. He watched Ben and Polly warily. They were odd-looking all right, he thought, odd enough to be friends of Noll Cromwell or those stinking Levellers. What reward might be his if they turned out to be Parliamentarian spies?

The brisk December wind was still whistling around the weathered stonework of the Commons as Colonel Pride struggled wearily onto his horse.

Lord Grey of Groby, already mounted, was slumped in his saddle, his face a mask of weighty responsibility. They were alone now, the ranks of troopers having been finally dismissed as the winter sun sank low over the rooftops.

Pride turned his face to the drifts of snow which draped the entrance like dustsheets. 'I shall return tomorrow,' he said at last. 'Our work is not yet done.'

Grey spoke without looking up. 'What news of Cromwell?'

Pride fastened the clasp of his cloak around his neck. 'He's returning from the North. I dare say today's events will not displease him.'

Grey nodded to himself. The cold was stinging his cheeks and he longed to rest his bones in his own bed, but there was a question he knew he had to ask of Pride. 'Well, Thomas,' he said, rising in his saddle. 'What now?'

Pride looked up, his milky eyes full of cold purpose. 'Now, My Lord? Now we must draw up a charge against the King so that the remains of this Parliament might vote it through.'

Grey shook his head with infinite sadness. 'A charge? What charge can we levy against our monarch?'

There was a sudden increase in the violence of the wind, as though a bottled tempest had been unleashed. Grey struggled to hold on to his hat and craned his neck as two horsemen appeared quite suddenly out of the wintry shadows.

The first was a young captain of perhaps twenty-five whom Grey knew to be Thomas Culpeper. The other, much older, spoke in a voice ringing with authority.

'We must cease to regard him as our monarch, My Lord.'

The speaker's horse clopped slowly forward, revealing its uniformed rider in the failing light of dusk. He was a stocky, powerful-looking man with a ruddy complexion and thinning, shoulder-length hair. His nose was bulbous and as warty as the rest of his skin but his brilliant-blue eyes marked him as very much out of the common.

'General Cromwell!' gasped Grey.

Cromwell nodded in greeting and turned in his saddle towards Pride. 'It is done then, Colonel?'

'Aye, General.'

Cromwell gave a small, affirmative grunt. 'Though I was not acquainted with this plan, I'm glad of it,' he said, unconsciously echoing Fairfax's prediction. 'This dissembling Parliament will not stand in the way of justice a moment longer.' He stared into space and the freezing wind blew his hair back off his high forehead. 'You were speaking of a charge, My Lord of Groby?' he said finally.

Grey nodded.

Cromwell raised himself up as though about to address Parliament itself. 'This King has waged a wicked war against his fellow countrymen. He has sought to rule as a tyrant. Charles Stuart must stand trial for nothing less than treason.'

Grey, Pride, and Culpeper were silent but Cromwell's florid face had taken on a fiery zeal. When he spoke again it was in a hoarse, dangerous whisper. 'I tell you this. We will cut off this King's head. Aye, with the crown upon it.'

They remained in silence for a long, terrible moment as though the hand of Death itself had closed around them. Then Cromwell turned his horse away and disappeared into the dusk.

The mist that covered the Thames was thickening as the Doctor and Jamie made their way towards the TARDIS. It was a little after sunset and already quite dark but the Doctor didn't seem to mind. He had contrived to fix a wreath of holly and mistletoe around his head and, as he skipped happily along the embankment, he looked for all the world like some ancient woodland spirit come to life. He rubbed his numbed hands together and hummed to himself a little tunelessly.

'Oh, I did enjoy that, Jamie,' he cried. 'Just the tonic we needed, wouldn't you say?'

Jamie, who was still feeling the effects of his festive drink, smiled and nodded. 'Aye. But we'd better hurry along. We're late as it is.'

The Doctor shivered and pulled his cloak tightly around his throat. 'Yes. I wonder what Ben and Polly have been getting up to. I hope they're not too tired. We have an appointment with our friend Scrope, remember?'

'I'm not going to forget a fellow like him,' said Jamie with a laugh.

As they began to move off, a bulky figure appeared out of the mist and blocked their path. He carried a vicious-looking pikestaff and was dressed in some kind of watchman's uniform, black tunic and breeches with a wide, plain white collar and big stovepipe hat jammed on to his head. His piggy eyes were screwed up in a frown of permanent suspicion.

'Now then,' he grunted, his three chins wobbling like a turkey's wattle. 'What do we have here?'

The Doctor looked worried. 'Oh, lor. The law.' He fixed a cheery grin on to his face. 'I beg your pardon?'

The newcomer looked the little man up and down. 'There's been a lot of queer things happens in this city of late. And I've been told to keep me eyes peeled for anything out of the common.'

'Well, we may be uncommon,' said the Doctor with a small smile, 'but there's nothing odd about us.'

'That's right,' chimed in Jamie. 'What is he, Doctor? A sheriff?'

'Something like that,' said the Doctor without switching off his smile. He pulled himself up to his full, not very considerable height and peered at the watchman. 'Now look here, my good fellow. We're late for an appointment.'

'An appointment?'

Jamie put on his most superior expression. 'Aye. We're meeting friends and then we have to see someone. On important matters of state.'

The watchman cocked his head to one side. 'You're a Scot, are you?'

Jamie folded his arms proudly. 'That I am.'

The Doctor sighed. 'Oh, dear.'

The watchman nodded to himself. 'I think you two'd better come with me.'

Holding up his hands in protest, the Doctor began to look about for a quick exit. 'Now don't do anything hasty. We're perfectly respectable.'

The watchman was decidedly unconvinced. He lowered his pikestaff so that the blade was uncomfortably close to the Doctor's throat. 'What's this important state business then?'

The Doctor hesitated a fraction too long and Jamie blurted out, 'We're to see Mr Nathaniel Scrope.'

The watchman looked at him as if he were mad and then burst out laughing, his florid smile widening like the spread of melting fat in a pan. 'Are you now?' he chuckled. 'Well, you come along with me and we'll see if we can't find Mr Scrope for you.'

The Doctor almost stamped his feet in frustration. 'But you don't understand,' he pleaded. 'Mr Scrope is engaged on vital Parliamentary matters!'

'Hold your tongue!' barked the watchman. 'Are you lunatic? Nat Scrope's a saltpetre man.'

'A what?'

'A saltpetre man!' shouted the watchman. 'He's paid to dig up the privies and chicken runs.'

Jamie frowned. 'That explains why he smells so bad.'

'Saltpetre, you say?' said the Doctor.

The watchman nodded. 'Of course. For the gunpowder. There's never enough.' He laughed again. 'Aye, that's state business, for sure!' He moved his pikestaff so it threatened both Jamie and the Doctor. 'Now move!'

The time travellers began to shuffle away from the river, their feet sinking deep into the snow drifts.

The Doctor held his hands above his head and sighed deeply. 'So much for our friends in high places.'

As the shadows had lengthened, the atmosphere in the inn improved considerably. The fire in the grate had been stoked up to huge proportions and an assortment of people warmed themselves around it. A couple of mangy-looking dogs had wandered inside and were snuffling under the tables in search of scraps and there was a not unpleasant haze of pipe smoke hanging in the air. Above all, there was chatter, some about the activity outside Parliament, some concerned with more mundane matters.

Polly tried to listen in as discreetly as she could while Ben sat by her side, sinking slowly into warm, rum-induced oblivion.

Turning away from the fire, Polly smiled and shook her head as she took in the slack, distant look on her companion's boyish face. 'I can't believe we've wasted the whole day in here,' she said with a sigh.

Ben let out a short chuckle and patted her hand affectionately. 'Don't fuss, Pol.'

She glanced over his shoulder and out of the mullioned window. She could see little in the darkness, just a few cold citizens struggling home. 'It's not everyone who gets a chance to walk around their own history. And what do we do? Spend the afternoon in the pub!'

Examining his empty glass, Ben shrugged. 'Well, it's a little bit of normality, innit, Duchess? You have to admit, it's not often we get to do something like this.'

Polly smiled. 'No. No, I suppose not. Anyway, drink up, you. It's time we were on our way.'

Ben nodded and sat up, disguising a burp with the back of his hand. He tossed a few coins onto the table and looked up at Polly. 'D'you reckon that's enough?'

'Probably the heaviest tip they've ever had,' said Polly, edging around the table and heading for the door.

Ben pulled on his cloak. 'I've always fancied running a pub.'

Polly opened the door of the inn and stepped out into the wintry darkness. Ben stopped her on the threshold. "Ere!' he cried happily. 'Maybe I could buy this one now and pick up the deeds when we get back to 1966.'

Laughing, Polly wagged her finger at him. 'I'm sure the Doctor would have something to say about that!'

They stepped outside. The narrow street seemed almost unnaturally peaceful under its thick blanket of snow. It was unlit save for the light spilling through the door of the inn and, with its pools of blue shadow under the drifts, it looked more like a pathway through a dark wood than a main thoroughfare.

Ben pointed along the street. 'That way, innit?'

As they moved off, one of the shadows on the wall of the inn detached itself and stood, breathing quietly, nearby. It was the same leathery-faced individual who had followed them earlier.

He watched as the couple began to make their way up the street. In his hand he carried a heavy cosh, a kind of cloth bag packed tight with hard sand. He tested its weight and slapped it against his palm, then cursed as it stung his skin.

Just as he was about to follow Ben and Polly, three other

men appeared from around the corner. All were burly and dressed in heavy winter coats which muffled their faces.

Ben and Polly stopped in their tracks, warily eyeing the strangers. Ben glanced quickly around and indicated that Polly should move behind him.

'All right, Pol,' he muttered out of the side of his mouth, 'don't panic. Let's see if we can make it back to the pub.'

The three men began to approach them and Ben immediately positioned himself in front of his friend. Polly let out a little shriek as the first of the men revealed a vicious-looking club from inside his coat, which he proceeded to swing to and fro like a pendulum.

Ben looked behind him and was just working out the odds of reaching the tantalisingly close door of Kemp's inn when the man with the club rushed at him.

Ben neatly sidestepped and tripped him up, sending him crashing into the snow. The second man ran across, threw himself at Ben, and landed a solid punch on his jaw. Ben staggered and fell to his knees.

'Run, Pol!' he gasped, as the first man came at him again, spitting snow and mud from his mouth and swinging the club high above his head.

'Not likely!' shouted Polly, hurling herself at Ben's attacker. She leapt onto his back and tried to wrestle the club from his hand but the third man dragged her off and pinioned her arms behind her back.

She called out for help just as the first man cracked Ben behind the ear with his club.

Ben felt a painful nausea rise in his belly and a white flash, like distant summer lightning, dazzle his eyes.

Just then, the leathery-faced man ran out from his hiding place, waving his own cosh and shouting for help.

Sensing that their game was up, the three attackers began

to withdraw, dragging Polly with them. She tried to cry out but a big, dirty hand was clamped over her mouth.

Ben struggled to his feet and then collapsed senseless, his mouth and nose slopping into the wet ground.

The three men moved off with Polly. She dug her heels into the soft ground, leaving furrows in the snow, struggling desperately. She could smell tobacco on her abductor's thick fingers and tried in vain to sink her teeth into his tough flesh.

In the blink of an eye, however, the three men had succeeded in spiriting her away.

Ben's rescuer watched them go and then strode swiftly towards the sailor, helping him to sit up.

'Are you well, mate?' he asked in a thick, West Country accent.

Ben tried to focus on the newcomer's tanned face but the image kept swimming in and out of focus. 'Polly…' he croaked. 'They've taken Polly. Help… me.'

The man patted Ben on the head as he sank back into unconsciousness. 'Don't you fret, my friend. You stick with Isaac Ashdown. All will be peachy. Just peachy.'

He smiled strangely and began to drag Ben to his feet.

Frances Kemp slipped out of the inn, her angelic features disguised beneath a long, grey, hooded cloak. Her cheeks were flushed from an evening spent helping her mother by the kitchen fire but there was an altogether more intangible warmth burning inside her. Something that made her forget the chill of the night altogether.

She made her way swiftly through the maze of narrow alleys which led off the main street, until she approached the baker's shop she knew so well.

Ever since she had been old enough, she had carried a hefty sack of flour from the shop to the inn twice weekly. Once it had been an onerous task, staggering back through the filthy lanes in all weathers, but now Frances did it with a glad heart.

Making her way around to the back of the darkened shop, she stood at the door and craned her neck to see the upstairs windows. One long, diamond-patterned pane was aglow with candlelight from within.

Frances bent down and, with her ungloved hands, pressed some snow together to form a ball. She carefully aimed it at the window and looked around quickly. Then she threw it and winced as it made a louder-than-expected thud on the leaded glass. Nothing happened.

She was preparing to throw another snowball when there was a noise just inside the shop and the heavy back door was opened.

A figure stood framed in the doorway for a moment and then two arms emerged and dragged Frances inside into a fervent embrace.

'Oh, Tom!' cried Frances ecstatically. 'Tom! Is it really you?'

The young man crushing her in his arms was a tall and striking figure. His face was strong and handsome with neat blond brows and grey eyes. His hair was cut quite short for the time, just curling under his ears.

'Yes, my little dove, it's me,' murmured Tom Culpeper, grinning.

Frances planted kisses on his hands and face. 'But when did you return? Your father told me this afternoon that they did not expect you back for a week!'

Tom clasped his hands over hers and pressed them to his chest. 'All is changing, Frances. The general brought me back with him. Something… something is afoot here in town.'

Frances leaned her face close to his, revelling in the warmth from his body. 'Whatever is happening, I am glad it has brought you back to me.'

Tom grinned again and kissed her. They gazed into each other's eyes until he finally spoke again. 'Does he know yet?'

Frances shook her head. 'Nor will he if God's willing.'

Tom let their hands drop. 'But he must one day, my dear. I mean to marry you. I am proud of you. I will not have this thing done in a corner.'

Looking down sadly, Frances's face was made even more pale and lovely in the soft glow of the candle. 'There is only one way you could earn my father's favour Tom,' she said quietly.

Tom looked long and hard at the woman he loved and then sighed heavily. Then he gathered Frances once again into his arms. They kissed with the passion of long-separated sweethearts until the candle flame sputtered and died.

The night sky was rolling over and over, the stars cartwheeling like a projection in a planetarium.

Ben looked up, vaguely aware that he was lying on his back on a broad, flat, wooden floor. The only light, a flaring orange glow, came from a flickering torch close by.

He knew he was outside and there was a strong odour of tar and salt. Trying to sit up, he felt nausea overwhelm him and a blinding pain leapt across his eyes.

Then there was a terrible drowsiness. If he could only sleep, he thought fuzzily, then everything would be peachy. Just peachy...

As he slipped into sleep once more, his instincts told him that something was very wrong. The wooden floor beneath him was rocking slowly back and forth...

The leathery-faced Isaac Ashdown appeared out of the darkness with a rough blanket. He threw it over Ben, smiled grimly and then sat back on the deck of the ship, a barrel at his back, looking over at the distant lights of London. The sound of the sea swell was oddly comforting.

Ashdown glanced down at Ben and gave a humourless chuckle. 'Well, my friend,' he muttered, 'that's the last either of us'll be seeing of old London for a while.'

Captain Stanislaus's ship ploughed on into the black night.

CHAPTER
3

Much to her surprise, Polly did not find herself taken to some den of Stuart iniquity, sold into slavery or, as she had half feared and half expected, burnt as a witch. Instead she was ferried around the corner of the inn, taken through the now-empty kitchen and upstairs to the chamber where Sir John Copper and Christopher Whyte sat alone.

As she was dragged in and pushed roughly down into a chair, she quickly looked about for an escape route. But the room was now so dark that she could make out little except the candlelit features of her captors.

The leader of the thugs who'd kidnapped her exchanged some whispered words with Copper and then held out his hand, palm upward.

Copper slid some coins over the table. The three men looked at Polly, laughed to themselves and, bending their burly frames, exited through the low door.

'What on earth do you think you're doing?' cried Polly indignantly.

Copper held up a neatly manicured hand. 'Patience, mistress,' he purred. 'We mean you no ill.'

'Oh really?' she almost shrieked. 'What about my friend back there?'

'He sustained a bump on the head, I gather. He'll be all right.'

Polly glared at him. 'Is that a professional opinion?'

Christopher Whyte leaned forward across the table and smiled at her. Despite herself, Polly couldn't help but feel slightly reassured by the handsome stranger.

'What's your name?' he asked gently.

'Why do you want to know?' She hoped she sounded defensive and strong but was rather afraid the question sounded almost flirtatious.

Copper steepled his fingers and looked up at the darkened eaves. 'You were overheard in the inn discussing... certain matters. Matters of interest to us.' He turned his cold eyes onto Polly. 'Now, what is your name?'

She sighed. It was going to be a long night. 'Polly. Polly Wright.' She smoothed back her hair with one hand.

Whyte's grin grew wider and he unconsciously ran his hand through his own long hair, as though preening himself.

Copper's face remained impassive. He leaned forward and pointed his finger at Polly in an uncompromisingly hostile manner. 'Now, Mistress Polly, you will tell us all you know about the King and exactly when Parliament intends to cut off his head!'

Jamie sat with his head sunk low on his chest, wondering why he seemed to spend an inordinate amount of time in dungeons of one sort or another.

The latest was an incredibly cramped affair of brown stone walls and ceiling that ran with unappealing, slimy green deposits. There were heaps of filthy straw clustered in the corners and big iron rings projecting from the walls themselves, their purpose unknown, their fastenings stained with rusty water.

The Doctor, who was sitting against the opposite wall

playing a repetitive tune on his recorder, had explained that the damp was caused by their cell's proximity to the river.

Jamie thought briefly of the happy time they had so recently spent on the same river, of the colourful mummers and the fire-eater. Then his thoughts drifted off into contemplation of warmth in general and of his own cosy, comfortable room back in the TARDIS.

With a start, he suddenly realised that he had begun to consider the eccentric time machine his home. He had grown used to its winding network of corridors and the surprises its infinite size had to offer. Polly, Ben, and the Doctor were his family now, even if they sometimes annoyed him, as families were wont to do.

He glanced over at the little man, who seemed entirely unconcerned at their current predicament. 'I dinnae believe this, Doctor,' he complained with a wry smile. 'We seem to get locked up everywhere we go.'

The Doctor tootled on his recorder. 'Occupational hazard,' he muttered between notes. 'They're just a bit jumpy.'

Jamie stood up and began pacing up and down the little cell. It was so small that it was hardly worth the effort. 'But why pick on us?'

The Doctor pocketed his recorder and stared up at the ceiling. 'I suppose we might look a bit unusual,' he conceded. 'And then there's the question of your nationality.'

Jamie frowned. 'What d'you mean?'

'Well, you see, the Scots fought on the King's side for much of the conflict. They've recently changed their minds, according to the book.'

He fished out the little volume and flicked rapidly through its pages. Jamie caught a glimpse of the yellowed pages with their faded colour plates showing horsemen, musketeers, and battling troopers. The Doctor nodded. 'Yes. The Scots have changed sides.' He clapped the book shut and looked up at Jamie worriedly. 'And nobody likes a turncoat, if you see what I mean.'

'I'm no turncoat!' protested Jamie.

'I know that,' said the Doctor, patiently 'but our captors don't.'

'So the English don't trust us?'

'In a nutshell, yes.'

Jamie smiled. 'Just like old times.'

Footsteps began to echo in the corridor beyond and then the door rattled as a key was slid into its massive iron lock.

Jamie and the Doctor looked up as the watchman slid his bulk through the narrow door, panting and gasping with the effort.

'Why did I put 'em here, I ask?' he muttered. 'I'm a fool to meself. Can't expect to go getting into these here cells if I care not how many gooseberry creams I have.' His little lecture to himself over, the watchman straightened up and fixed his prisoners with a baleful glare.

Behind him came a small, hatchet-faced man with brutally cropped hair and a large, livid scar across his forehead. He slipped easily and quickly through the door like a ferret.

'Well, my fine fellows,' said the watchman. 'I fear we've had no luck with your friend Master Scrope.'

'Scrope, no,' said his companion with a strange, high-pitched giggle.

'But there's another gentleman here who wants to ask you a few questions.'

The cropped-haired man moved forward, brandishing a long and vicious-looking knife. 'Questions, yes,' he hissed, grinning all over his sinister face.

The Doctor and Jamie exchanged worried glances.

*

In the room above the inn, Polly was beginning to feel the effects of her afternoon spent with Ben. A kind of drowsy numbness was warming the back of her skull and she wanted nothing so much as to lie back in her chair in the dark room and go to sleep.

Her captors seemed amiable enough and, apart from their incessant questions, didn't seem to constitute too much of a threat. She had to admit she quite enjoyed sparring with the younger one. In fact, if she'd run into him back at the Inferno Club in Chelsea, she might have considered him quite a dish.

Smiling to herself at this incongruous thought, she forced herself to concentrate and began again. 'Look, I've told you. We were just talking. I don't know anything about any plots, real or imagined.'

Copper's eyes narrowed. 'Do not play pell-mell with us, mistress. Your companion was heard to say something about cutting off His Majesty's head.'

Polly thought quickly. 'Well... isn't that what they're bound to do? I mean, there were soldiers outside Parliament this morning turning people away. Everyone knows something's going on.'

Copper seemed to consider this.

Whyte flashed her his most winning smile. 'Your speech is strange, Mistress Polly. Where are you from?'

'Chelsea, as it happens. But I've... I've been away. Out of the country, you might say.'

Copper laid a finger to his lip and tapped it thoughtfully, then turned to his companion. 'She's no common woman.'

'Indeed, no,' purred Whyte.

Copper turned back to Polly. 'Do you have contacts in France? With the Queen, perhaps?'

Polly sighed. 'I wish I did. She might get me out of here. But, no. I've been travelling some time. Great distances.'

'Have you indeed?' said Copper. He inclined his head towards Whyte and they spoke in whispers for several moments, the older man occasionally nodding.

'Well, Mistress Polly,' he said at last. 'I have decided to let you go.'

'That's very magnanimous of you,' said Polly sharply.

'But I would advise you and your friend to keep your tongues still in future. These are dangerous times.'

Polly stood up. 'You're telling me. What did you do with Ben?'

Whyte frowned. 'Your companion? Nothing. He was left where he fell.'

Polly was appalled. 'What? I thought you must have kidnapped him too!'

'Nay, my dear,' said Whyte, genuinely concerned. 'I'm sorry.'

Polly ran to the doorway. 'I've got to find him!' she cried, throwing open the door and clattering downstairs to the inn.

Copper looked at Whyte. 'Well, Chris?'

Whyte smiled and held up his hands. 'She's a strange one, indeed. But harmless, I'm sure of it.'

Copper stroked his silvery beard. 'Perhaps, but I think it can do no harm to follow her for a while.' He nodded towards the door.

Whyte picked up his hat. 'It will not be an onerous task,' he said, bowing low and then slipping out of the door after Polly.

Copper crossed to the window and sat down on the sill. He saw Polly emerge into the street and begin to look wildly around. Then Whyte stole outside and concealed himself within a doorway, his attention fixed on Polly.

Copper grunted, satisfied, and turned back to the table and the sheaf of documents that covered its surface. On the uppermost one was drawn a large, detailed map of a fortified building, the thin body of water that snaked by it etched out in thick black ink.

'It's the bull's pizzle for you!' laughed the watchman. 'Or maybe the Water House.' He swung round to face his small, scarred jailer companion. 'What say you, Jem? Or are such things too good for 'em?'

The man with the knife giggled horribly. 'Too good for 'em, yes,' he repeated.

The Doctor was practically hopping with frustration. He stood at Jamie's side while Jem the jailer threatened the young Scot with the vicious-looking blade.

'Look—' began the Doctor.

''E can speak for 'isself, can't 'e?' spat the jailer, his yellowy eyes blazing.

The Doctor held up his hands. 'Well, naturally. But, you know, with all the confusion…'

The jailer frowned, and his brows sank unpleasantly over his eyes. 'Confusion? Who are you anyway?'

'I'm… I'm his doctor,' said the Doctor sheepishly.

The watchman pressed his fat body back against the door of the cell. 'It's not catching, is it?'

'No, no,' smiled the Doctor, 'nothing like that.'

'Right, then. Shut your face,' said the jailer, turning back to Jamie. 'Now then, master Scotchman. You tell me what you're doing in London?'

Jamie shot a look of desperate appeal at the Doctor but the little man just shrugged helplessly, raising his hands, palms upward.

'There's nothing to tell,' announced Jamie boldly. 'We're just… visiting.'

'Visiting?' spat the jailer. 'I say you're a deserter!'

'No!'

But the jailer pressed on. 'Couldn't stomach your nasty Scots friends making up with Parliament. That's it, isn't it?'

Jamie was angry now. 'No!' he bellowed. 'I'm no deserter!'

The watchman came forward, his chins wobbling excitedly. 'But you admit you're a soldier?'

'Look—' said the Doctor again.

'Silence!' screamed the jailer. He peered at Jamie. 'Are you a soldier?'

Jamie shifted his weight and looked down at his boots. 'I... I was.'

'Oh, Jamie,' said the Doctor sadly.

The jailer stood up straight and fixed Jamie with a penetrating stare. 'Was?'

Jamie shook his head. 'Och, it's too difficult to explain. You'd never believe me, anyway.'

'That's for me to decide, my young buck,' said the jailer quietly.

The watchman took the knife from him and laid it against the bare flesh of Jamie's throat as though taking his turn at interrogation was part of the fun. 'You heard the gentleman. Explain yourself!'

Jamie shot another desperate look at the Doctor. 'I—'

The jailer spun round and glared at the Doctor. 'Get that little one out of here!' he roared. 'I want to talk to the Scotsman alone.'

The watchman began to bustle the protesting Doctor from the cell.

The jailer turned back to Jamie and the young man recoiled from his sour breath. 'Now then?'

Jamie sighed. 'I fought... I was fighting for the Prince?'

'Which Prince? Prince Rupert?'

'No,' said Jamie carefully. 'Prince Charles.'

The jailer frowned, causing deep furrows to spring up on

his pockmarked forehead. 'The Kings son!' he said. 'Were you part of his lifeguard?'

Jamie shook his head wearily. 'No. You've got it all wrong. Another Prince Charles. One that... that hasn't been born yet.'

The jailer knew he should have had some smart retort to that one but all he could think to say was 'Eh?'

The watchman, who had opened the door of the cell and was holding the Doctor by the scruff of the neck, turned. 'What did he say?'

The Doctor glanced at Jamie, gave a quick smile, and then extricated himself from the watchman's grip. With astonishing speed, he raced across the room to stand by Jamie's side and began to speak rapidly in a bizarre Scandinavian accent.

'Ah! The secret is out, my boy,' he announced. 'We will have to tell them now!'

The jailer scowled. 'What secret?'

'The secret of second sight,' cried the Doctor, warming to his theme. 'My friend, the McCrimmon of... er, Culloden, is a powerful seer. He can foretell the future. He can see how the winding pathways of the future may twist and turn!'

The watchman raised a fat, threatening fist. 'What are you on about?'

The Doctor stood behind Jamie and raised his arms above the young man's head. 'Do you not see, man?' he said appealingly. 'The McCrimmon can tell you what fate will befall this warring land of yours. He can tell you whether the forces of Parliament will ultimately be victorious. You must listen to him!' He poked Jamie in the back. 'Isn't that right, McCrimmon?'

Jamie frowned. 'Eh? Oh. Aye.' At once he assumed a glassy expression and moaned softly as though possessed. To add to the effect he raised his hands and began to wiggle his fingers.

The jailer moved closer again. 'What trickery is this?'

'Tell us something, then', said the watchman, folding his arms and grinning. 'If you're so clever.'

The Doctor cleared his throat and thought desperately of the little book concealed in his pocket. What had he seen there that might be useful? He nodded to himself then bent his lips to Jamie's ear. 'Oh, great McCrimmon,' he whispered. 'Tell us! Tell us of the time to come!'

Jamie rolled his head from side to side and began to breathe in short, gulping rasps, the way he had once seen a wise woman in the Highlands behave. Finally, he whispered in the Doctor's ear and the little man straightened up, smiling.

'Well?' said the jailer.

The Doctor clasped his hands over his chest and spoke with as much gravitas as he could muster. 'The McCrimmon tells me that the King has been moved from his prison on the Isle of Wight and is to stand trial for treason.'

The watchman and the jailer exchanged shocked glances.

'Nobody knows the King's been moved!' hissed the latter.

'The McCrimmon knows!' said the Doctor. 'The McCrimmon knows all.'

The jailer leaned forward, his chin jutting out threateningly. 'Aye. Maybe you know because you're a Royalist spy!'

The watchman, who had been superstitious ever since, as a boy, he'd seen a three-headed lamb delivered on his family's farm, laid a hand on his colleague's shoulder. 'No, no, Jem. Peace. I think we'd better tell someone about this.'

Uneasy, the jailer bit his lip. 'Very well. But who?'

The watchman regarded their two charges with renewed interest. 'I can get a message to John Thurloe,' he mused. 'Who knows? Even General Cromwell may be interested.'

The Doctor's eyes flashed with excitement.

The jailer moved to the door. 'We will return,' he muttered.

The Doctor nodded his head sagely. 'Very well. The McCrimmon and I will await you.'

The two men backed out of the room, the jailer cannoning into the watchman as he squeezed his massive buttocks through the doorway. They both cast final, fearful glances at their prisoners through the little barred window in the door and then, after turning the key in the lock, vanished.

At once the Doctor began to laugh cheerfully and rubbed his hands together. He took out his recorder from his coat pocket and began playing a little jig.

'Oh, Doctor,' lamented Jamie, 'what did you want to go and say all that nonsense for? If they think we're important, we'll never get away.'

The Doctor looked slightly affronted. 'Well, I had to do something, didn't I, Jamie? And I think we'll have a far better chance of pleading our case to Cromwell than to those two thugs. Besides –' he gave a mischievous smile – 'I've always wanted to meet him.'

The standard fell. Fell and was trampled into the mud, its supporting pole snapped beneath the feet of the advancing Roundhead force. Its motto was obscured but its pictures still plain enough: a Bible, the countryside, a sword, a laurel wreath, a crown...

They swept forward, pikes bristling like huge wooden fangs before them, bellowing their battle cry, as men seethed and fought around them.

Their armour glinted dully in the daylight, dazzling those they faced whose eyes were already confused by the riot of colour. Here, the broad orange sashes that were tied around the soldiers' waists. There, the belching black smoke of exploding powder kegs. Elsewhere, the livid crimson of spilled blood, soaking into the Yorkshire earth.

Hot now it was. Summery hot with woodsmoke smells mingling with the stink of the dog daisies that covered the field of battle.

The constant thrum-thrum of the drums was like blood pounding in the ears. Or the sound of the troopers' mud-caked boots as they ran at full pelt across the field.

Horses thundered by, musket shots rang out, and the horses fell, whinnying in pain, crashing to the hard soil, crushing their riders.

And now here was a new sound. Unexpected, eerie, almost beautiful. It was singing. The Roundheads were singing psalms as their dragoons roared into the Royalist flank.

The boy stepped bravely forward, facing the Roundhead troopers, the red sash around his waist a proud symbol of his Royalist allegiance. He thrust his pike forward and charged, his mouth stretching into an 'O', his throat already hoarse from shouting.

The musket ball seared the air as though it were a comet, striking the boy cleanly between the eyes. He stood stock still for a moment, his senses too shocked to realise that he was already dead.

The pike slid from his grip and he toppled backward into the mud. At once, the troopers advanced over him, their feet smashing his delicate face into bloodied pulp...

William Kemp jerked awake and almost fell out of the narrow bed. He was breathing as though he'd run a mile and his calico nightshirt was drenched in sweat.

He put his head in his hands and tried to focus his eyes in the pitch-dark room.

Beside him, Sarah slept on, but Kemp could see nothing but the boy's face. The boy from the dream. His own boy, Arthur.

He had been a brave little soldier – all who knew him had said – and had joined the King's side without a moment's hesitation, despite his youth. His commander had been a man called Sir Harry Cooke who had nothing but praise for the young Kemp, something that filled his father with pride.

But it had all come to an end. All of it. On a field called Marston Moor, hundreds of miles from home.

The Roundhead musket ball had taken away Kemp's son but created something else. Inside William Kemp, a hard, black ball of bitter poison had begun to grow.

Pitch and roll... pitch and roll.

As dawn broke, Ben slept on, seemingly oblivious of the sickening, lurching movement of the ship in the heaving winter sea.

Beneath his rough blanket, he turned on his side, his mouth hanging slackly open until, out of nowhere, a torrent of sea water splashed over the ship's rail onto his face.

He woke with a cry, spluttering and gasping, then looked rapidly around, trying to orientate himself.

In quick succession he saw the rolling grey sea, the deck, the full, billowing sails, and the two dozen or so men who were streaming over the ship, working busily at ropes, pumps and stores.

Ben groaned as he recalled the events of the previous night. How on earth had he got himself into this mess? He rubbed his weary brow and sighed.

The leathery-faced Isaac Ashdown walked carefully across the wet deck towards him, a pleasant smile on his tanned face. 'Ah,' he said. 'So now you know, my lad.'

Ben managed to struggle to his feet, despite the dull pain in his head. 'Know? Know what?'

Ashdown shrugged. 'Where you are.'

Ben gave a short, humourless laugh. 'That's pretty obvious, isn't it? Even if I wasn't a sailor.'

Ashdown looked delighted. 'You're a sailor already! That's a novelty indeed. The scum we usually get are somewhat unsuited to life at sea.' He rubbed his chin thoughtfully. 'At first.'

Ben repositioned himself so that his legs were wider apart. Trying to stand upright on the deck was proving difficult. 'You can't force me to stay here, you know,' he shouted above the noise of the spray. 'I haven't taken the Queen's sh – the King's shilling or anything.'

Ashdown clapped him on the shoulder. 'What's your name, son?'

'Ben Jackson.'

'Well, Ben Jackson, don't you fret. Captain Stanislaus was just a bit short for this voyage. I was in charge of... er... recruitment last night. I saw you with your lady and I thought, aye, aye, there's a likely lad if ever the opportunity should come my way. Which, as you know, it did. And you were hardly in a position to refuse, were you now?'

Ben shook his head and scowled as a sharp pain scorched through his brow.

Ashdown smiled kindly. 'You're free to go when we reach land.'

A little reassured, Ben turned his mind to Polly. 'What happened to the girl? The one I was with. Did you see?'

Ashdown looked away evasively. 'Can't say as I did, lad. When I found you, you was lying in the road.'

Ben nodded to himself. 'I have to get back as soon as I can. Anything could've happened to her.' He turned back to Ashdown. 'You say I can get off at our first port of call?'

Ashdown gave a sly smile. 'Aye.'

'And where's that?'

Ashdown began to chuckle. 'Amsterdam,' he said.

*

The London morning was cold and unpleasant, a fine rain blowing in sheets from the river and pocking the snow that still lay all around. The swans and geese that squawked and waddled through St James's Park did not seem overly concerned, however, emerging into the light and sliding comically over the thick sheets of ice that covered the park's waterways. There were cattle, too, huddled together at one end of the park, shifting miserably from hoof to hoof.

Emerging from his hiding place, Christopher Whyte stretched and groaned, feeling the muscles in his back pop and strain. His evening's vigil had been more than a little unpleasant. He had followed the woman Polly around what seemed like half the capital, yet she had seemed to have little idea where she was going.

At first she had made straight for the street outside the inn where her friend had last been seen but, finding nothing, had then run like a mad thing towards a narrow alley some way off. She had waited there for the best part of an hour before giving up and, finding herself near the park, had managed to grab a few hours' sleep in one of the small gardeners' shelters.

Whyte had followed at a discreet distance. More than once he had wanted to intercede, to offer her food and a comfortable lodging for the night, but his job was to keep an eye on the woman, not woo her. She might yet prove to know more than she was saying and no interference could be tolerated with Copper's plans at such an advanced stage.

Rubbing his stiff neck, Whyte kept a weather eye on the sleeping Polly and tried to ignore his grumbling belly. He had stayed awake much of the night, as keen to avoid the attentions of the young Ganymedes who frequented the park as to ensure Polly did not elude him.

He had spent much of this time contemplating the current situation. Unlike Sir John Copper, he was no disgruntled

Parliamentarian. He had fought bravely for the King throughout the conflict as a captain. Wounded at the Battle of Edgehill, he had carried on the Royalist cause as best he could, as an agent for His Majesty, travelling incognito about London and bringing back his reports to the Royalist base in Oxford. It was while going about his secretive business that Sir John Copper had approached him, almost as a molly might in the park, thought Whyte with a smile. Though initially suspicious, he had soon warmed to the older man's rhetoric. Copper feared that the army had gone too far, that they would tilt the land into utter chaos unless the sensible thing was done and the King restored to his throne.

To his surprise, Whyte found that not so much separated them as he would have thought. War made strange bedfellows.

On the mildewed bench inside the gardeners' shelter, Polly stirred and Whyte dropped back into the foliage out of sight. The young woman stretched and blinked, then grimaced, obviously recalling where she was.

Swinging her legs off the bench, she got unsteadily to her feet and pulled her cloak tightly around her. Then, with a quick look around, she set off to face the day.

Christopher Whyte waited a few moments and then followed close behind her.

The Doctor threw up his hands in exasperation. 'Do pay attention, Jamie,' he sighed. 'You're supposed to be an oracle.'

'I am?' said Jamie with a frown. 'I thought that was a kind of wee boat.'

'No, no. An oracle. A fount of wisdom. And it'll do us a fat lot of good if Cromwell turns up and finds that you know next to nothing about the Civil Wars.'

Jamie folded his arms defensively. The schoolboy's book lay on the cold stone floor at his feet. 'I know what Polly said.

About the King ruling without Parliament.'

The Doctor gave a soothing smile. 'That's right. And he did it, too. For eleven years until he ran out of money.'

Jamie nodded. 'What did he need the money for?'

The Doctor looked up at the low ceiling of the cell. 'Oh, a war against the Scots.'

Jamie let out a snort of disbelief. 'Hang on, Doctor. I thought you said the Scots were on his side.'

'Yes. But that was later on. This was before the wars broke out.'

Jamie slid glumly down the wall. 'Och, I'll never get it. Why couldn't you be the oracle?'

The Doctor clasped his hands together. 'Yes, well, we weren't fortunate there, were we?'

The cell door rattled and then creaked open, revealing the bulky form of the watchman. He didn't seem keen to come any nearer to his prisoners and looked at them with something like fear. 'Very well, you two,' he said. 'They're ready for you.'

It was, Ben thought, the very definition of a motley crew. Aside from Isaac Ashdown, the rest of the ship's complement seemed united by only one thing: their oddness. There were Moors, Turks, a hook-handed African and a vast, flame-haired Irishman called O'Kane who seemed to put the fear of God into the rest of them.

Most were now assembled in a sweating, heaving line as they pulled with great effort on one of the ship's tarred ropes. With a cry of satisfaction, the topsail they'd been hoisting slotted into place, flapping in the stiff North Sea wind.

At their head squatted Ben and Ashdown, brows speckled with beads of perspiration.

Ben fell back on to the deck with a groan and rubbed his aching arms. Struggling to speak between heaving breaths, he turned to Ashdown. 'What's our cargo, mate?'

The older sailor shrugged. 'Wool. Flour. Suet. Odds and sods.'

Ben let his gaze range over the deck and out across the wild grey sea. 'And the ship is definitely coming back to London?'

'Certainly. Eventually,' said Ashdown with a smile. 'But that's for the captain to decide, ain't it?' He got up and pointed to a thick coil of rope which ran through an iron ring fixed to the side of the ship. ''Ere, grab a hold of that, Ben. And tie it up on the capstan yonder.'

Ben did as he was instructed, hauling on the thick rope and feeling its rough texture against his hands. As he grappled with the rope, he glanced over the ship's rail and his eye caught a name etched carefully into the woodwork of the hull. It was painted gold on black in a highly ornate style that was almost Elizabethan. It said 'Teazer'.

Ben started to laugh, quietly at first and then with increasing force.

Ashdown looked puzzled. 'What ails you?'

Ben laughed loudly. 'Oh, you wouldn't understand, mate. It's a long story. It's pretty ironic, that's all.'

Ashdown frowned. 'What do you mean?'

Ben glanced at the ship's name again and shook his head. 'I've been trying to get back to my ship all this time... This isn't exactly what I had in mind.'

He thought briefly of his own *Teazer*, sleek, grey, metal, the peak of modern twentieth-century naval warfare. How these lads would gasp if she were to appear out of the North Sea fog banks now.

At that moment, a cabin door opened and Captain Stanislaus emerged, wolfishly handsome even in the cold light of the morning.

O'Kane, the Irishman, stood upright and stiffened. 'Captain

on deck!' he yelled.

The entire crew, with the exception of Ben, stood to attention. Ashdown leaned over and jabbed Ben in the stomach.

Realising his folly, Ben straightened up just as Stanislaus walked by him, his red coat flapping in the wind.

He looked right through Ben and walked towards another cabin, pausing on the threshold, blinking in the bleak daylight. He turned back, scanning the crew with cold eyes, and nodded. 'Thank you, Master O'Kane. Carry on.' He tapped gently on the cabin door.

'That's Stanislaus?' whispered Ben.

Ashdown kept his head down. 'Aye,' he hissed out of the corner of his mouth. 'Look busy, or there'll be hell to pay.'

Stanislaus knocked again. 'Mr Godley?' he said, his voice deep, his accent thick and guttural. 'Mr Godley, sir. Are you awake?'

The door opened to reveal an even more exotic sight than the vulpine captain.

Godley emerged, his noble bearing disguised in plain, spartan black. He was carrying a monkey on his shoulder. It was a tiny, spindly thing, all limbs and tail, its bright eyes like beads of blood in its fragile skull. It chittered and scuttled over Godley's shoulder as he stepped out on deck.

Stanislaus recoiled from the pet instantly and took an involuntary step backward as Godley steadied himself on the rolling deck.

'Good day, Captain,' said Godley with a small, tight smile.

Stanislaus nodded. 'I trust you slept well.'

Godley patted his stomach. 'I've never been the best of sailors, I fear.'

The monkey hopped from Godley's shoulder and scampered over the deck towards a tin dish which had been set aside for it. It began to feast on the beef and fish scraps inside the bowl, looking up and down from its food to the crew with nervous speed.

Taking his passenger gently by the arm, Captain Stanislaus began to move towards the stern of the vessel.

'How is all progressing?' asked Godley.

Stanislaus looked around as they walked. He seemed a little more nervous and anxious than before, his head jerking about like Godley's monkey. 'All my communications are favourable, Mr Godley,' he said, struggling to be heard over the sound of the swell.

Godley cocked his head inquisitively. 'And the package?'

'Is safe in Amsterdam,' said the captain. 'Come.'

He steered Godley away and they disappeared around the corner.

A big wave crashed over the deck and Ashdown prodded Ben. 'Come on, my friend. Don't slacken. The captain sees everything.'

Ben frowned. 'What was all that about?'

Ashdown shook his head. 'Best not to know. This is not a ship for inquisitive men.'

'I wonder what they're bringing back from Amsterdam,' said Ben, looking down the length of the ship.

Ashdown shook his head then bent down and busied himself.

Ben smiled. 'Oh, well. Maybe it's just tulips.'

'Please do not say it again, Father,' pleaded the young man. 'I do not think I could stand it.'

Oliver Cromwell pinched the bridge of his bulbous nose and sighed. A very bad, thudding headache was lurking in the back of his brain. 'Say what again, Richard?'

The boy was in his twenties, long-haired and rather thin

with a pale, waxy complexion. He looked appealingly at his father. 'That I… I disappoint you.'

Cromwell looked around him at the spacious, panelled apartment in which he did most of his business. It was a pleasant room, with high windows and a floor tiled in black and white geometric shapes. There was a heavy old globe in the corner, surrounded by books, ledgers, and the masses of papers with which the general had to deal on a daily basis.

Sighing, Cromwell wished that his son were not there to bother him, that he could have a moment of simple, unqualified peace. Normally, the room would be crowded with men. Advisers would be advising, soldiers would be scheming, and John Thurloe, his most trusted aide, would be doing his best to keep the general from drowning under a tide of bureaucratic waffle.

For once, though, the room was empty. Empty save for the thin boy who was proving, as he said, such a disappointment to his father.

Cromwell sank back into his chair and cleared his throat, looking away evasively.

'It is not that, Son,' he said patiently. 'Only that I fear for your future. Look at these.' He rapped the papers strewn over his knee. 'Debts and debts on top of them! How I raised such a profligate spender is quite beyond me.' He closed his eyes and scratched the bristles on his inexpertly shaved chin. 'What do you do all day, Richard?'

'Well—' the boy began.

Cromwell held up his hand. 'Nay, spare me. I do not wish to know the details of your shopping.' He opened his blue eyes and glared at Richard. 'But do it less!' he thundered.

Richard dabbed his mouth with a lace handkerchief and nodded quickly. 'Yes, Father. May I—'

'Yes,' drawled Cromwell wearily. 'Please go.'

Richard bowed and shambled out of the room, his sword, which seemed to hang too low on his belt, scraping over the tiles.

Cromwell sighed and closed his eyes again. What had he done to deserve such a poltroon as an heir. Had his beloved Oliver not died...

But there was no sense in raking all that up again.

He sank back, grateful for the cushions that nursed the painful boil on his buttock.

For a long moment, he saw nothing but darkness beneath his closed eyelids but, gradually, faint images, like translucences in a church window, began to swim into his mind. He was a boy again. A boy, playing in the broad, flat fields of his father's estate in Cambridgeshire. The day was warm and fine, just as the summers of one's childhood always were. He saw again the heat haze sparkling over the crops, the old weather vane creaking, turning stiffly in the breeze. And the young lad with the huge spaniel eyes who had come to visit.

Cromwell had been too young to appreciate the importance of this particular visit and this particular, small, grave-looking boy. To him, he was just another playmate, an eight-year-old come to clash wooden swords with him, or play tag out among the swaying wheat.

There had been whispering in the house for weeks, he recalled, but not a word was spoken to him or his sisters. Not until the day of the visit, and then – oh! – a ceremony of such pomp, young Cromwell thought that Christmas had come early.

The two young boys had sat together by a pond, idly dropping stones into its depths and listening to the lovely, satisfying gloop they made as they entered the water.

Cromwell had smiled at the boy but the newcomer did not smile back. He seemed preoccupied and tense, almost old beyond his years. Trying again, Cromwell opened his coat and produced the puppy which had been a present from his dear mother only weeks before. Surely this would cheer the boy up?

But the boy turned his sad eyes away from Cromwell and looked back towards the large, grey rectangle of the house. He seemed to perk up as a young woman approached, her long, full skirts brushing over the dusty ground.

She scooped the boy up into her arms and he smiled delightedly. 'There now, my boy,' she said. 'It is time for your bed. Say goodbye to Master Oliver.'

The boy frowned and shook his head.

The woman wagged her finger at him. 'Say goodbye, now, Charles.'

He buried his head in her breast and, muffled by her apron, he stammered, 'G-goodbye.'

The nurse smiled, shook her head and gave Cromwell a little wave and turned back towards the house.

Cromwell remembered thinking the boy was very rude indeed.

He had no thought then – how could he? – that one day he would be putting that boy, that prince, on trial for his life.

Opening his eyes, Cromwell found John Thurloe standing before him.

'Yes, John?'

Thurloe, a middle-sized, extremely neat man with a horsy face and sparse beard, gave a little bow. 'They have arrived, General.'

'Who?' frowned Cromwell.

Thurloe coughed into his gloved hand. 'The prisoners. The… er, seer and his doctor.'

Cromwell's face lit up. He felt immensely cheered already. 'Oh! Yes. Yes, bring them in.'

He rubbed his hands together. For a rational, God-fearing man Cromwell was inordinately fond of the mystical. He had recently taken much notice of a wise woman from Cornwall who had predicted that the whole of London would be destroyed by a plague of angry cats within the century. She had been very convincing.

Cromwell adopted his most sagacious-looking pose on the chair and let his chin rest on his hand. No, no, no, too contrived, he thought.

He sat back and opened his legs, resting his hands on the heavily carved arms of the chair. Too regal.

He heard Thurloe returning and made a snap decision to stand by the globe. He set it spinning and then leaned over it, his lower lip jutting out thoughtfully, his hands behind his back.

Thurloe swept in moments later with a young man and a funny-looking fellow with untidy black hair. Both wore long black cloaks and had a somewhat sheepish air about them.

Cromwell looked up and tapped his finger against his chin. 'Well now,' he mused. 'What do we have here?'

The fire was burning a little low in the kitchen grate when Frances Kemp entered the room. She made straight for the range, ignoring the hunched figure of her father, who was staring broodingly into the flames. There was a large tray of ale and cheese on the table before him, covered by a fresh cloth.

Frances set to work at once to revive the fire, twisting to avoid the spits on which four suckling pigs were skewered.

Kemp turned his head and scowled at her. 'Do you not have a word for your father, girl?'

Frances reflected wryly that she had several words for him, but none that he would like. 'Good afternoon,' she said at last.

Kemp grunted. 'A good afternoon is it that sees a king to be put on trial for his life?'

'I meant—'

'I know what you meant,' growled Kemp, hawking up a ball of phlegm and spitting into the fire.

Frances tugged nervously at her knuckles. 'The King is to stand trial, then?'

Kemp nodded and then raised his head a little arrogantly. 'I have it on the best authority.'

Frances looked up at the ceiling. 'From your friends upstairs?'

With sudden and startling ferocity, Kemp leapt to his feet and grabbed his daughter by the front of her dress. He pushed her against the kitchen wall and pressed his face close to hers, his eyes flashing with menace.

'You would be well advised, daughter, to keep all thoughts of my visitors out of your head.' Frances felt herself shaking and cowered from Kemp's wrath. 'Is that understood?' he hissed.

She nodded and Kemp let her go, stumbling to his chair.

Frances rapidly rearranged her clothes just as a bell began to clatter in the corner of the kitchen. Kemp looked up and then shot a dangerous glance at Frances. He got to his feet, picked up the tray, and backed towards the door, exiting without another word.

Frances sat down heavily and rubbed her throat. She felt tender and vulnerable. The funny stinging sensation in her palms told her she was close to tears.

What made everything worse was that she knew it had not always been like this. Her father had always been a supporter of the Crown, of course, but not with this strange, stupid, blinding passion.

He had been a wonderful father, too. Gentle and funny,

quick-witted and popular with his customers and adored by his wife.

But that was before Marston Moor and the loss of his beloved Arthur.

Now William Kemp was like a man possessed by an angry ghost. He could not, would not, spare a kind word for anybody. And gradually life in the inn had changed beyond all recognition.

The wrong kind of person came there now – rough and unsavoury people who didn't care that their landlord spoke not two words to them all evening.

Odd, thought Frances, that it should be called the World Turn'd Upside Down.

And now there was Thomas. The timing could not have been worse. With the King about to be tried, her love for a Roundhead would be like pouring salt into her father's gaping wound.

She glanced up at the bell, which was still gently tinkling. What was going on in that upstairs room?

The Doctor walked boldly up to Cromwell and gave a very deep bow. 'General Cromwell,' he said. 'This is a pleasure.'

Cromwell nodded slightly and spun the globe again. 'No doubt.' He stuck out a big, thick finger and stopped the spinning. 'You're a doctor, I hear.'

'The,' said the Doctor without a trace of immodesty.

Cromwell grunted. 'That good, eh? Well, Doctor, what do you know of boils? I'm a martyr to them, sir, a martyr.'

The Doctor shrugged. 'Alas, General, it is not quite within my purview.'

Cromwell shrugged, disappointed, and made his way back to the chair. 'You have some connection with this lad, then?'

The Doctor pushed Jamie forward. 'May I present the

90

McCrimmon of Culloden, for whom I have the honour to act as… er… spiritual sextant.'

Cromwell frowned. 'A what?'

The Doctor waved his hands airily. 'I guide him through the highways and byways of the other world.'

Cromwell nodded and sat down, shifting his weight and grunting as his boil connected with the cushions. He beckoned Jamie towards him. 'Is it true, lad? Can you see beyond this mortal veil?'

Jamie looked at the Doctor, who nodded discreetly. Then he drew himself up boldly. 'Yes,' he stated simply. 'That I can.'

Thurloe came to stand by Cromwell's side, raising an eyebrow suspiciously and coughing lightly, as though trying to clear a small blockage from his throat. 'The jailer tells me you know of the King's imprisonment.'

'Oh yes,' said the Doctor.

Thurloe folded his arms over his tightly buttoned black tunic. 'Information that any Royalist spy might have wrung out of a loyal Parliamentarian.'

'Oh, no, no, no,' cried the Doctor. 'The McCrimmon saw it in a vision.'

Cromwell seemed to consider this. He thought again of the Cornish woman and the plague of cats. Then of the plague they all knew too well, that had ravaged the city only twenty years before. And then of his memory of the little prince with the sad eyes. There was so much he wanted to know.

'Well, then,' he said at last. 'Will there be more visions? What can you tell us of the future?'

The Doctor frowned. 'Well—'

'These are mad and fast times, Doctor,' interrupted Cromwell. 'The world is giddy about our ears. And great matters are being decided.'

'Yes,' said the Doctor gravely, 'I know.'

91

'Then,' said Cromwell grandly, 'tell us what we must do. Tell us how we may best serve the Lord our God and heal this wounded land of ours.'

The Doctor smiled pleasantly. 'Ask away.'

Cromwell looked at Thurloe, who coughed again into his glove.

'What of the King?'

Jamie began to follow the usual procedure, moaning softly to himself and waving his hands about close to his ears. Then, after a great bellow of pain he announced, 'I see a vacant throne!'

'And a vacant hat!' put in the Doctor, enjoying the theatricalities immensely.

Cromwell and Thurloe looked quickly at each other. 'I should cut off his head, then?' asked Cromwell with ponderous gravity.

Jamie cleared his throat, aware that any answers he might give could have historical repercussions. 'You must look to your own... conscience, Oliver Cromwell. And seek the counsel of the Lord.'

The Doctor smiled and whispered, 'Very good.'

Cromwell did not react for a moment, then his ruddy face broke into a broad smile. 'Good. Good!' he said happily. 'I would talk more with this remarkable pair, John. Let them be given quarter here until I need to consult them again.'

He rose and bowed to the Doctor and Jamie, then clamped his hand over his backside, grunting with the pain from his boil. Muttering to himself, he stomped out of the chamber.

Thurloe clicked his fingers and a young secretary came running inside. With a suspicious glance at the time travellers, he whispered in the secretary's ear and then turned to the Doctor and Jamie.

'Very well, then. You shall be quartered here until the

general decides to see you again. I hope we can make you comfortable.'

He gave a short, incredulous laugh and strode out, his cloak trailing behind him.

Jamie stuck out his tongue at Thurloe's back and noticed that the secretary was already leading the Doctor away. He raced after them into a long, dark, panelled corridor which led into another, much smaller apartment.

As the secretary opened the door, the Doctor moved to let him pass and there was a minor collision.

The Doctor apologised profusely but the secretary told him to think nothing of it. He ushered them inside.

The room was plainly and functionally furnished with two beds, a dresser, and a long mirror on a stand.

The secretary bowed and exited. As soon as they were alone, Jamie jumped onto the bed and lay down, sighing with contentment. The Doctor made straight for the door and tried the heavy iron handle.

He turned to Jamie and frowned. 'It's locked.'

Richard Cromwell was making his way down the corridor the Doctor and Jamie had just passed through. He gazed absently at the paintings that hung from the panelled walls, though they held no interest for him. The battle of this, the siege of that. It was all so tiresome. He couldn't understand what his father saw in it.

He yawned. Perhaps he would go outside and see the snow. Yes, that would be splendid. A walk in the gardens and then dinner.

Suddenly happy, Richard walked on. As he passed the door to the Doctor and Jamie's room, he pulled up sharply.

There was something lying on the floor, a smooth, rectangular shape with a picture on it. It looked like a book, but Richard had never seen such a book before.

He bent down on one knee and gingerly picked up *Every Boy's Book of the English Civil Wars*.

CHAPTER
4

The small man with the huge brown eyes ate the last of his breakfast and pushed the china plate away from him. He dabbed at the corners of his mouth with a richly brocaded handkerchief, wiping away the traces of the plain and not very pleasant meal.

Water would be good now, he thought. Perhaps he should call for some.

He lifted his hand and then, with a small, sad cluck in his throat, dropped it heavily to his lap. How easy it was to forget. There were no servants around him now. No one to anticipate his every whim. No one to execute his orders.

Execute.

The word seemed to ring around his mind like the echo of a sharp knife against a flint wheel. He closed his eyes and sighed deeply.

King Charles was not used to such treatment. From birth, he had been pampered and indulged, both by his father, the slovenly James, and his elder brother, Prince Henry. Then, after Henry's unexpected death, the beloved and wonderful Duke of Buckingham had taken the underdeveloped, rather sombre Charles and groomed him for the throne.

Thus it was he who had taken on the burden of ruling the

kingdom, as fairly, he judged, as his father or any monarch before him.

For many years his had seemed a perfect state. His marriage to the Queen, Henrietta Maria, was, after a difficult start, solid and loving. He had wonderful children and perhaps the most elegant and sophisticated court in Europe. The country was prosperous and seemingly content. Nothing could spoil things. Nothing except Parliament.

Of course, they were a necessary evil. After all, he had to raise taxes and get his money from somewhere. But they refused to accept that only the King could summon such an assembly into being and dissolve it just as easily. He had done without the rabble for eleven whole years before those bothersome, uncontrollable Scots had forced him to raise an army against them.

But Parliament had struck, struck like a viper to his heart, suddenly demanding all kinds of reforms. They wanted to take control of the Army away from him. Away from the King! Charles remembered his own words, thundering through the Palace of Whitehall that far-off day. 'By God, not for an hour! You ask of me what was never asked of any king!'

And they were not content with that, oh no. Now they wanted religious reform. They objected to the beautification of his country's lovely churches undertaken by Archbishop Laud. Should worship really be as plain as a milkmaid's face?

Aye, the Puritans demanded and Charles had lost Laud to them. Lost him to charges of crypto-papistry, and they had cut off his head to prove their point.

And then there was Strafford, who had fought so loyally for the King in Ireland and urged him to take on his rebellious Parliament, else he be no King at all.

Charles laid a trembling hand across his brow. They had taken Strafford's head too and Charles had felt the death almost as though it were his own. It was too cruel a blow. Too cruel.

And so the wars had come. There was no way to avoid them. It was either King, with a mandate to rule which came from God himself, or Parliament, with a much more parochial mandate altogether.

Charles rose from his chair and crossed to the great window. His rooms were small but comfortable. Thickly carpeted with rugs which had been a present to his late father from some exotic potentate and hung with tapestries from the royal collection.

Through the thick glass, the dreary course of the Solent could be seen, winding past the castle like a gigantic grey snake.

Charles watched the water in silence, the December light bleaching the colour from his grave, noble face, creating dark hollows in his cheeks and making him look far older than his forty-eight years.

Well, well, he thought. It seemed that God had made up His mind. The Royalist armies had been roundly defeated and now he, the King, was a prisoner. He didn't doubt that soon the Roundheads would be calling for his head.

Execute.

Charles felt a pang of terror grip at his bowels. He sank down to the floor and clasped his hands together in prayer. There was little else left for him to do.

Polly stood by the banks of the Thames, enjoying the feel of the cold drizzle on her face. She breathed in and the air felt crisp and good. What would a lungful of air be like inhaled in the same spot three hundred or so years from now? she thought absently. Filthy, acrid, polluted.

Yet there was terrible degradation here, too. She had seen

it as she made her way through the city – the squalor, the filth and the back-breaking labour that seemed to be the common lot of most of the inhabitants of Stuart England.

Polly rubbed her face and eyes and shook her head as though to clear it. Her fine, straight hair was becoming matted and rather greasy and she longed for a hot bath. But the TARDIS and the Doctor seemed a long way off. She was no nearer to finding anyone or anything she knew.

A wheezing splutter close by made her turn and she stepped back as two men struggled by at each end of an ornate sedan chair. Their faces were almost purple with effort, sweat streaming into their eyes. Polly caught a brief glimpse of an exquisitely dressed man, all burnt-orange velvet and frills, gazing absently out of the chair's little window. He seemed bored and completely unaware of the efforts being made to keep him out of the mud.

Polly scowled but then checked herself. Was it any different from someone of her own time having a chauffeur? Perhaps it was just a shock to her twentieth-century sensibilities. After all, this place was as alien as another planet, despite the superficial similarities to her own time. There was a monarch and Parliament but...

She froze a moment as a thought occurred to her. If she knew the Doctor, he wouldn't be content to hang around waiting for her and Ben to turn up. He'd be doing something. Using the opportunity to get a closer look at this period of earth's history. And, given the tumultuous time they had landed in, he would trying to get close to either the Royalists or the Roundheads. Yes! Surely that was it. She'd lay odds that even now the little man would be close to the centre of some kind of power, probably dragging a protesting Jamie in tow. She smiled to herself, a little cheered, and crossed the snowy road, jumping over the muddy furrows scored into it by passing traffic.

Where could she turn for help, though? It would be unwise to go around asking strange questions – the Doctor had warned them all to be circumspect, as had the man at the inn.

Polly stopped in her tracks and let out a little chuckle, delighted at her second revelation of the morning. The men at the inn, particularly the rather handsome young one, had been fairly kind to her. She could tell they felt some guilt over Ben's disappearance. Perhaps she could use that to get them to ask around about the Doctor and Jamie. Restored to her friends, she felt sure they could find Ben. With a gladdened heart, Polly set off for Kemp's inn at a brisk run.

She moved so swiftly, indeed, that Christopher Whyte had trouble keeping up with her.

Making her way stealthily along the corridor, Frances Kemp held her breath. The shadows were lengthening and the inn was beginning to lose itself in darkness. Soon her mother would be flitting about the place, lighting the lamps and preparing for the evening's custom. But perhaps Frances could take advantage of this dim hour to find out what was going on and the identity of her father's guests.

She was close to the room now and could see the old door rattle as her father spoke urgently with his mysterious visitors.

Frances crept over the bare boards and gently pressed her ear against the door, straining to hear the conversation within. Several voices reached her but she couldn't separate them. Only her father's low grumble seemed recognisable. A point was being debated, she could tell from the rising tone of his voice. But what was it, and why all this secrecy?

After a time, some conclusion seemed to be reached and the voices became more audible and conversational. Chairs were scraped back and Frances ran swiftly to the other side of the corridor, closing her hand on the doorknob of her own room.

But she had not quite managed to slip inside when her father appeared from the opposite chamber. Turning back towards him, she closed her eyes and braced herself for his wrath.

'Frances?'

She spoke without turning round. 'I'm fetching darning thread for Mother,' she said quickly.

'Yes, yes,' said Kemp with a chuckle. 'Good girl.'

She turned to face him and was astonished to see a broad smile plastered over his face. She hadn't seen her father look so happy in years. What could the men in the room have done to effect such an unlikely transformation?

Kemp patted her fondly on the head and turned away. 'Now then, we have an inn to run, do we not?' he cried happily, and set off down the corridor.

Frances frowned and cast another curious glance at the closed door opposite.

Lamps were lit the length of the Commons chamber, the sound of their flickering flames combining to produce a faint whispering sound, as though the debating chamber beyond were still full of honourable members.

This place, set off the main room, was a brown, heavily panelled area, so stained with age that the whole atmosphere seemed affected by it. A sepia tinge hung over the assembled men, giving their concentrated faces a pallor like tobacco stain.

Around the table, like knights at a solemn Camelot, sat a fair proportion of the members of Parliament not recently expelled by Colonel Pride.

The soldier himself and Lord Grey of Groby were there, along with the others of like mind, determined to press for the King's head. The Presbyterians had been purged, as had John Lilburne and his troublesome Levellers. Now this 'Rump' remained, and the Rump would see justice was done, Cromwell was sure of it.

The general sat at the head of the table, Thurloe by his side, riddling with his none-too-clean collar and scanning an impressive document spread out before him. Something about the portentously elaborate style of the writing betrayed its purpose as an instrument of state. Cromwell read it over in his head several times, before running a hand through his thinning grey hair.

'Well, gentlemen?' he said at last.

Groby held up a gloved hand. 'By your leave, General, I think I speak for us all when I ask that the charge be read aloud.'

Cromwell shifted in his seat, uncomfortable because of the boil on his buttock, but also because he was almost painfully aware that he was not only living through a moment of great historical import, but actually creating it.

There was no joy, however, no triumph in his voice as he lifted the paper closer to his eyes and began to speak.

'Charles Stuart,' he began, 'the now King of England, is accused of entertaining a wicked design totally to subvert the ancient and fundamental laws and liberties of this nation, and in their place to introduce an arbitrary and tyrannical government.'

Cromwell paused and looked down the length of the table. To a man, the members sat with heads bowed.

'And that, besides all other evil ways and means to bring his design to pass, he hath prosecuted it with fire and sword, levied and maintained a cruel war in the land.'

Cromwell stopped again, letting the impact of his words sink in. The room was hushed, save for the sputtering of the lamp flames.

Then, as though from miles away, the sound of approaching footsteps became audible. They were coming from the adjacent corridor and their owner was in something of a hurry. His boots rang off the stone floor.

Cromwell looked up expectantly as the double doors were thrown open and Sir Thomas Fairfax stood framed there, his arms spread wide.

'So this is where it is done, Oliver?' he spat. 'In the shadows, like knaves?'

Cromwell didn't react at first. His heavy, warty face remained impassive and then, with a sniff, he looked at Fairfax with something like pity. 'I can think of few places more public than this chamber,' he said quietly. 'With Parliament close by.'

Fairfax shot a look at Colonel Pride and laughed derisively. 'Aye, what's left of it.'

Cromwell looked at the floor and then glanced at Thurloe, who indicated, with a small movement of his hand, that it was perhaps wise for the other members to leave.

When Cromwell and Fairfax were alone, they stood in brooding, angry silence. Then Cromwell dragged the charge sheet across the table and thrust it under Fairfax's nose. 'You would object to what this document says?'

Fairfax shook his head. 'It is true. I know it.'

Cromwell's blue eyes blazed with righteous ire. 'Then what ails you?'

The commander sighed. 'It is all true. But we have gone too far, Oliver. We cannot... we must not kill our King.'

Cromwell rolled the document up and held it in his hand like a dagger. 'We gave him every chance, Thomas, every chance. He chose to repay our trust with the basest treachery.'

Fairfax looked pleadingly into Cromwell's face. 'But there must still be another way—'

'There is no other way,' said Cromwell in a dangerous whisper. 'If we let him slip again, our cause is finished, Thomas. We might as well call ourselves serfs and have done with it. We must cut out this poison at its source.'

Fairfax shook his head. 'And have history condemn us as regicides?'

Cromwell turned away. 'I have no care for history. I am concerned with the present.'

Fairfax looked at his old friend, the soldier alongside whom he had fought so long and so bravely. He let out a long sigh that was more like the last breath of a dying man. 'Then you must face the consequences alone, my friend. I shall have none of it.'

He turned smartly and went out of the room without looking back.

Evening came fast and, as the *Teazer* approached the winking lights of Amsterdam, Ben shivered. Ahead, he could just make out a rather splendid skyline of tall public buildings, churches, and, inevitably, windmills.

Ashdown and the other men were busy making fast the sails as the ship lurched into the harbour, the black water slopping like oil around her hull.

Aware that to tarry would attract attention, Ben set to work, doing his best not to eavesdrop as Captain Stanislaus and Godley emerged from their cabins.

The passenger straightened his clothes and donned a broad, black, feathered hat as the captain approached him.

'We are safe,' murmured Godley.

The Captain smiled, his teeth glinting in the glow of the lamps. 'Unlike some I could mention,' he said quietly.

Godley's monkey chose that moment to leap from the cabin and land on his master's shoulder, making both men turn and become aware that Ben was leaning just a little too close to them.

Godley caught sight of him, frowned, and jerked his head rapidly upward as a sign to Stanislaus. Ben was immediately grabbed by the scruff of the neck.

'What is this?' hissed the captain. 'Do we have a spy aboard, Master Ashdown?'

Ashdown hurried across the deck, flapping his arms placatingly. 'Oh, no, no, Captain,' he cried. 'This is the new lad, sir, the new lad. He's just getting to know the ropes. Expect he's curious about what you and the gentlemen are doing here.'

Stanislaus gave Ashdown a dark look. 'I should not worry about that, sir. This gentleman's business is no concern of yours. You content yourself with the workings of this ship, is that clear?'

Ashdown and Ben nodded silently.

Stanislaus let Ben go and smoothed down his cravat. 'Or else you'll all get to know the ropes. Intimately.'

He glared at his crew and set a free rope that hung from the sail swinging, leaving no doubt as to his threat.

The rope cast a snaking shadow over the men as Godley and Stanislaus made their way down the creaking gangplank and on to the shore.

There were already sounds of uproar and general merriment coming from the port and, after a moment's silence to make sure the captain and his passenger had gone, Ashdown gave Ben a friendly pat on the arm.

'We were lucky there, Ben,' he said. 'The captain's got a terrible temper on him. I've known him flog the skin off a man for less.'

Ben peered after the retreating Stanislaus and Godley. 'Wonder why he didn't. And who's that bloke?'

Ashdown smote his forehead. 'Will you not listen, man? The captain has told us not to pry and we must not. Now, what say we finish our work and then spend a few hours on shore, eh?'

But Ben was far more interested in what he had heard. 'They said something about a package…'

Ashdown began to lead Ben by the elbow. 'I know a girl with hair like spun gold,' he said lyrically. 'And lips like a rosebud…'

Ben laughed. 'All right, mate. You've convinced me. Come on.'

They went back to their work and for another hour or so laboured at readying the ship for sail.

Finally, bone-weary but anxious for distraction, the crew of the *Teazer* slipped ashore into the cold Amsterdam night.

The King was dreaming of faraway days at Hampton Court when a sound outside his door made him stir. He opened his heavy lids and blinked up at the ceiling, his ears pricked. But all was silent, save for the sound of his own breath and the ticking sound of saliva on his parted lips as he opened his mouth.

He sat up in the darkness and listened attentively.

The room was black except for the tiny oil flame that burned by his bed and a sliver of light from the corridor beyond that seemed to bob and weave, throwing strange shadows into the room, as though someone with a candle were hovering indecisively outside.

Charles pulled back the bedclothes as quietly as he could and stole across the room in his bare feet. He crouched down and tried to make out any sound in the corridor beyond, but he heard nothing.

The light under the door moved again and then diminished.

Charles waited a moment or two, fiddling with the coils of his long hair, and then crept back towards the bed. He found a wax taper, which he lit from the flame close by. Then, after lighting a candle, he went back to the door.

There was a square of folded paper lying on the elegant rug. Carefully, Charles stooped and picked it up. He walked back to the bed and sat down on the counterpane.

Holding the candle in one slightly shaky hand, he unfolded the paper and peered at the message it contained.

A short time later, an unaccustomed smile found its way on to his grave features. He paused, lost in thought, tapping the paper against his chin, then he let the candle flame catch at its edge.

Soon the paper was alight and he dropped it carefully to the floor and watched it burn, the red-orange flames licking satisfyingly at the parchment, then curling it up into a black ball.

Charles slid back into bed, pulled the blankets over himself and extinguished the candle with his fingers.

It was, Ben decided, only fair that he allow himself a little relaxation. The past couple of days had been trying, to say the least, and, as he knew there was no opportunity of returning to England until the morning, he decided to enjoy himself.

Ashdown led him through the streets of Amsterdam, talking nineteen to the dozen about the strange and wonderful sights that awaited them.

'Your Dutch, you see, are a queer breed,' he expounded, gesticulating as he walked. 'They're prone to drunkenness 'cause of them having to live among all the stinking vapours and chills of these here bogs.'

Ben laughed. 'Is that what it is? I thought they just knew how to have a good time.'

Ashdown cackled merrily. 'That they do, Ben, that they do. I know a place where they have a great tun, a barrel that you can sit in! Aye, with thirty-odd of your fellows and they keep the ale coming from dawn to dusk!'

Ben didn't reply. He was too caught up in the very real beauty of the city, which was different again from the narrow, cramped streets of old London.

They walked through streets that still bustled, despite the lateness of the hour. The houses seemed new, almost freshly minted, and imposingly tall. Some were three or four storeys high and topped with the familiar Dutch gable. Surrounding them were shops of every description, their entrances clustered with fine porcelain, silks, and linen. Fat cheeses and churns of buttery milk were set out on the pavement, like bait to entrap the salivating visitor.

Ben found himself smiling. It was just like the sensation he had visiting any new port with his own ship, full of new sights and smells and an exciting expectation of what might be to come.

They had entered a vast, open space which was bordered at two sides by rows of elegant houses and trees. In the centre stood a huge new building with a dome, a spire, and a clock which seemed to Ben like a glorious folly made up of the most familiar parts of a town hall, a cathedral, and a bell tower.

Ashdown explained that it was the new church on the Botermarkt and that it meant they were close to a certain establishment of his acquaintance. The church, like the houses and roads that surrounded it, was wet and sparkling with new rain and Ben was grateful that Amsterdam was at least a little warmer than London.

They passed through a cross street and Ben looked up to see the tiled nameplate which identified it as the Heiligeway, whatever that might be.

He became aware of a strange sound, a sort of combined grumbling and moaning, as though he'd accidentally stumbled on the entrance to purgatory.

Ben stopped dead and listened. The sound was desperate, so awful that it made the hair on the back of his neck stand up.

He grabbed Ashdown s shoulder and turned him round. 'What's that?'

Ashdown looked glum and shook his head. 'Don't you pay no mind to that, Ben. It ain't a thing to think about too hard.'

Ben looked across the street. The sound seemed to be coming from a big, red-roofed building with a large, columned portico as its entrance. Above this was cut a bas-relief showing a charioteer viciously lashing at his bridled team of lions and wolves. A motto in Latin was inscribed below it.

'*Virtutis est domare quaecuncti pavent,*' read Ben slowly.

He turned to Ashdown, hoping for enlightenment, and, to his astonishment, the sailor translated, looking down at the ground as though in fear. '"It is a virtue to subdue those before whom all go in dread",' he said, his face set into a frown.

'How do you know that?' asked Ben.

Ashdown fixed him with a miserable glare which made him shrink. 'Because I have been shut up in there, my friend. 'Tis the Tugthuis. The House of Correction.'

Ben felt suddenly humbled and wanted to offer some words of comfort to Ashdown, but the sailor merely grinned and patted him on the shoulder. 'But come, lad. Are we not on pleasure bent?'

Ashdown marched off ahead, cackling and in high spirits, though Ben detected a strong desire to put as much distance as possible between himself and the fearsome Tugthuis.

Polly sat down heavily on the bench by the bar of Kemp's inn. After her initial enthusiasm, she had been systematically worn down by a whole day of disappointments. First, she had great trouble locating the inn among the maze of filthy, decrepit buildings which made up the city. It would be a good thing for one and all, she thought, when the Great Fire came and cleared all those slums away. Then her questions about the men who had captured her had been met with blank incomprehension and then downright hostility from the surly customers.

She had asked to speak to the landlord but was told he was unavailable and his wife denied the inn even possessed an upstairs room, never mind had guests there.

Dejected and alone, Polly had traipsed off and spent another fruitless day searching for her missing friends. She had eaten well, at least, after finding a few of the coins from Ben's purse rattling around in the pockets of her cloak. She had found a stall selling oysters and gorged herself on a dozen or so. They were delicious, salty and fresh with a hint of nutmeg and thyme. She topped this with several hunks of good brown bread and now she was back at the inn, washing it all down with a kind of hot toddy that took the edge off her loneliness.

The place was noisy with the clatterings and clangings of pots as food and ale were dished out to the rough clientele. Men with foamy beer dribbling down their beards and onto their collars were laughing and shouting, occasionally taking the chance to grab at a passing girl.

Polly glanced anxiously across the crowded room at the little niche recently occupied by her and Ben. It wasn't safe for her to remain here alone.

Suddenly, and to her own great surprise, she began to cry. Looking down at her dress to avoid prying eyes, she heaved a great sigh and let the hot, salty tears drop onto her lap. She wanted nothing more than to be away from this place. To see Ben, Jamie and the Doctor again.

Her next breath came out as a ragged sob and she hastily wiped her eyes. What was wrong with her, for goodness' sake? Couldn't she even manage one day alone?

She thought of what her old friend Rosie would say now. They had both worked in an office in Bond Street what seemed like an eternity ago and had become great pals. The older Rosie, tall and striking with a jet-black Twenties-style bob, was heavily involved with the fledgling Women's Liberation Movement and had taken Polly under her wing, transforming the shy young girl into something of a swinger.

Polly could picture Rosie now, looking at her the day she had left to become Professor Brett's secretary at the Post Office Tower. Rosie had given her a big hug and then held her out at arm's length. 'Let me look at my monster,' she'd said, with a sad smile. 'Yes. You'll do.' Then they'd walked together arm in arm to the entrance to the great shining new building. 'You keep your chin up, girl,' Rosie had said. 'Remember, you can manage on your own. I know you can.'

Polly let the images of that warm day wash over her – the flashy cars and ozone stink of Oxford Street, the Tower glittering in the sunlight, Rosie standing before her.

She seemed to be standing there right now, but, as Polly shook her head, she realised another girl was next to her and that she was still in the crowded, heaving inn.

The newcomer was very pretty and rather delicate-looking, wearing a heavy blue woollen dress with an apron over it and her blonde hair was tucked up into a little lacy cap. She was frowning concernedly.

'Are you well?' she asked gently.

Polly put on her bravest face and nodded.

The girl sat down next to her and took her hand. It was warm and reassuring and Polly felt instantly comforted. She wiped her eyes again.

'I must look such a state,' she laughed. 'I'm never usually like this.'

Her new companion smiled kindly. 'My name's Frances,' she said. Polly introduced herself and then looked around the busy inn. 'Not the sort of place I'd expect to find a demure young lady like you.'

Frances shrugged. 'Nor you.'

Polly laughed. 'Quite right.'

Frances laid her hands in her lap. 'My father is the innkeeper,' she said. 'I have to spend most of my evenings in here, trying to fight off the brutes this place attracts.'

Polly leaned forward. 'Is your father that one over there?'

She pointed across the room at Kemp, who had emerged from upstairs and was hard at work. He still seemed much more cheerful than normal and the customers, at first bemused but then delighted, had noticed and were carousing raucously.

Frances nodded. 'That's him. Though I can't see what has come over him this evening. He's quite the life and soul.'

Polly grimaced. 'I tried to speak to him earlier but he was… unavailable.'

'Why did you wish to speak to him?' asked Frances.

'Oh, it's a long story,' muttered Polly, waving her hand dismissively. But then she frowned and moved closer to the young woman. 'But maybe you can help me. I've lost my friends, you see.'

Frances swept some tankards across the table and shuffled closer. 'Go on.'

'My friend Ben and I were supposed to meet up with two others last night at sunset. But we were attacked. I don't know what happened to Ben but I was taken back here. To a room upstairs.'

Frances's eyebrows shot up. 'The room above the inn?'

111

Polly nodded.

Frances swallowed excitedly. 'Who took you there?'

'Some paid goons…'

'Some what?' asked Frances with a puzzled frown.

Polly shrugged. 'Hired men. The people inside were quite different. There was a very handso- er… quite a distinguished-looking young man and a much older one with a white beard. They thought I knew something about the King.'

Frances sat back, suddenly afraid. 'The King?'

Polly nodded. 'They overheard my friend and me talking and got suspicious.'

'Do you know anything about the King?' Frances's face was a picture of wariness.

Polly smiled. 'No more than anyone else.'

Frances chewed her lip thoughtfully and folded her arms.

Polly sat back. 'Look, you don't know me, but I'd really appreciate a little help. I can't find my friends and I'm honestly in big trouble if they stay lost. Couldn't you let me see upstairs? If I could just talk to those people again, I'm sure they'd help me.'

Frances shook her head. 'I'm sorry, Polly. It's out of the question. My father won't let anyone near that room. I've tried myself.' She suddenly smiled, a lovely, enchanting smile. 'But I do know someone who might be able to help you.'

Frances stood up and pointed towards the door of the inn. 'Come on.'

Polly got up and gratefully followed Frances out.

Christopher Whyte lifted the brim of his wide velvet hat from over his eyes and watched them go. Then, laying a few coins on the table, he jumped up and made his way outside into the freezing night.

The unmistakable sound of drunken laughter led Ben and

112

Ashdown to a lopsided, cheerful-looking hostelry, on the far side of the Botermarkt.

They had to bend low to enter and were immediately confronted by a scene of wild and wonderful chaos. The room beyond was packed with sailors from all corners of the earth, just like an enlarged version of Stanislaus's crew.

There were Moors and Turks again, their ears studded with silver hoops. But there were other exotics too. An enormously fat woman who seemed ready to eat the little fellow she had perched on her lap. Two Chinamen, dressed in gorgeously ornate, jade-coloured robes, were standing by the fireplace, laughing and chattering in a high-pitched staccato. A black dwarf, his pudgy hands festooned with rings and silver bangles, was scuttling around the tables trying to sell his wares.

The tavern itself was crammed with cooking meats and slopping ale and Ben felt suddenly, ravenously hungry. The sweet smell of fresh bread and roast beef assailed his senses.

'Welcome,' said Ashdown with an elaborate bow. 'Welcome to the Dolphin. The worst stew in all Amsterdam!'

Ben couldn't help grinning at his friend's enthusiasm. He began to move forward, his feet crunching on the shattered eggs and empty mussel shells that littered the stone floor.

Sailors were grouped around every table, talking and cackling and making lewd gestures at the serving girls, who were struggling through, carrying foaming flagons of ale.

Ashdown clapped Ben on the shoulder. 'What did I tell 'ee?' he said with a laugh. 'There's no finer place in all Europe!'

So saying, he threw himself bodily into the heaving crowd and was quickly swallowed up.

Ben smiled indulgently and fought his way to a table. It was already crowded but one stool remained free, possibly because its former occupant was lying in a drunken stupor on the filthy floor. Ben sat down and tried to attract the attention of one of the girls. He almost shouted 'Waitress!' but then thought better of it.

What should he call them? Wenches? Or was that only in films?

He was spared further embarrassment by a tap on the shoulder from the woman sitting opposite him – a huge, big-bosomed figure in a stained green velvet coat. Her hair was long, black, and matted and she had an embroidered patch over one eye. In fact, she was so completely the image of a pirate that Ben almost laughed.

The strange woman smiled at him, showing off brown teeth like stained fence posts. Then Ben noticed something else, something curious about the woman's nose. Peering closer through the haze of tobacco fumes, he realised with a start that the nose was made of silver and had been screwed tightly into the bone.

She let out a whoop of laughter and slammed her glass down onto the table. 'Quite summat, ain't she, mate?'

Ben looked a little worried. 'Sorry?'

The woman tapped her nose, which made a bright, sharp clang like a bell. 'This little beauty always gets people talking. It's a great conversation piece.'

'Yes,' said Ben, 'I don't wonder.'

The woman folded her arms and leaned forward conversationally. 'Now, tell me. What would a pretty lad like you find here for his pleasure? There's plenty of girls who'd see you right for a guilder. Or the odd ingle upstairs, if that's your fancy.'

Ben did not understand but thought it best not to inquire further. He looked round, still anxious to find himself a drink. 'I wouldn't mind some beer to start with.'

'Oh,' said the woman flatly.

She sounded so disappointed that Ben had not been excited by her list of the Dolphin's wares that he turned back to her with a smile. 'Sorry, love. I've had a hard day, that's all.'

'They're all hard, these days,' said the woman philosophically. She extended a grubby hand. 'Sal Winter, with the *Demeter*.'

Ben shook her hand. 'Ben Jackson, with the *Teazer*.'

Winter frowned deeply and a flush rose in her thick skin, which had the unmistakable signs of black powder burns etched into it.

'The *Teazer*?' she growled. 'You're with the Pole's ship?'

'Captain Stanislaus, you mean?' said Ben.

Winter nodded vigorously. 'That's the cove.'

She sank back into her chair and looked broodingly into her empty glass. Then she clicked her fingers and, at once, a girl was by her side, refilling the glass with a strong, amber-coloured ale. Winter pointed at Ben and the girl fetched him a flagon of the same malty stuff.

'You know him?' asked Ben conversationally.

Winter's voice dropped to a low grumble. 'Aye, I know him.'

Ben leaned forward, intrigued, blinking as the light of the tavern glinted off Winter's artificial nose. 'Tell me more.'

Jamie was smiling peacefully, sound asleep, his head sunk in a fat, feathery pillow, when the Doctor shook his shoulder.

'Eh? What?' muttered Jamie, waking. 'What is it?'

The Doctor was sitting on the edge of the bed, holding a candlestick in his hand. The wispy light gave his face an almost supernatural glow.

'Jamie,' he whispered urgently. 'The book. Have you got it?'

Jamie groaned. 'What? Och, Doctor, can't it wait till morning?'

The Doctor shook his head. 'No, no. You don't understand. I don't want to look at it. I can't find it.'

Jamie shrugged and sank back onto the bed. 'Well, you had it last. Don't fret. You probably dropped it somewhere.'

The Doctor shook him again, somewhat crossly. 'Oh, Jamie, don't you understand? If I have lost it somewhere, the consequences could be terrible.'

'I'll get you another one.'

The Doctor jumped up, frustrated. 'It's not the book itself. It's what it represents. Can't you see? If someone gets hold of it they'll know what's going to happen for the next twenty years!'

Jamie sat up and leaned on his elbow. 'Oh,' he mumbled. 'I see what you mean.'

The Doctor sat down again glumly. 'Quite apart from the fact that it was published almost three hundred years in the future! Why did I ever pick up the stupid thing?' He crossed his arms and thrust out his lower lip sulkily.

Jamie thought for a moment. 'So what can we do?'

'I have absolutely no idea. Not until we get out of here, anyway.'

Jamie nodded, turned over again, and plumped his pillow. 'Aye. Right. So why don't you just forget about it until the morning and get some sleep?'

The Doctor shook his head. 'No, no. I'm far too worried about the book. And Ben and Polly.'

Jamie's voice was muffled by the pillow. 'They'll be all right. They'll have gone back to the TARDIS and, when we didn't turn up, they'll have found somewhere to spend the night.'

The Doctor's face looked grave in the light of the candle. 'I hope so, Jamie. I hope so.' He brandished a piece of paper which he'd torn from his diary. 'I've written down descriptions of them. I thought perhaps we could persuade Cromwell to

116

instigate some sort of search. Perhaps we could…' He trailed off and wrinkled his nose. 'Can you smell something?'

Jamie sat up straight and sniffed. 'Aye… It's like… it's like—'

They both turned at a noise from outside the windows. The smell was stronger here and the Doctor wrenched back the curtain to peer out into the gardens below.

It was a frosty night and a bone-white moon illuminated the snow-covered grounds of the building.

The Doctor managed to open the diamond-patterned window and poke his head out. He smiled as the smell intensified and he caught sight of a familiar figure, shuffling through drifts, a lantern in one hand and an ominous sack slung over his shoulder.

'Mr Scrope!' hissed the Doctor.

The wizened old man looked up in surprise and then waved to the Doctor. 'Hello to thee!' he called. 'I heard you was about.'

The Doctor frowned. 'What are you doing here?'

Scrope crunched his way through the drifts so that he was directly below the high window, some three storeys up. 'I said I had state business, didn't I?' he muttered, sounding rather affronted.

The Doctor noticed the sack on his shoulder and nodded. 'Oh yes. Yes, of course.'

'Well, then, state business brings me to Parliament's precincts and to you. How're they treating you?'

Jamie came to the window and covered his nose, grateful that the semi-darkness hid him. 'You know they've got us locked up in here?'

Scrope cackled. 'I hear you're a wizard, lad. Is that true?'

The Doctor set his candle down on the sill. 'Look, Mr Scrope, could we ask you a favour?'

Scrope set down his sack, which made an unpleasant squelching sound as it hit the snow. 'Ask away, friend. I'm still in your debt.'

The Doctor chewed his lip thoughtfully. 'A gentleman such as yourself must have... certain contacts.'

'Contacts?'

The Doctor nodded. 'Yes. Eyes and ears everywhere.'

Scrope nodded vigorously. 'Aye. I have to. You have to keep alert in this game.'

'Quite,' said the Doctor. 'Now, I was wondering if you might put some of those contacts at our disposal?'

Scrope nodded and grinned. 'You lost something?'

'Aye,' said Jamie. 'Two friends.'

Scrope frowned. 'Oh. Well, happens a lot these days. In the wars, was it?'

The Doctor shook his head. 'Oh, no. Nothing like that. They were with us quite recently but our little excursion here has made us miss them. Do you think you might be able to track them down?'

Scrope picked up the sack again. It had left a large yellow stain in the snow. 'It'll be a pleasure, sir, a pleasure.' He tapped his nose. 'Nothing gets past this.'

Jamie grunted. 'Obviously.'

The Doctor leaned further out of the window and tried to speak as clearly as possible without raising his voice. 'The girl's name is Polly Wright, the boy's Ben Jackson. I've written down descriptions for you...' The Doctor stopped, holding the piece of paper out in front of him. 'You can... er.. you can...?'

'Course I can read!' snapped Scrope, raising his hand.

The Doctor threw the paper from the window and it sailed down, landing at Scrope's feet.

The old man picked it up looked at it briefly by the light of

118

his lamp. 'Very well. If they're in London, I shall find them for you. Now I must be off.' He turned and then spoke over his shoulder. 'I'll bring news as soon as I can. Goodnight to you, sirs.'

The Doctor and Jamie watched him trudge off through the drifts.

Jamie sat down the wooden sill. 'We should've asked him to help us get out of here.'

'No,' said the Doctor. 'We've got to put our minds to retrieving that book. Everything else can wait.'

The streets of old Amsterdam were beginning to glaze with frost as Ben and Sal Winter staggered along them. Their pace was slow, partly because of the amount of ale they had imbibed and partly because, as Ben had discovered to his delight, Winter had a false leg as well as a false nose, completing her extraordinary appearance.

They had left Ashdown in a heap of snoring bodies inside the inn. Ben had been quite tempted to press-gang the sailor onto another ship as a bit of revenge but Ashdown had been kind to him and, anyway, he wasn't having such a bad time of things.

Ben laughed hysterically as Winter came to the end of another of her seemingly endless supply of filthy anecdotes and slapped the wood-and-iron peg jutting from the hem of her ragged trousers. 'A twenty-five-footer!' she bellowed. 'And it took the lot in one snap!'

Ben's cherubic face was creased into a broad, astonished grin. 'What... what about the nose?'

Winter cackled mischievously and stopped, striking a pose with her wooden leg. 'Ah, now, Master Jackson. I think I'll have to know you a little better before we get to that tale.'

She smiled coquettishly and Ben felt himself blush.

Rapidly, he changed the subject. The thought of having to somehow get back to London sobered him. He explained his situation to Winter.

'Then you'll come with me,' she said. 'The *Demeter* sails on the morning tide.'

Ben was delighted. 'Are you sure? Will the captain mind?'

Winter let out a huge laugh, her massive chest fairly shaking till the silver buttons on her velvet coat rattled. 'Mind? Mind? I am the captain of the *Demeter*!'

Ben was stopped in his tracks. 'Oh.' He frowned and then burst out laughing himself. 'I'll work my passage,' he said at last.

Winter shook her head. 'You'll do no such thing. You are my guest. And if you've been working under that cur Stanislaus, I'll wager you need a rest.'

Ben nodded. 'That reminds me, Sal. You never did finish telling me about him.'

Winter's face fell. She suddenly seemed grave and introspective, as though dredging up some particularly unpleasant memories. 'He's a fellow of the night. A dark soul. I wonder the bastard can sleep.'

Ben was intrigued. 'Why? What's he done?'

Winter cocked her head and one good eye glinted in the starlight. She was about to speak when she looked past Ben, started, and then grabbed the young man by the hem of his cloak. She slammed her bulk back into an alcove and pulled Ben in beside her, laying a fat finger against his lip to silence any protest. Then she nodded towards the end of the street.

To Ben's astonishment, both Captain Stanislaus and his mysterious passenger, Godley, were making their way down the narrow alley towards them. Neither spoke but they were walking quickly, as though anxious to keep an appointment.

Winter let the two men pass before she and Ben moved carefully and silently from their hiding place.

'That was the passenger you told me of?' asked Winter.

Ben nodded.

Winter scowled and slammed her fist into her palm. 'By Christ, that man. He vexes me like a plague of boils. I have tracked him these twenty years but never had the chance of a proper reckoning.'

Ben frowned. 'A reckoning? For what?'

Winter prodded her silver nose. 'For this, Ben. It was that scurvy knave who took it from me.'

Ben let out a low whistle. 'I see.' He folded his arms and thought hard. 'Well, maybe this is your chance, Sal. Stanislaus is up to no good. Maybe we can nail him and get your revenge at the same time.'

Winter smiled. 'I like your thinking, lad. But what game is he at now? Lord knows, he's glutted himself on every pirate's trick there is.'

'What're his politics?' asked Ben with sudden inspiration.

Winter shrugged. 'He's no friend to Parliament, that I do know.' She squared her shoulders and ran both hands through her mane of greasy hair. 'Come along, Master Ben Jackson. I think you and I had better find out what Captain Stanislaus is up to.'

Ben nodded eagerly, and the big woman and the skinny sailor set off, keeping a safe distance from their quarry.

CHAPTER
5

Polly and Frances approached the bakery laughing like little girls. Despite Frances's rather frail appearance, she had proved to be great fun and Polly found herself much cheered by her presence. They had fallen to discussing Frances's impending engagement and she had said something of the problems that faced her. Then Polly had spoken of her strange experience in the room above the inn and Frances found herself intrigued by Polly's account of the charming stranger.

'What was his name?' she whispered as they made their way through the snow towards the door.

'I don't know,' said Polly with a giggle. 'But he was terribly handsome.'

Frances pulled a face. 'Not as handsome as my Tom, I'll bet.'

'Oh,' said Polly. 'It's Tom, is it?'

Frances produced a long, spindly key from her apron pocket. 'Thomas Lemuel Culpeper,' she announced grandly.

'It's a fine name,' said Polly.

'He's a fine man,' responded Frances proudly. 'As fine a man as ever served in the service of Parliament.'

She bent down, inserted the key in the door, and turned it, then beckoned to Polly, and they both entered the bakery.

Polly looked about the pleasant room, taking in the

comforting clutter of pans and trays. It was still very warm from the heat of the ovens and instantly she felt a sweat break out on her forehead. She took off her cloak and laid it on the chair.

Frances closed and locked the door and then turned round, her jaw dropping open as she saw Polly's minidress and boots for the first time. She waved her hand up and down, struggling to find words. 'Do you… do you not feel the cold, Polly?'

Polly laughed. 'That I do. You couldn't fix me up with something when we get back to the inn, could you?'

'Surely.' Frances shook her head in disbelief. How could a lady dress so indecently? She sighed and moved to the table. 'But first we must leave the message for my Tom.'

She found some paper, a quill and a bottle of ink and sat down to write.

Polly glanced at the window and, for a moment, thought she caught sight of a face, pressed to the glass. Then she realised it was her own bedraggled reflection and grimaced. 'Oh, what I wouldn't give for a hot bath.'

Frances didn't look up. She was concentrating hard on the note.

Polly sat down and rubbed at her grimy face. 'If Tom's doing so well, then what's the problem?' said Polly.

'The problem is the King, or, rather, my father's allegiance to him,' murmured Frances.

'But the King's been defeated, hasn't he?'

Frances nodded. 'That he has. And is like to die before long. But domestic affairs do not change, Polly. I would require my father's permission to marry. And he would never grant it to one of Cromwell's lieutenants.'

Polly looked impressed. 'Goodness. Your Tom is doing well.'

Frances paused in her writing and stared into space. 'I

almost wish he were not,' she lamented. 'A commoner man might be less of a problem.' She smiled suddenly as though to disguise her fears. 'But at least it means he may be able to help you.'

Picking up the note, she folded it in half and, crossing the room, hid it inside a large brown jar. 'He will return tonight. This is where we always leave our little letters.'

Polly thought this very touching. 'And he'll keep an eye out for my friends?'

Frances nodded. 'If any strangers have come into Cromwell's circle, then Tom will know about it. Come, let's get back to the inn before my father misses me.'

Polly leaned over the table and squeezed her hand. 'Thank you, Frances.'

Frances shook her head. ''Tis nothing. People should be kinder to one another. If they were, then we would not have to suffer as we have done.' A look of profound sadness swept over her lovely face and she turned away quickly towards the door.

Polly grabbed her cloak and followed her out of the bakery.

The warm room remained undisturbed for several minutes until a loud cracking sound began to come from the relocked door. The woodwork around the mechanism splintered and, in a matter of seconds, the door was forced open.

Christopher Whyte swept boldly inside and looked rapidly around the room. He had been watching Polly and Frances through the window and went straight to the jar, which he tipped upside down. Frances's note fluttered out.

Whyte put the jar back where he had found it, then rapidly read the note. Without hesitation, he slipped it inside his coat and marched swiftly outside, leaving the bakery door swinging loosely on broken hinges.

*

Hands shaking and mouth hanging open, Richard Cromwell turned the brittle pages of the book on his knee.

He was lying in his bedchamber, the coverlet drawn up to his chest, a lamp burning brightly at his side.

After finding the book, he had hurried back to his chambers, where some tiresome state business had kept him occupied for almost four hours. It was only when absolutely sure that he would remain undisturbed that he had retired to bed and taken the strange book from his coat.

He spent a long time simply stroking the smooth cover and marvelling at the picture which, by some alchemy, had been printed there. It showed a Cavalier and a Roundhead fighting, each on horseback, one with a pistol, the other a sword.

Richard traced his finger over the title and then carefully opened the book, marvelling at once at the quality of its pages and the neat, precise way in which the words were set out. Even the best-printed works he knew were rough affairs, their pages mismatched and ragged, their print higgledy-piggledy and erratically spaced.

When, at last, he had recovered from the sheer novelty of the thing, Richard set himself to begin reading.

It was not an easy matter. Although there were many words which were familiar to him, the spelling was very strange and he squinted as he tried to make sense of it.

Deciding that it was wiser to start with the easy bits, he flicked through the book and looked at the pictures.

Almost at once he came upon a picture of his father – a rather splendid etched print which showed Oliver in armour, standing before the massed ranks of his New Model Army.

Below his outstretched arm lay the royal arms, a laurel-wreath crown, a felled stag and a mask, as used in dramatic entertainments.

The symbolism of all this eluded Richard but there were

words inscribed upon the objects and Richard traced them, speaking each letter in turn in his head before repeating them out loud.

'Oliver Cromwell,' he murmured, '1599 to 1658.'

Richard looked up, astonished, and then scrutinised the page again to make sure he had read it correctly. He mouthed the dates and gulped nervously. According to the strange book, his father would die in ten years' time!

Quickly, he read on. 'Lord Protec- Lord Protector of England, Scotland and Ireland.'

Richard felt his pulse quicken and a strange, buzzing in his ears. His father, then, would rule the kingdom, alone. As something called Lord Protector.

Richard laid the book down on the blanket and shivered. What could it mean? Where had the strange volume come from?

'Perhaps some prophecy,' he muttered to himself.

He picked up the book again. It was unlike anything he had ever set eyes on before. He knew that it was somehow special.

A fragment of some conversation sprang into his mind. Of course! The Scotch seer and his doctor. He had heard of the strangers Thurloe had uncovered. Perhaps the book had something to do with them.

Resolving to investigate further in the morning, Richard was about to put the book aside and go to sleep when a thought struck him.

Gingerly, he began to leaf through the pages. What if he were in there, too?

Captain Sal Winter's peg leg made a hollow clopping sound on the cobbles as she and Ben followed Stanislaus and Godley.

Ben gritted his teeth, convinced that the noise would be heard, but they kept their distance through the labyrinthine streets and, though more than once they thought they had lost the two men, they eventually came to a halt in a small, tumbledown courtyard.

It was dominated by a vast, sloping roof which came down from the highest building in the yard and continued to the ground, a kind of rough barn having been erected in its shelter.

Next to this was a collection of ramshackle houses with high gables and broken lead guttering. One of these, smaller than the rest with elaborate but faded blue tiles on its walls, had a lamp burning in a window.

Ben and Winter kept well back, crouching down by the barn and watching as Stanislaus approached the house.

He looked behind him furtively and then laid his hand on a wire bell pull. There was a soft, resounding tinkle and the sound of someone stirring within. Godley swept his hat from his head and he too looked back the way they had come, his big brown eyes shining in the starlight.

After a moment a bolt was drawn back and the door opened, revealing an extraordinarily tall figure standing in the porchway. From their vantage point at the entrance to the courtyard, Ben and Winter could make out nothing of the man's features. He inclined his head slightly, as though in greeting, and Stanislaus and Godley went inside.

As soon as the door was closed behind them, Ben crept out from his hiding place and, keeping close to the walls of the houses, made his way to the tiled residence.

Once he was below the window he sat down on the cold ground and beckoned urgently to Winter. The woman began to hobble across the courtyard and Ben winced at the steady clatter of her false leg.

Winter gasped as she slid her bulk down next to Ben and the young man held up his finger in a gesture of silence. There was more light coming from within the house now and they could see the shadows of the three men moving about.

After a time, all three sat down and Ben pricked his ears in the hope of catching a fragment of their conversation. If only the weather had been warmer, he thought ruefully, perhaps the window would have been propped open. But it was cold now and he drew his cloak closely about him as the night air grew ever more chill.

Ben beckoned to Winter, who slid across the cobbles on her voluminous backside.

'What else do you know about this Stanislaus bloke?' asked Ben in a low whisper.

Winter's huge shoulders contracted in a shrug. 'He's no better than a pirate,' she spat. 'And treats his men no better than beasts.'

Ben frowned. 'Then why do they stay with him?'

Winter grunted. 'Pirates pay well. They get to supplement their wage with whatever booty they can strip off other ships.'

Ben nodded to himself. 'But if he's just a kind of mercenary, why's he so loyal to the King?'

Winter smiled. 'He fancies he has blue blood himself, do you see? Claims to have been sired by the King of Poland.'

Without thinking, the big captain let out a loud chortle.

Ben clamped his hand over Winter's mouth but it was too late. Shadows moved inside the house and footsteps hurried to the door.

Ben hauled Winter to her feet and they clattered as fast as they could across the courtyard and around the corner of the barn.

The door of the house flew open and Stanislaus stood framed there. His head moved from side to side like that of a great lizard as he scanned the darkness.

Ben and Winter pressed themselves flat against the wall, scarcely daring to breathe.

Then Ben's concentration shifted as he felt a strange, heavy warmth on his foot. He looked down but couldn't make anything out in the darkness. He almost gasped as he felt a warm, furry something brush past his leg.

Looking down hard, he make out a shape, a patch of blackness that was distinct from the night. There was a gentle, insistent clicking and Ben felt a shudder run through him. Whatever it was was gnawing at his shoe.

Suddenly, some way off, a lamp was lit in another house, providing the exterior of the barn with just enough illumination for Ben to see that a big black rat was sitting on his foot.

It was incredibly long, obscenely fat, and sleek with moisture. Its scaly black tail was wrapped around Ben's heel.

He let his breath stream out through his teeth, feeling his stomach flip over.

If only he could kick out his leg and throw the thing off… But he knew that would be fatal. Stanislaus would see them and the game would be up.

The next breath he took, he held, as the rat began to draw closer to his trouser leg. He could feel its bristly fur poking through the material of his trousers and his hair stood on end at the horror of it.

He rolled his eyes and bit into his lower lip, screaming silently inside. If the rat got any closer he would have to cry out, have to smash the vile thing against the wall, anything to get it away from him.

The horrid weight on his foot shifted as the rat sat up on its hind legs and sniffed at Ben's shin, its whiskers twitching.

Ben steadied himself. There was nothing he could do. No choice. He had to be rid of the disgusting creature…

Suddenly he saw the iron-capped end of Winter's leg hove into view. The captain took aim and then swung her leg in a vicious kick which sent the rat flying across the courtyard.

It hit the ground squealing and scurried instantly into the darkest recesses of the place.

Stanislaus saw it and smiled grimly. He nodded to himself, then withdrew into the house, apparently satisfied. The door was closed and bolted after him.

Ben turned and winked at Winter. Then he sank back against the wall, sweat dribbling down his face.

Christopher Whyte swept his hat from his head and entered the room above the inn, a rectangle of yellowy light from the corridor spilling inside and revealing Sir John Copper, sitting in the darkness. Whyte hovered in the doorway until Copper spoke.

'I am not asleep, Chris. Come inside. Quickly.'

Whyte closed the door and moved swiftly across the room while Copper lit the lamp. The older man looked up inquisitively.

'Well?'

Whyte threw himself down in a chair and sighed. 'I've had quite a day,' he said with a grin, flinging his hat into the corner and lifting his weary legs onto the table.

Copper smoothed his white moustache. 'The girl?'

Whyte nodded. 'She spent the night in St James's Park and then wandered around like a lost thing until she came back here.'

'Here?'

'Aye. She ran into our landlord's daughter and they went off on a little errand.'

Copper frowned and leaned forward. 'Does she know anything?'

Whyte's face fell a little. 'I don't know. She certainly hasn't found that friend of hers, whoever he was.' He closed his eyes

131

and smiled. 'You don't know how hard it was not to offer her a bed last night.'

Copper grinned himself. 'The ladies can wait until we've saved the King, my lad.'

He rose and paced the room, hands behind his back. 'I'm sorry to have sent you out on a fool's errand, Chris. I thought we might be on to something.'

Whyte's eyes flicked open and he flashed Copper his most charming smile. 'Ah, but we might be.'

Copper stopped and turned. 'What do you mean?'

Whyte took Frances's note from his tunic and laid it down on the table. 'Do we know a… Thomas Culpeper?'

Copper shook his head. 'Should we?'

'He's only one of Cromwell's lieutenants,' said Whyte.

Copper nodded. 'The name is familiar now you say it. One of Henry Ireton's cronies, is he not?'

Whyte shrugged.

'Well, what of him?' asked Copper, puzzled.

Whyte stretched out his legs and dug his hands into the pockets of his breeches. 'Our friend Mistress Polly may or may not be all innocence, but her friend, the landlord's daughter, is engaged in an… *affaire du cœur* with said Master Culpeper. What do you think about that?'

Copper sank down into a chair and swallowed, his eyes blazing with excitement. 'Go on.'

'Well,' said Whyte, relaxing into his story. 'Young Frances Kemp left a note for her dearest, asking if he has heard anything about the whereabouts of Polly's friends. He's obviously close to the general. I wonder if we can't make use of it.'

Copper nodded eagerly. 'I think we can. Where are they now? The women, I mean?'

Whyte pointed to the floor. 'They're here. I think Mistress Polly intends to rest her bones in the tavern for the night.'

Copper rubbed his chin. 'I must consider this news, Chris. The link with the boy Culpeper could prove decisive. You must bring Frances to me later. She must be made to understand her duty to the King.'

Whyte nodded slowly. 'And we still go ahead as planned?'

'Of course,' said Copper. 'Our first priority must be to free His Majesty. All other considerations are secondary.'

Whyte dragged his feet from the table and stood up. 'Very well. I'll bring the girl once the household is asleep. What about Polly?'

Copper smiled. 'Well, you did say something about a bed for the night…'

Whyte smiled and turned on his heel.

Thurloe entered Cromwell's apartments to find the general still awake, poring over a letter. His eyes were moist with tears and a strange grin was fixed on his flushed face.

Remaining in the doorway, his cloak swaying in the breeze from the open window, Thurloe reflected on the strange contradictions of the great man to whom he was so loyal. It was extraordinary but one who invoked such awe and fear, one so determined and single-minded, could yet be reduced to weeping by the slightest act of tenderness. Thurloe had seen the general with tears rolling down his cheeks as he listened, utterly transported, to some passage of sweet music. And he had wept when he had witnessed the King's reunion with his royal children, moved beyond words by the King's emotion.

Perhaps it was his own losses that made him so tender-hearted in that direction.

Cromwell looked up and beckoned to him, wiping the tears from his eyes with the back of his hand. 'John. Here a moment.' He thrust the letter under Thurloe's nose. 'It's from my daughter, Bridget.'

Thurloe nodded, not a bit surprised. 'All's well, I trust?'

Cromwell nodded and smiled. 'Oh, yes, yes. And that husband of hers is giving no trouble. Not that Bridget would ever let him, eh?'

He chortled merrily and Thurloe smiled back. 'You desired to see me, General?'

'Mmm,' said Cromwell, placing his arm on Thurloe's shoulder. 'Please sit down.'

Thurloe did so in a high-backed, uncomfortable chair.

Cromwell took his accustomed seat, adjusting the cushions to take account of his bothersome boil, and sat forward, holding his hands together as though in prayer. 'John, I am most vexed by what Sir Thomas Fairfax has said.'

'Vexed?'

'Aye,' said Cromwell with a frown. 'And he is not alone in saying that we can't walk about cutting off our monarch's head.'

Thurloe sighed. 'With respect to Sir Thomas, General, the King has not yet stood trial.'

'Oh, fie, John!' cried Cromwell. 'The King will be found guilty, we all know that. Damn it, we all want that.'

'All but Sir Thomas Fairfax, it seems,' said Thurloe quietly.

Cromwell waved his hand. 'There is no treachery, John. You have been too long among spies and agents. Fairfax is as brave and honourable man as ever I have known. And I listen to him because of that.'

Thurloe pinched the bridge of his nose wearily. 'We gave the King every chance to come to an honourable peace, sir. You now that better than any other. Yet, whilst he pretended to study our demands, did he not make secret plans to bring in foreign troops to shore up his discredited throne?'

Cromwell's large head nodded slowly. 'And now we say he must pay with his life. But what then, John?'

Thurloe looked up. 'Then?'

'I am no Republican. You know that,' said Cromwell. 'What are we to have if we have no King?'

Thurloe was becoming concerned. 'A council of state, as we proposed. Then no more will we be ruled by the whim of one man.'

Cromwell stared into space. 'This seer and his Doctor. They see an empty throne.'

'Naturally.'

'But I must know more,' said Cromwell urgently. 'Will the throne remain empty, or will one of Charles's heirs snatch it back within the twelvemonth?'

Thurloe smiled. 'You must ask them, not me.'

'I will, John, I will.'

Thurloe shifted his weight on the uncomfortable chair. 'Am I to understand that you think a council of state an inadequate replacement for Charles Stuart?'

'Nay,' said Cromwell abruptly. 'But to govern… to govern this land of ours is a Herculean labour. Some say it must have a figurehead. Of sorts.'

Thurloe looked Cromwell directly in the eye. 'Who says this?'

Cromwell's eyes dropped evasively. 'I have many advisers, John. You know that.'

Thurloe slapped his hand across his knee. 'It's Henry Ireton, is it not? And that lad Culpeper?'

Cromwell nodded and held up the letter. 'My Bridget's letter is full of it. She says her Henry talks of nothing else.'

Thurloe rose crossly to his feet. 'I may not have any influence over your son-in-law, sir, but I would certainly argue the toss with Culpeper. He thinks far too highly of himself and gives you ill counsel.'

Cromwell said nothing, merely staring into space.

Thurloe bent towards him, his face right by the general's ear. 'Ruling this country is, as you say, a Herculean labour, General. And we must ensure we are up to the job.'

He bowed and swept from the room, leaving Cromwell staring broodingly into the fire.

Much to her relief, Polly was able to bathe and change once she returned to the inn. Frances made her very welcome in her little bedroom and, though the bath was a tiny, cramped, tin affair placed in front of the fire, the hot water was a blessed relief.

She lay and soaked in it for as long as she dared and then changed into a simple white nightdress. The clean, fresh material was like a soothing balm.

Frances had gone down to help her mother clear up in the kitchen and Polly was just eyeing the large, soft bed with its plump pillows when there was a quiet knock at the door.

Not quite sure what to do, Polly hesitated. The knock came again and she moved swiftly to the door. She opened it just enough to see that her handsome stranger was on the other side.

Christopher Whyte averted his eyes at once. 'Oh, forgive me, mistress,' he mumbled apologetically.

Polly looked down at her nightdress and smiled. If only such chivalry still existed in 1966!

'Just a sec,' she said and closed the door. She quickly slipped on the green woollen dress which Frances had laid out for her, and then opened the door wide.

Whyte smiled broadly, looking her up and down with an appreciative eye. 'Forgive me, Mistress Polly…'

'That's all right,' said Polly with a smile. 'And you can just call me Polly.'

'Can I?' He seemed astonished. 'Oh. Very well.'

Polly stepped to one side. 'Come in.'

Whyte shook his head. 'Nay, that would be improper.'

Polly frowned, rather disappointedly. 'Oh, yes. I suppose it would. Well, what can I do for you, Mr…?'

He swept his hat from his head and bowed, his shining hair falling forward in curls. 'I am Christopher Whyte, lady.'

Polly was enchanted. 'What can I do for you, Christopher Whyte?'

Whyte cleared his throat. 'It is rather more what I can do for you.'

Polly smiled cheekily. 'Oh, yes?'

'Yes. You see, I have news of your friends.'

Polly almost seized him by the collar. 'You do? Where? Where are they?'

Whyte smoothed down his tunic and stepped back a little. 'I have word that they are close by. In a castle on the Solent.'

Polly's mouth turned downward. 'On the Solent? What are they doing there?'

Whyte shrugged. 'I know no more. But I can take you to them. Tomorrow.'

'Why not now?'

Whyte shook his head and his hair rustled over his lacy collar. 'No, no. It's far too late. But they are safe, I swear to it. You will see them tomorrow.'

Polly seemed dissatisfied with this, but gradually her expression softened. 'Very well. As long as they're safe.' She glanced longingly at the comfortable bed. 'I must admit, I wouldn't mind getting my head down.'

Whyte laughed. 'Getting your head down where?'

'You know. Sleep.'

Whyte smiled. 'Ah, yes. Sleep.' He too cast his eye towards the bed but with a different look on his face altogether. He looked back to Polly and cocked his head. 'Polly, you are like no woman I have ever known.'

'I should hope not,' she said with a giggle. Then she leaned forward and kissed him gently on the cheek. 'Goodnight, Christopher Whyte. And thank you.'

He held her gaze for a moment and then bowed. 'Good night, Polly.'

Putting his hat back on his handsome head, he left the room, closing the door after him.

He lingered in the corridor for a moment, his face set in a deep frown, conflicting emotions chasing over his features. Then he made his way up the stairs towards Sir John Copper's chamber.

Ben flung himself back against the wall of the ramshackle barn as Stanislaus and Godley exited into the courtyard and made their way towards the street.

They seemed noticeably more relaxed and Godley clapped Stanislaus on the shoulder in a friendly fashion.

The captain flinched and scowled at Godley, who shrugged and removed his hand.

'Well, friend,' he said in a determinedly cheerful fashion, 'that's that. What say we have ourselves a little sport before turning in?'

Stanislaus's face remained impassive until, slowly and almost unwillingly, a rather cruel smile crept over his features. 'Why not? I know of a place. A place where we can buy... entertainment for a few guilders.'

Godley was delighted and clapped his gloved hands together. 'Excellent!' He ushered Stanislaus forward. 'Onward, my dear Captain. Onward!'

They strolled away.

When the coast was clear, Ben stepped boldly back on to the street and peered through the darkness after the retreating figures.

'Well,' said Winter, chewing her lip. 'They carried naught that I could see.'

Ben shook his head. 'No. No package.' He turned to the buxom captain. 'What now? Should we follow them?'

Winter shook her head. 'They're on pleasure bent,' she said. 'And God help the Judies the Pole lays his claws upon.' She thought for a moment, rubbing her silver nose as though for inspiration. 'We'd best be getting aboard the *Demeter*, friend. She sails at dawn.'

Ben nodded. 'Will we reach London first?' he inquired anxiously.

'God willing,' said Winter. 'It depends on all manner of things. Tide. Wind.'

'Oh,' said Ben disappointedly.

'And the fact that I was a better captain at three years old than the Pole will be in all his lifetime!' cackled Winter. 'Of course we'll get there before 'em. But what's your plan, Ben?'

Ben shrugged. 'I just want to find my friends, that's all.'

Winter eyed him interestedly, her one eye twinkling. 'And what of this mystery?'

Ben shrugged and then grinned.

'Ha! You're a card, Ben Jackson,' cried Winter, her fat face shaking. 'I can read you like a book. You think there's dirty work afoot, yes?'

Ben nodded urgently. 'All I know is I've got a funny feeling that lot are up to something big. And I think we should find out what it is, don't you?'

Winter drew herself up to her full, imposing height. 'Naturally I do. Sal Winter never runs from a fight. Especially if it's with that damned Pole and his gang of cutthroats!'

Ben chuckled to himself. 'I'm glad to hear it. Now, how about this? Why don't we try and get aboard the *Teazer* and have a root around? Maybe there's something in Stanislaus's cabin that'll give us a clue to this whole thing.'

Winter gave an enthusiastic nod. 'Aye. If we hurry we might just steal a march on every man jack of 'em.'

Keeping close to the walls, the incongruous pair set off at a swift pace for the docks.

The first dreary streaks of dawn were spreading through the sky when the door to the Doctor and Jamie's quarters was opened. The key turned silently in the lock and a figure stole inside, his long black coat, which hung almost down to his boots, whispering around his legs. He scanned the room carefully.

There was the boy, sound asleep on top of the bed. Next to him, the curve of the Doctor's shoulder could be made out. The boy was snoring gently.

The newcomer was about to step closer when the Doctor's voice came out of nowhere.

'Shall I shed a little light on things, Mr Thurloe? There's really no need for all this skulduggery.'

Thurloe whirled around in surprise. The Doctor's voice was coming from the window casement. A match was struck and a candle lit, revealing the little man, in shirtsleeves, sitting cross-legged on the sill and smiling.

He nodded towards the bed and the bundle he had made from a pillow and his frock coat. 'It's an obvious ruse, I know,' he said. 'But they're often the most effective.'

Thurloe gave a small, grudging smile. 'Well versed in the arts of espionage, Doctor?'

'Oh, I dabble,' said the Doctor. 'But aren't you the spymaster around these parts?'

Thurloe crossed the room and, lifting the skirts of his coat, sat down opposite the Doctor. He looked out of the window onto the snowy gardens outside. He could see the outlines of hedges and leafless trees beginning to emerge.

'You know that I am not as easily taken in by portents and prophecies as is the general,' he stated flatly.

The Doctor looked at him interestedly. 'I'd be disappointed if you were.'

Thurloe turned and caught the Doctor's gaze. His face was thrown into stark relief by the dawn light and the sputtering candle flame. 'You'll be more closely questioned tomorrow, I can assure you.'

The Doctor nodded. 'And of course it's your job to protect the general from any charlatans or enemies of the state who seek to… er… bamboozle him?'

'Precisely!' cried Thurloe. 'Charlatans or enemies of the state. You put it very succinctly, Doctor.'

The Doctor looked over towards Jamie. 'We don't mean any harm, you know. We're just travellers. And he's scarcely more than a boy.'

Thurloe nodded slowly and then looked away. 'There is darkness all around us, Doctor,' he said at last.

The Doctor looked out of the window. 'Not really. I think it might be quite a pleasant day,' he said brightly.

Thurloe shook his head. 'That is not what I meant.'

The Doctor frowned and the lines on his face grew deeper. 'Oh. I see.'

Thurloe folded his arms and suddenly began to speak very rapidly. 'Parliament will shortly vote through the trial of the King. If he is executed there will be a new order in this land. I do not doubt that the kingmakers will attempt to place the crown upon the general's head.'

The Doctor nodded, with an expression of feigned ignorance on his face.

'I am completely loyal to the general, you must understand that,' continued Thurloe.

The Doctor nodded again.

'But I fear that the mood of the people may turn his head. He is a God-fearing man, but there could be such clamour for him to take the crown.' Thurloe looked levelly at the Doctor. 'I do not think this should happen. Cromwell did not want to destroy the monarchy. The monarchy has destroyed itself. And if that is the way it must be, it must remain destroyed.'

The Doctor cleared his throat. 'What do you want me to do?'

Thurloe examined his fingernails in the candlelight.

'The general sets much store by seers and wise folk. If you can... say something that will plant a seed of doubt, chafe away at the back of his mind to make him... think carefully should the throne ever be offered him, then I would be grateful.'

'How grateful?' said the Doctor evenly.

'Your freedom,' said Thurloe. 'Money.'

The Doctor waved his hand impatiently and the candle flame flickered in the draught. 'I don't want money. But I would like to ask a favour.'

Thurloe rose from the casement. 'We will discuss this later. First you have to convince the general that you and the boy are the genuine article.'

He moved back across the room and disappeared into the darkness. A man of the shadows, thought the Doctor. Yes, that's where he belongs.

Thurloe's voice drifted back as he opened the door. 'Charlatan or enemy of the state. As to which of these you are, Doctor, we shall see upon the morn.'

The door closed behind him with a solid thud.

Polly was sound asleep, her curled back rising and falling gently.

Frances was lying next to her, but the landlord's daughter

was awake, blinking slowly in the darkness, her mind fizzing with thoughts.

The room was chilly now, its fire long since extinguished, and Frances was grateful for the thick blankets and the warmth of her new friend, lying beside her. She wondered longingly how it might feel to have Thomas's arms around her now, holding her tightly, pressing her to his chest.

Unconsciously, she folded her arms over her own body and squeezed herself, imagining the pressure of her love's strong body. But would such a day ever come? How could there ever be a reconciliation between her father's views and those of Thomas? There could be only one outcome to this: a final and devastating schism between herself and William Kemp.

At least her mother understood. She knew how a young girl's heart could melt and be enslaved by a noble creature like Thomas Culpeper. Hadn't she said as much about the days her father had spent courting her? Sometimes Frances found it hard to believe that her parents had ever been young, that they had spent lovely, carefree days simply enjoying each other's company. Her father must have been handsome then, full of fun and vigour, not the bitter, misanthropic figure Frances had come to loathe.

There was a soft creak of wood from close by and Frances suddenly knew she was not alone in the room. She reached out to clasp Polly's arm but a broad, warm hand was suddenly clamped across her mouth. She looked round wildly in the darkness and started as her father's voice hissed out.

'Don't be afraid, my dove. But get up now. Your father has business for you.'

He moved his hand from her face and Frances hastily drew on a gown and slippers.

'What is it, Father?' she asked in trepidation. 'Is something the matter?'

She could see her father's bulk looming in the darkness. 'Nothing's wrong, Frances. Just be quick now and follow me.'

He opened the door and crept out into the corridor.

Frances felt a thrill of fear run through her. And yet her father had been in such a different mood all day. Perhaps this had something to do with it.

As she followed her father, Frances heard a distant church bell toll three in the morning.

Keeping close behind Kemp, she realised they were ascending the stairs towards the upper room, the room she had so wanted to see inside. Now she desired none of it, wanted only to run back to bed and hide beneath the blankets. What if the men Polly had spoken about were still there? Might they question her too?

Kemp knocked gently on the door and a man's voice told him to enter.

The room she saw was lit by three or four candles and Frances found herself shivering in the unaccustomed brightness.

An imposing-looking man with a white beard sat at the top end of the table, studying a sheaf of papers. He didn't look up as Frances entered but the other occupant of the chamber did.

He was every bit as handsome as Polly had said and smiled kindly as Kemp led Frances to a chair.

'Father,' she said quietly. 'What is it? What's amiss?'

Kemp laid a heavy hand on her shoulder. 'Hush, child,' he said testily.

Frances felt her heart begin to pound. She watched the older man reading for a while, then he looked up and stared at her. His eyes were cold, malicious.

'Mistress Kemp,' he said at last, 'you know a man named Thomas Culpeper?'

The name went like a dagger to Frances's heart. She felt a

cold sweat spring out on her forehead.

'Tom? Yes, of course. He was the baker's lad. I used to see him often. When I was a girl. I've been running errands there for years.'

She glanced up at her father, seeking confirmation, but Kemp's blank expression didn't alter.

Christopher Whyte took his turn. 'He left his father's service and went to war.'

Frances frowned. 'He did? I hope he is well.'

Whyte smiled, charmed by her play-acting. 'He is. In fact, he's done rather well for himself. He's been appointed to General Cromwell's lifeguard.'

'Really?' said Frances, stifling a yawn.

Copper tossed a square of paper across the table. 'Did you write this?'

Frances did not have to look at the letter to know. A wave of cold terror washed over her. Was everything discovered? Her relationship with Thomas? Their secret trysts?

'Well?' hissed Kemp, looming over his daughter like a vengeful giant.

Frances clasped her hands together. 'What am I accused of? Is this a star chamber that I am brought to—'

Kemp lashed out with his big hand and slapped her across the cheek. She yelled as she felt the impact sting her soft skin.

'Slut!' barked Kemp. 'I have toiled to save my King's life whilst my own daughter ruts with his enemies!'

He raised his hand to strike her again but Whyte shot to his feet and grabbed Kemp's arm.

'Enough, Kemp! This is no time for recriminations. There's too much to be done.'

Kemp swung away, his back ramrod straight, boiling with fury.

Copper regarded Frances steadily as tears rolled down her

cheeks. 'My dear,' he said quietly, 'we don't seek to blame you. Heaven only knows where the heart may lead us. But what we ask of you now is to help us.'

Frances could hardly think straight. 'What do you mean?'

Copper looked up at the ceiling and stroked his beard. 'You are in an invaluable position, lady. You have the heart and, therefore, the ear of one of Cromwell's closest aides. We only ask that you acquire a little… information for us.'

Frances was aghast. 'And betray Thomas? Never!'

Kemp swung back and raised his hand threateningly. 'You'll do as you're instructed, girl or—'

This time Whyte's sword flashed from its scabbard and he pointed it menacingly towards the landlord's throat. 'I've warned you, Kemp. I'll not tolerate such behaviour. Your daughter may be of use to us, but you are eminently dispensable. Is that understood?'

Kemp glowered, his hand still raised.

'Is it?' hissed Whyte.

Kemp nodded slowly and lowered his arm. Whyte sheathed his sword and resumed his place, huffing with repressed fury.

Sir John Copper gave a small sigh and continued, as though the incident had been a minor distraction.

'It is not a question of betrayal, Frances. We merely wish to know certain dates and times. How we put this information to use is our own business. Besides –' he arched an eyebrow mockingly – 'have you not betrayed your father and your King already?'

Frances set her jaw determinedly. 'I will not do it.'

Copper returned to his examination of the papers. 'You'll find that you will, my dear. In the morning.'

He waved her away. Kemp put his brawny arms around Frances and dragged her to her feet. Kicking and protesting, she was hustled out of the room.

Copper turned at once to Whyte. 'This is heaven-sent, Chris,' he smiled. 'Through Culpeper we might find out the duty times of the King's guards. It will make the whole operation much easier.'

Whyte nodded. 'It would still be better if we had someone on the inside.'

Copper considered this. 'What of the serving girl? At Hurst Castle?'

Whyte grimaced. 'Unreliable. I would hate to stake my life on her cooperation. No, better that we substitute another.'

Copper's face contracted into a smile. 'You have someone in mind?'

Whyte nodded slowly. 'I do. A rare woman indeed.'

CHAPTER
6

The *Teazer* creaked and shuddered as she scraped alongside the other ships in the harbour.

Ben and Winter had clambered aboard. There was only one man on watch and he was sleeping soundly, his huge chest rising and falling like the bellows of a pipe organ.

Winter looked rapidly about. 'I can't think why I've not done this before,' she said, shaking her head. 'Lord knows I've had opportunity enough.'

'You just needed someone to spur you on,' whispered Ben. 'Now, come on, let's get to his cabin.'

The captain nodded and thrust her peg leg forward. Ben went ahead, crossing the deck on which he had so recently toiled. As stealthily as possible and keeping flat against the woodwork, the two made their way to what was Stanislaus's cabin.

Winter turned up her nose in disgust. 'I can smell him from here,' she spat. With a nod to Ben, and a sharp intake of breath, she kicked open the door and swaggered inside.

Ben followed a little more sheepishly.

The cabin was large and handsomely furnished. Rich red velvet drapes shrouded Stanislaus's narrow bed, which occupied the whole of one corner. There were brass navigation instruments on every surface and a broad oak desk covered in papers. A brass chandelier which was hanging from the low ceiling swung gently back and forth in time to the ship's gentle movement.

Winter cursed and spat a great black gobbet of tobacco onto the bare floor.

Ben glanced through the mullioned window at the rapidly lightening sky. 'We'd better get a shift on,' he muttered.

Winter leaned over the desk and peered at the papers. 'Now then, before we start looking for whatever it is we hope to find, you keep your eyes peeled for a strongbox.'

Ben was puzzled. 'What do you mean?'

Winter began pulling books and charts from shelves, scanning the room with an intensity that was almost feverish. 'The Pole has a strongbox somewhere,' she insisted. 'There's something of mine in it that I want back.'

Ben looked a little sick and fluttered his hand over his face. 'It's not…?'

Winter turned and laughed loudly. 'No, Lord bless, it ain't my nose!' Still cackling, she began to sift through the charts and maps that were stacked in the corner of the cabin.

Ben joined in, though he was more concerned with the paperwork, hoping to find something that would give them a clue to the mystery. 'So Stanislaus is sort of your Moby-Dick?' he said absently.

Winter did not pause in her search. 'My what?'

'Nothing,' said Ben, moving back towards the door. 'Found anything?'

Winter shook her head, hands grabbing at everything that wasn't screwed down. 'A moment, Ben. I've been waiting many years for this.'

Suddenly the door creaked and slammed shut, revealing a figure who had been hiding behind it the whole time.

Ben and Winter turned to see two pistols levelled at their chests.

The Doctor gazed at his reflection in the frosted-over bowl of water and then, with a resigned shrug, shattered the ice with his elbow. He rolled up his sleeves and splashed cold water over his face.

There was no towel about and he stumbled over to the bed, water dripping into his eyes, until he found his frock coat. He wiped his face dry with it and then stumbled backward onto Jamie's bed.

The young Scot sat up with a cry and the Doctor flashed him an apologetic smile.

'Sorry to wake you, Jamie.'

Jamie rubbed his eyes and stretched. 'What time is it?'

'Sixteen forty-eight,' said the Doctor cheekily.

Jamie tutted and buried his head in the pillow.

The Doctor got up and struggled into his coat. 'It's about six in the morning. I think we should be ready for an early audience with Cromwell.'

Jamie groaned. 'Och, do I have to go through all that again?'

'I'm afraid so,' said the Doctor sheepishly. 'And it's even more important now. We had a visitor last night.'

'Yon smelly fella?'

The Doctor shook his head. 'No. Mr Thurloe. He wanted to strike a bargain.'

Jamie sat up, interested. 'What kind of bargain?'

Chuckling, the Doctor began to pace the room. 'Well, he's worried about the future, you see.'

Jamie nodded. 'And he wants us to predict how things'll come out? Aye, well, that's easy enough.'

'No, no, no,' muttered the Doctor. 'He sees right through us, I'm sure. The point is, Cromwell might well believe that you're the McCrimmon of Culloden. And that could prove very useful to Mr Thurloe.'

Jamie frowned. 'How?'

'Well, I'll explain. But first we must find that book. Apart from everything else, we need to get our facts straight. Now, let me see, it's Christmas 1648. What happens next, I wonder?'

What happened next was that a key turned in the lock and a guard entered the room. He looked at the Doctor and Jamie and then stepped back, ushering in the slight, unprepossessing figure of Richard Cromwell.

He blinked repeatedly as though the grey morning light disagreed with him, then turned and waved the guard out. He stood in silence for a long moment, and the Doctor decided to take the initiative.

'Hello,' he said. 'Can we help you?'

Richard looked at him with real fear, his mouth trembling. 'My name is Richard Cromwell,' he said, glancing at Jamie out of the corner of his eye. 'And I shall die a hopeless failure in 1712.'

The Doctor fiddled with his hands. 'Oh dear,' he said.

Someone was crying, Polly could tell. In her mind's eye, she saw it as a little girl on a garden swing, fists screwed up close to her eyes, bawling her little heart out. Hot tears ran over her plump little cheeks and splashed onto her little summer dress. Polly heard the poor thing sobbing and moved to help.

She opened her eyes and found that she was reaching out into empty space.

Blinking, she began to reorientate herself and found that the sobbing was real. She turned over in bed. Frances was gone. But the sound of her crying was distinctly audible from downstairs.

Polly frowned concernedly and jumped out of bed. Hastily,

she put on her green dress, petticoats, and soft leather shoes. A little white mobcap had been laid out too and she swiftly clapped it on to her head and tucked her hair inside it.

Satisfied that she now looked every inch a Stuart girl, she moved to the door and tried to open it. It wouldn't budge.

Frowning, Polly tried again. This time she rammed her shoulder against the woodwork in case the door was jammed. But it refused to open.

With a little huff of irritation, she began to hammer on the door with the heel of her palm. There was no response and she could still hear Frances's sobs coming through the floor below. There was another sound too, a sort of comforting cooing which Polly took to be Frances's mother. What on earth could have happened to make her so upset?

She raised her hand to bang again when there was a scrabbling sound in the lock and the door swung open.

Christopher Whyte was framed in the doorway, the key dangling from his gloved hand. 'A trifle more respectable than when last we met, eh, Polly?' he said saucily.

Suddenly Polly didn't like his attitude and regretted having given him permission to use her first name like that. She snatched the key from him. 'Am I a prisoner?'

Whyte held up his hands. 'Nay, lady. It's for your own protection. An inn is no place for one such as yourself to sleep. Your slumbers may have been… disturbed.'

Polly sighed. 'Are you going to take me to see my friends now?'

Whyte smiled happily. 'Yes. Yes, of course. We'll begin the ride at once. I have horses outside.'

Polly picked up her mud-splashed cloak and swung it over shoulders. 'Right. I'll just say goodbye to Frances and we can be on our way.'

Whyte shook his head and moved to bar the way down the

stairs. 'No. There isn't time.'

Polly looked at him oddly. 'It'll only take a minute. I think she's upset.'

'Yes. She is. There's been some bad news. A death in the family,' said Whyte quickly.

Polly's face fell. 'Oh, how awful. Who?'

Whyte looked momentarily flummoxed. 'It was her brother. Yes. Her brother, I'm afraid.'

Polly made a little sympathetic cluck and shook her head. 'Poor girl. And I suppose they all want to be left alone?'

Whyte nodded hastily. 'Aye. Now, the horses?'

He led her down a separate stairway that led directly to the back of the inn.

Two horses, puffing and stamping in the cold, were tethered to a wooden rail. Whyte jumped athletically onto one and helped Polly onto the other.

She sank back on to the saddle in silence.

Whyte looked at her oddly. 'Is all well, Polly?'

Polly nodded and smiled and urged him forward. She trotted behind him as they moved off and stared at his back, suddenly full of suspicions. Frances had told her about her brother. Dead the past four years.

The figure behind the door of Stanislaus's cabin stepped out into a beam of dusty dawn light and Ben let out a huge sigh of relief. It was Ashdown.

'Am I glad to see you!' chirped Ben.

But his relief was short-lived. Ashdown's pistols remained levelled at both him and Winter.

'What are you doing here?' barked Ashdown.

Winter put her hands on her hips and threw her head back defiantly. 'What do you think, you sot? We've come to find that blasted captain of yours and run the bugger through!'

Ben rolled his eyes. 'Look, mate. You've got to help us. Stanislaus is bringing something back to London. A package from Holland.'

Ashdown nodded. 'Aye. And what's it to do with you?'

Ben indicated Winter. 'We reckon he's up to some mischief.'

Ashdown smiled grimly. 'He wouldn't be Captain Stanislaus if he weren't up to mischief.'

Ben held out his hands placatingly. 'This is different, mate. He could be up to something… treasonable.'

Ashdown frowned but his grip on the pistols didn't falter. 'Like what?'

Winter let her fat tongue protrude out over her lip. 'Well, mate,' she said slyly, 'that's what we're here to find out.'

Ben looked the sailor in the eye. 'Come on. You owe me one, remember? If it wasn't for you I'd be safe in London.'

'In London, but hardly safe, Ben,' chuckled Ashdown. 'I found you slugged in the road if I remember aright.'

Ben grinned. 'So you did. But help us now, can't you? We must know what him and that Godley fella are bringing back home.'

Ashdown sighed. 'I confess, some of us have been worried for a while. These constant trips to France.'

'France?' queried Ben.

Winter nodded. 'Aye. I've kept an eye on that. The Pole seems inordinately fond of the French these days.' She looked towards Ashdown, her ruddy face creasing into a horrible smile. 'Now, lad, if you're loyal to the new order, you'll help us get to the root of all this.'

Ashdown grimaced bitterly. 'I remember a time when a man was loyal to no one but his King.'

Winter threw up her hands in agitation. 'Was that not what we fought for, oaf? Would you now restore Charles Stuart to his bloody throne? Nay, if we are good Englishmen… well, good English anyway, we must see this thing through, and bring to justice any enemy of Parliament!'

Ben nodded to himself, thinking that an orator like Winter wouldn't make a bad politician herself.

Ashdown lowered his pistols a little. 'I don't see what I can rightly do.'

Ben turned his hand palm upward, pleadingly. 'You can start by letting us get off this ship, Isaac. And then have a sniff about. Then, when we get back to London, we can compare notes.'

Ashdown thought for a long moment, looking first at Ben and then at the huge, bizarre figure of Sal Winter. Finally he nodded. 'Very well. I have a few scores to settle with Stanislaus myself—'

He stopped abruptly as Winter leapt forward and retrieved a small wood-and-iron chest from beneath the desk.

With a cry of triumph, she slammed it onto the desk, pulled a knife from her filthy velvet coat, and prised the lock open with the blade.

The lid sprang back and Winter rooted hastily about inside.

'Well, well,' she murmured in surprise. 'The old dog kept his word.'

So saying, she pulled a bundle of what looked like letters, tied with a mauve ribbon, from the box and stuffed them into her pocket.

'What are those?' asked Ben.

Winter winked and tapped the tip of her silver nose. 'Never you mind, Ben Jackson. Now, let's away to the *Demeter*. We sail with the tide!' Ignoring Ashdown, she stomped out of the cabin.

Ben shrugged apologetically. 'See you in London,' he said and raced from the room.

Ashdown watched them go and then, with a huge sigh,

began to tidy up the captain's cabin.

'Now, Mr Cromwell,' said the Doctor soothingly. 'You mustn't go around believing everything you read in books…'

Richard toyed miserably with the hem of his coat. 'Then it's not true?'

Jamie decided he had better say something, being the McCrimmon of Culloden and all. 'It's just a wee fancy,' he said. 'We bought it for a shilling in a bookshop in Edinburgh.'

Richard frowned. 'It says on the first page that it comes from London.' He looked up and to the side, as though summoning a spirit, and recited from memory: '"Made and printed in England for the publishers B.T. Batsford Limited, London and… Malvern Wells by Unwin Brothers Limited, the Gresham Press, Woking, Surrey".'

The Doctor opened his mouth to interrupt but Richard continued.

'"First impression, October 1919.This impression, November 1920".'

Jamie sidled over to the Doctor and bent to whisper in his ears. 'We're in trouble, aren't we?'

The Doctor nodded. 'And it's true.'

'What is?'

'First impressions last,' said the Doctor with a smile.

Jamie shook his head and sat down on the edge of the bed as the Doctor approached Richard Cromwell.

'Look,' he said. 'You know who we are. Speculating about the future is our business. We have to keep an eye on the… er… competition. And that's what that book is. Just a silly bit of fluff by one of the McCrimmon's rivals.' The Doctor frowned suddenly. 'You haven't got it with you, by any chance?'

Richard looked up. 'What?'

'The book?' said the Doctor hopefully.

Richard shook his head. 'It is in my bedchamber.'

The Doctor smiled at Jamie and breathed a relieved sigh. 'I wouldn't go showing it to anybody else. It could upset them.'

'It's upset me!' cried Richard. 'It says I will be known as "Tumbledown Dick"! That I shall rule for only a few scant months after my father's death and I shall never be half the man he is!' He sobbed bitterly into his lacy handkerchief.

The Doctor stepped forward and put a soothing hand on his shoulder. 'There, there. There's no need to worry. As I said, it's pure speculation. A fake designed to fool the gullible.'

Richard looked up with red-rimmed eyes. 'Then what will become of me? Of all of us? If you really are what you say, then tell me the future! Tell me, or I shall have my father string you from Tyburn's gibbet!'

The Doctor folded his arms and rubbed his eyes. This was going to be difficult.

The spray hit Ben full in the face and he closed his eyes as the *Demeter* ploughed forward into the waves. The ship, as old and hoary as its disreputable captain, was nevertheless a pleasant little vessel, her oaken planks stained almost black with age. Ice hung in the stiff, knotted rigging.

Ben stood on the prow of the vessel, holding tightly to a forward mast as the ship plunged and rose on the heavy swell. The salty air in his lungs made him feel glad and, after the events of the previous night, somewhat grateful to be alive.

Around him, Captain Winter's crew worked steadily. They were a strange collection, almost as motley as the customers at the Dutch tavern, and had clearly been drawn from many different lands. But they seemed noticeably more cheerful than the crew of the *Teazer* and Ben was happy to have joined their company.

Now they were speeding back towards London and, Ben

was confident, a reunion with his friends.

He frowned as he thought of them. He knew the Doctor and Jamie would be all right, but what about Polly? When he'd last seen her she was being dragged away by that gang of men. Ben knew what kind of things people got up to in Stuart England and didn't fancy Polly's chances of getting through it with her modesty, and possibly her sanity, intact.

He let the wind blow through his blond hair and over his face for a few moments more and then turned back towards the main body of the ship.

Making his way through the sweating ranks of the crew, who all spared him curious but friendly glances, he banged his fist on the door of Winter's cabin.

'What?' came the growling response from within.

Ben opened the door and stepped inside into a narrow, low-ceilinged room. There was a large, mullioned window at the back and a vast old table occupying most of the space, but there was none of the elegance of Stanislaus's cabin. Clothes and discarded bottles littered the floor and there was a pervasive smell of rum.

Winter sat in her chair, poring over a ledger. Piles of scrolls and charts littered the rug beneath her wooden leg. She looked up and the sun streaming through the window sparkled off the end of her silver nose.

'Ah, Ben!' she cackled. 'A better voyage than last time, I'll wager?'

Ben cracked a big smile. 'That it is, Sal.' He looked down at the desk. 'What've you got there?'

Winter swivelled the ledger round on the table and planted a thick finger on a two-page entry. 'There,' she said. 'That's my account of our Polish friend and his deeds.'

Ben scanned the pages quickly, then turned over. And over. Finally, he looked up in amazement.

'Makes fine reading, doesn't it?' said Winter with a twinkle.

Ben shook his head and whistled. 'Looks like he's looted half the ships in the North Sea. How come they've never nabbed him?'

'They?'

Ben shrugged. 'Well, the authorities. Surely they try and keep this kind of stuff under control?'

Winter slumped down in her chair and slammed her wooden leg onto the table, dislodging half a dozen filthy metal plates. 'Ha! The Revenue men take a cut, of course. And there's few richer than Stanislaus. He'd pauper us all if he got the chance. But look you here.' Winter leaned over the ledger and turned to the final page of the Stanislaus entry. 'It was what your friend said last night that got me thinking.'

Ben was intrigued. 'Oh yeah?'

Winter nodded and her mangy hair fell forward into her eyes. 'These last few voyages of his I have on record. He's been a-toing and froing to France like a top on a string.'

'And that's unusual, is it?' queried Ben.

Winter thumped the table. 'I'll say it is. He plies the route to Holland and back and that's an end to it. I've never known him go across to France, not in all my years.'

Ben sat down. 'Well, perhaps he's trying out new territory. I mean, if everyone knows he does the Amsterdam route, they might steer clear of him.'

Winter held up a finger. 'Aye. That they do. But my ledgers tell me that he's not been attacking any ships on his way to France. I have eyes and ears everywhere, see, Ben. Even that Pole can't outwit me.'

Ben folded his arms and looked up at the beamed ceiling. 'So he's just been visiting France?'

Winter tapped the ledger again. 'I count six times in the last two months. Now why is that?'

'Maybe he's got a French sweetheart?'

Winter let out a thick, rasping laugh. 'What? That dried-up old poltroon? Nay, lad, he's less between his legs than a maiden girl.' She began to fiddle with the ragged ends of her hair, momentarily lost in thought. Then she snapped out of it and grinned at Ben. 'But you may not be far wrong. There might be a lady who's captured our man's heart.'

'Who?'

Winter leaned back in her chair until it creaked under her bulk.

'The Queen,' she murmured at last.

Before Ben could reply, the door was flung open and a young boy raced inside. His adolescent face was flushed with fear and excitement. 'Captain!' he gasped. 'Captain, ma'am!'

Winter looked up. 'What's amiss, young Hugh?'

The boy caught his breath and looked wildly between Ben and the captain. 'A ship, ma'am! There's a ship approaching fast.'

'Well?' said Ben. 'What of it?'

Hugh was frantically wringing his slender hands. 'I think they're pirates, sir!'

Sitting in a pair of comfortable chairs, the Doctor and Jamie faced Oliver Cromwell with benign smiles. They had been temporarily spared Richard's inquisition by Thurloe's arrival, to tell them that the general required their presence at once.

For the best part of an hour they had been fending questions with what the Doctor thought was great skill, not saying too much and not too little.

Now the general sat with his chin on his hand, peering up at the ceiling as he framed yet another inquiry.

John Thurloe stood close by Cromwell's chair, regarding the two strangers with cool interest, while Richard sat in the corner, anxious to see how the mystics performed.

'Say that England be a republic, then,' said Cromwell airily. 'In that event, should we strive for closer links with our cousins?'

The Doctor cocked his head. 'Cousins?'

'Aye,' said Cromwell. 'Our Protestant allies across the sea.'

'Oh, them,' murmured the Doctor. 'Well, what did you have in mind?'

Thurloe rolled his eyes heavenward. 'We have spoken of this before, General. It could never happen.'

Cromwell thumped his fist against the arm of his chair. 'But why not? Surely it is only logical.'

Jamie was puzzled. 'What could never happen?'

Thurloe sighed. 'The general thinks that closer integration with our neighbours is desirable.'

Cromwell pointed to his aide. 'John here will have none of it, but I say why not? An England allied to… the Low Countries, say, would be far more of a force on the international stage.'

The Doctor steepled his fingers. 'European integration, eh? It's a nice idea.'

Cromwell pointed to Jamie. 'What say you, McCrimmon? Will it happen?'

Jamie looked a little worried but, as usual, leaned towards the Doctor and whispered nonsense in his ear.

The Doctor nodded slowly, as though receiving information of the utmost sagacity. Finally, he sat up, clearing his throat. 'The McCrimmon says it is almost inevitable. But not for a very long time. And there'll always be trouble with Euro-sceptics.'

Cromwell frowned. 'With what?'

The Doctor folded his arms across his chest. 'A figure of speech, General. It means an… er… irritant, a bothersome thing.'

Cromwell nodded his understanding. 'Like Lilburne and his Levellers,' he said sourly. 'God, they afflict me like the piles.' He smiled cheerily. 'What say you, Doctor? Are these urrosceptics of yours not like winnets on a man's backside?'

The Doctor smiled tightly. 'Quite.'

Cromwell laughed and smacked his knee. 'Now then, I must away. There is much work to do in preparation for the King's trial.' His face suddenly darkened and his tone became serious. 'I must ask you one thing, finally.'

The Doctor and Jamie nodded simultaneously.

Cromwell chose his words carefully. 'If the King dies, who should rule in his place?'

Thurloe shot a look at the Doctor, which the little man did his best to avoid. He rotated his thumbs and glanced at Jamie, who was trying to shrink back in his chair.

At last, the Doctor spoke. 'Such a question demands time, General. There are many twisting pathways that the future might take. I should hate for the McCrimmon to give you bad advice.'

Cromwell nodded. 'There's much wisdom in your words, Doctor. You shall have all the time you require.' He rose and bowed to them and then walked swiftly from the room.

Thurloe looked at the Doctor again, a quizzical expression on his long, horsy face. 'Yes, Doctor, take your time, but not too long. And please don't disappoint me with your answer.'

With that, he swept from the room, leaving the Doctor and Jamie alone with Richard.

'Ha!' he exclaimed. 'You did not say one thing that was not fudge and fumble!'

'Oh, I don't know…' said the Doctor.

Richard got up and stalked towards them. 'Now, Doctor, tell me the truth. Will this nation be a republic? And will my father be its sole ruler?'

The Doctor decided to change tack. He assumed a rather fearsome expression which somehow seemed all the more frightening to Richard on such an unassuming little man.

'Richard Cromwell,' he said gravely, 'you must take us to your chambers and deliver unto us this strange book.'

Richard swallowed nervously. 'I must?'

The Doctor nodded slowly. 'Then – and only then – will all the mysteries of time be opened to you.'

Richard licked his dry lips and nodded to the guard, who had come to escort the Doctor and Jamie back to their room. 'Very well. Come with me. I'll speak to my father. Try to get responsibility for you.' He led the way out of the room.

'"Come into my custody," said the spider to the fly,' whispered the Doctor to Jamie.

The young Scot was not amused. 'What're we going to do now?'

The Doctor put his hands behind his back. 'Don't worry. I've got an idea. If that works out, then…'

'Then?'

The Doctor ran his hand through his untidy black hair. 'Then I think it's time we got out of here.'

Ben and Winter raced across the rolling deck, the latter clutching at Ben's arm to prevent herself toppling over.

The crew of the *Demeter* were already racing to their stations as their captain pulled a battered telescope from her huge green coat and jammed it against her eye. She squinted, then nodded feverishly. 'I see her.'

Ben leaned over the side and peered through the spray. 'Pirates?'

Winter offered him the telescope. 'Talk of the devil.'

Squinting to see through the crude instrument, Ben made out the lines of an all-too-familiar ship, racing through the waves towards them. 'It's the *Teazer*!' he gasped.

Winter nodded her massive head. 'Aye, Ben. It seems the Pole's not content with this secret package. He wants to return to port with booty from us!'

Ben handed her back the telescope. 'What do we do?'

Winter looked at him in surprise. 'Do? Do, lad? We do what any self-respecting mariner does in times such as these. We fight!'

Ben swallowed nervously. 'Yeah, I thought you were going to say that.'

Winter swung round, her great bosom jostling, her coat flapping like a sail around her. 'To your posts, men!' she bellowed. 'Let's give 'em a taste of our cannon!'

So saying, she drew her sword and tottered off across the deck, her wooden leg hammering on the planks. She pulled open the door of her cabin and emerged a moment later with a brace of cutlasses. Tossing one to Ben, she made for the entrance to the lower deck, where the cannons were located.

Ben caught the sword and tested its weight in his hands. It was surprisingly heavy and he curled both hands around its hilt to give himself courage.

There was a loud report close by, followed by a plume of white water as the *Teazer*'s cannons fired their first salvo.

Ben raced down the wooden stairs to the second deck, where Winter and her men were already hard at work. Hugh, the cabin boy, was ramming wadding and powder into the closest of the great iron guns while a small man, stripped to the waist, was doing the same with its twin.

Winter clapped the telescope to her eye again and thrust it out of the square porthole that enclosed the cannon. 'She's fast. I'll give her that!'

There was another tremendous boom and Ben felt the *Demeter* rock as the percussion echoed around her hull.

Winter staggered and almost fell, then, with a twinkle in her eye, struck a flint and lit the fuse of the first cannon.

'Back!' she roared and Ben jumped out of the way as the fuse hissed and spluttered.

Then the cannon reared backwards, a great cloud of smoke and fire belching from its mouth.

Ben raced to the porthole and looked out. The cannonball had missed Stanislaus's ship by a wide margin. Winter cursed and flapped her great arm at the next cannon along.

Fire!' she croaked. 'Keep firing until we get the bastards!'

The second cannon spoke with a belching roar but this time Winter didn't wait for the outcome. Spinning around on her wooden leg like a crazed ballerina, she began to hobble back up the stairs to the top deck, brandishing her cutlass and bellowing with rage.

Instinctively, Ben followed, resisting the urge to carry his own cutlass between his teeth. He pulled at the handholds and propelled himself up the stairs.

On the deck, all was confusion. Smoke from both ships' cannons enveloped everything and Ben could only just make out the crew, tearing from point to point on the slippery surface.

The *Demeter* rolled again as another cannon shot from the enemy vessel thundered into the sea by her side.

Winter clattered towards the ship's wheel and pushed the pilot out of the way with a tremendous shove.

'By God!' she screeched, her grizzled hair almost bristling with energy. 'That Pole will not have my ship!'

She spun the wheel around and the *Demeter* began to respond, lurching and creaking at the sudden change of direction.

Ben joined her on the poop deck and glanced anxiously at the increasingly close Teazer.

'Why risk this when his mission's so important?' he bellowed above the din.

Winter kept a tight hold of the wheel, her silver nose flashing in the winter sun.

'Ah, the arrogance of the nobility!' she spat. 'He thinks he's untouchable, the cur. But we'll outrun him, or sink him. I stake my life on it.'

Ben was not so sure. The masts of the enemy ship were heaving perilously close into view. He could already see the crew lining up to board them.

'Ben!' cried Winter. 'Get those cannons firing, will you, or, by God's wounds, they'll be upon us.'

Racing across the deck, Ben couldn't help but wonder at the irony of finding himself in the middle of such a scene. 'Funny,' he muttered to himself. 'I always wanted to be a pirate.'

He took the stairs down to the lower deck three at a time and found a state of utter devastation. A blast from the *Teazer*'s cannon had scored a direct hit, knocking out the deck's armoury completely.

'Oh blimey!' groaned Ben, looking around at the dead and wounded that littered the room.

He found young Hugh unconscious on a pile of sacking and slapped the boy's pale, smoke-blackened face until he came round. 'Hugh!' he barked. 'Come on! I need your help.'

The boy looked dazed, then focused on Ben's face and nodded.

Ben grabbed his skinny arm and dragged him back up the stairs to the upper deck. He bent down to the boy's level. 'Now look, son, you're going to have to steer the ship while me and the captain take on those pirates, all right?'

Hugh looked dumbfounded but then found his voice. 'Me, sir? The wheel?'

Ben held the boy's face between his hands. 'You can do it.

You know you can. Now get up there and tell the captain I need her down here.'

Hugh nodded and grinned, his teeth showing white through the grime that covered his face. He raced up to the poop deck.

Ben turned and raised his cutlass.

The *Teazer* was right by them now, scraping alongside the hull, its crew ready to jump ship.

Ben took a deep breath and waited for them to come.

'You're insane!' screeched Godley, forcing himself back against the walls of Stanislaus's cabin and clutching his cloak around him.

Stanislaus sat in his chair, unperturbed by the booming cannon fire which shook the room.

'Do not distress yourself, my friend,' he said in his heavily accented voice. "Tis no matter. We have the package and now we will have a little sport before we return to London.'

Godley shook his handsome head, his features blanched with fury and nausea. 'This is hardly the time, Captain. You know the urgency of our plan. What if something were to go wrong? What if this ship is sunk? What then?'

Stanislaus smiled coolly and leaned back in his chair. 'The *Teazer* will not sink, sir. I promise you that. Besides, we know that we had visitors last night. One glance at my strongbox and the information provided by our friend Ashdown tell us that it was that sluttish captain, Winter. It would be better for all of us if she were not involved in this… adventure at all.'

Godley groaned. 'To risk everything for some pathetic vendetta! 'Sblood, there will be a reckoning if this ever gets out!'

'Then it must not get out,' said Stanislaus firmly. 'Eh, Mr van Leeuwenhoek?'

He turned to face the third occupant of the room, a bald, almost skeletally thin man, swathed entirely in black like a huge, malevolent bird. His skin was dry and cracked like old parchment and when he smiled, as he did now, his mouth appeared more like a blackened maw. He let out a throaty chuckle and then his mouth sealed again like a rat trap.

Stanislaus laughed too and glanced towards the window. 'Well,' he said, rising to his feet. 'I suppose I had better go out and win the day.'

With a tremendous tearing screech, the *Teazer* slammed against the hull of Captain Winter's ship as though they were two great wooden whales in conflict.

A great cheer went up and Stanislaus's disreputable crew began to pour onto the decks of the *Demeter*. They teemed everywhere, clambering up the rigging and swarming like rats into the cabins and below decks.

From his vantage point behind a pile of coiled wet rope and a stack of gunpowder barrels, Ben swallowed nervously. The cutlass in his hand was shaking as he contemplated jumping out and facing the pirates head on.

The *Demeter*'s crew began their fight-back at once, swords clattering against the enemy's as men executed frantic manoeuvres across the decks, looking like gaily dressed crabs as they scuttled about and executed their dance of death.

Right before Ben, a swarthy chestnut-haired man was bravely fending off a much bigger and more fearsome pirate whom Ben recognised as O'Kane.

The Irishman's bright-green eyes and vast, knotted red beard that spilled almost down to his waist seemed to blaze with energy. He laughed to himself as he forced the smaller man to jump hither and thither over the deck.

Ben was on the point of leaping out to his crewmate's

rescue when O'Kane ducked a blow and brought his cutlass swinging round to pierce the other's belly. There was a dreadful popping sound and the sailor's innards spilled from him like a cork from a bottle.

Thrusting his fist into his mouth to stop himself from gagging, Ben sank back behind the coiled rope and closed his eyes.

O'Kane, meanwhile, stood ankle deep in the other man's steaming guts as they spread in a red pool over the deck. He looked about, anxious for another fight, and was just about to move off towards the action when the sound of retching stopped him in his tracks.

Moving carefully towards the pile of rope, his broad head moving from side to side and his green eyes flashing dangerously, he followed the pool of gore.

At last, he came upon Ben, who was being violently sick as the blood sloshed around his feet.

'What's this!' bellowed the pirate. 'Not found your sea legs yet, my young buck?'

He laughed horribly and kicked Ben in the stomach. Ben rolled across the deck, clutching his shaking body, retching again as nausea swept over him. He managed to stand and lifted his cutlass high above his head, gritting his teeth as he faced O'Kane.

It was only now that he saw that the pirate had tiny twists of gunpowder knotted into his beard. They were each alight and flaring with an unhealthy green phosphorescence, as though he were some crazed Celtic demon brought to chuckling life.

Ben tossed his cutlass from hand to hand, the way he remembered Errol Flynn doing in countless Hollywood films. But this fight was real, he told himself desperately, and the huge man facing him would spill his insides as cheerfully as he had the other unfortunate sailor's.

Suddenly, O'Kane frowned and peered at Ben through the drifting smoke of the battle.

'I knows you!' he said, incredulously. 'Were you not the lad Ashdown brought aboard on the way to Dutchland?'

Ben felt suddenly cheered. 'That I am, mate. So we've no quarrel.'

O'Kane laughed his terrifying laugh, his fizzling beard shaking. 'No quarrel? You've deserted our ship, you swine! And, besides, the captain tortured the truth out of Ashdown this morning. He knows all about your little visit last night.'

Ben swallowed fearfully.

O'Kane raised his cutlass. 'I'll slice you open from your guts to your windpipe, so help me!'

He dashed forward, his cutlass trained on Ben's chest. But Ben was nimble and neatly sidestepped, jumping on top of the pile of coiled rope as the red-bearded pirate swung round to attack again.

Their swords clashed and Ben felt a sickening vibration pass through his arm at the force of O'Kane's blow.

Immediately he riposted O'Kane's attack but the massive man was ready for him, smashing against Ben's cutlass and thrusting his great arm forward. The sword pierced Ben's striped T-shirt and ripped it apart along the shoulder.

O'Kane brought his cutlass to bear again at once and Ben ducked down as the great steel blade sliced through the air above his head.

He jumped down from the rope and grabbed desperately at its tarred end. Keeping low, he managed to loop it around O'Kane's legs and pulled with all his strength.

The pirate crashed to the deck with a roar of anger.

At once, Ben snatched up his cutlass and raced forward, clutching the hilt in both hands. Beneath him lay O'Kane, his big face pale and sweating. Still, the gunpowder in his beard sizzled and burnt, but he looked somehow pathetic, like a great sun god brought to earth. His expression was filled with dumb appeal and Ben hesitated as he prepared to thrust his cutlass into the pirate's throat.

It was the chance O'Kane needed.

He slid across the wet planks and got to his feet with surprising agility, hurled the rope around Ben's neck, and dragged him to the deck.

Ben let out a throaty gurgle as he fell and was instantly winded.

O'Kane appeared, towering above him, his glittering cutlass poised to deliver a killing blow. Ben closed his eyes, seeing, for an instant, images of Polly, Jamie, and the Doctor. He would never see them now, never have a chance to say goodbye...

There was a deep percussive crash and Ben's eyes flicked open.

Captain Winter was swinging on a rope from the mast and had landed her feet squarely in O'Kane's back.

'Sal!' cried Ben delightedly, struggling to his feet.

Winter dropped from the rope and gave Ben a reassuring smile. Then her cutlass flashed from its sheath and she advanced on O'Kane, who was on his knees, his head sunk on his chest, breathing stertorously.

'Get up!' barked Winter, jabbing O'Kane in the back with her sword.

The pirate got slowly to his feet and placed his hands upon his greasy red hair.

Winter and Ben positioned themselves some distance away, next to the gunpowder barrels, before Winter instructed O'Kane to turn around.

'Now,' bellowed Winter. 'Tell us what your captain has brought back from Amsterdam.'

O'Kane merely grunted and looked out across the decks,

which still hummed with battling men.

'Tell us!' barked Winter. 'Or, so help me, I'll have your lights for supper!'

O'Kane smiled ghoulishly. 'Nay, lass. That's a delicacy not fit for the likes of you!'

With a roar, he propelled himself forward. Caught off guard, Ben still managed to lash out with his cutlass, cutting O'Kane across the hamstring. The pirate howled with pain as he tried to get his big hands around Winter's throat.

Winter smashed her fist into the pirate's face and pushed him across the deck.

O'Kane tottered, slipped, and fell headlong into one of the open gunpowder barrels.

Ben looked at Winter. They paused for a second and then hared away towards the poop deck just as O'Kane's sparking beard connected with the deadly powder.

There was a colossal explosion and barrel staves flashed through the air like curved wooden javelins.

Ben and Winter ducked down and waited for the smoke to clear. When it did, there was a big, headless pirate slumped on the deck beneath them.

Winter let out one of her characteristic throaty laughs and got to her feet.

'We've not beaten them yet, Sal,' croaked Ben. 'Come on!'

He began to move off but Winter held him back. The big woman scanned the deck with her good eye and frowned. 'Hold on a moment, Ben,' she muttered. 'My crew is battling well and young Hugh has the ship arights. What say you and me nip over to the *Teazer* to see what we may see?'

Ben was astonished. 'Are you mad? Your ship's being attacked! If we go over there we might not have anything to come back to!'

Winter tapped the end of her silver nose. 'I have a score to settle with Stanislaus, my lad. Everything else can go hang!'

'And what about the package from Amsterdam? We know they're up to something. We can't just let it go because you want Stanislaus's guts for garters.'

Winter considered this, her beady black eye disappearing under her furrowed brow. 'His guts would have to be wide to clap around these thighs!' she cackled. Then she laid her hand on Ben's arm and spoke more quietly. 'I might never get a better chance, Ben. Me against him. On the open sea!' She gestured expansively.

Ben clapped her on the shoulder. 'Look, Sal. If we lose the *Demeter*, then we'll have nothing but open sea to look forward to for the rest of our very short lives. OK?'

Winter's face was a mask of concentration. Through the drifting fog of gunpowder she could make out her men valiantly fending off Stanislaus's gang of cutthroats.

She turned to Ben. 'I hear you, mate,' she said at last. 'But I wonder whether we might not be able to kill two birds with one stone.'

She raised her cutlass and fixed Ben with her remaining eye. 'Are you game?'

CHAPTER
7

The depressingly short winter day was fading fast, darkness creeping in from the horizon like a chill curtain. The cold sun, sinking into the embrace of the hills, was perfectly mirrored in the broad, still waters of the Solent.

Hurst Castle stood in a bend of the river, as grim and unwelcoming as any place in the kingdom, its old walls broken with age, its façade peppered with nesting rooks. Their harsh cries echoed through the eerie stillness as Sir John Copper and his men advanced along the shore.

Copper reigned in his horse and swung down from the saddle, never taking his eye off the gloomy fortress nearby.

Benedict Moor walked over to Copper's side. "Tis time, then?' he muttered anxiously.

Copper turned his cold grey eyes on him. 'Almost. But there is still much to be done. When Whyte arrives – ah!'

He paused as two figures on horseback emerged from the gathering dusk. The sound of hooves hammering on the frost-hardened ground echoed like a drumbeat through the quiet.

Whyte's and Polly's mounts slowed to a halt and trotted side by side, but the handsome Cavalier was the first to dismount.

He nodded to Copper and Moor before raising his hands to help Polly down.

She waved him away and dropped from the saddle, shooting Whyte another suspicious look.

Copper took her hand and kissed it. 'A pleasure to see you again, lady,' he said, smiling sweetly. 'I am glad to renew our acquaintance in happier circumstances.'

Polly did not return his smile. 'You have news of my friends?'

Whyte intervened. 'I have explained to Mistress Polly that the man known as the Doctor has been sighted within the walls of this castle.'

Copper nodded. 'That is so. But we must use all our guile to get him out, my dear. You see, the castle is well guarded.'

Polly looked at the men who surrounded her. 'Is the Doctor in trouble?' It would be surprising if he weren't, she thought ruefully.

Copper waved his hand airily. 'Our intelligence only extends to his presence in this place.'

Whyte shot her a reassuring grin, which Polly didn't altogether like. She thought again of his blatant lie about Frances Kemp's brother.

'What's your plan?' she asked plainly.

Copper pointed across the river to Hurst Castle. 'We have contacts within, you understand? An arrangement has been made to substitute a serving girl. Our spy will make contact with your friend the Doctor and then you can slip in and be reunited.'

Polly frowned. 'And who's the substitute?' Copper's elegant digit turned to point to her. 'Me?' she cried.

Whyte moved closer to her. 'But you're the natural choice, my dear.'

Polly folded her arms defiantly. 'And what do you get out of this?'

Copper smiled benignly. 'The chance to help a lady whom

we have wronged.'

Polly let out a snorting laugh. 'And?'

Whyte grimaced, sensing the game was up. 'And we would be terribly grateful if you could help the King escape while you're in there.'

'The King? He's in there too?'

Copper and Whyte nodded slowly. Then the older man gently took Polly's hand in his own.

'Will you help us, my dear? This is our beloved monarch's last chance. For, as sure as I stand here, Parliament will cut off his head before this damned year is out.'

Polly looked away. Surely, Parliament would do that no matter what her decision. But wasn't the Doctor always going on about the Web of Time? That history might be changed at any one of a number of points? Maybe what she, insignificant Polly Wright, did now would have massive repercussions for the whole of the future.

Then she thought about seeing the Doctor and Jamie again and maybe even Ben. She knew that together they could sort out any mess. And the Doctor was her only hope of escape from this strange world.

She nodded quickly. 'All right. What do you want me to do?'

Whyte came suddenly forward and kissed her on the cheek. She almost stepped back, still not trusting him, surprised by his sudden warmth and the tingle that raced through her body.

Copper opened his saddlebag and produced the map of the castle, which he had been studying back at the inn. Moor stepped forward with a lantern and the four of them stooped to examine the parchment by its pale glow.

Jamie shot the Doctor an anxious look and felt a cold wave of fear wash over him. 'Are you sure about this, Doctor?'

The Doctor stood on the window ledge outside their room, trying not to look down, his boots scraping on the frosty stonework.

'We can't wait for Richard Cromwell's permission any longer, Jamie,' he said with regret. 'I have to get that book back from him no matter what. The consequences are unthinkable. We could be in terrible trouble.'

He glanced down and saw the snow-covered ornamental gardens spread out like a doily pattern below. He snapped his eyes shut and flattened himself against the bricks. 'Possibly terminal trouble,' he added.

Jamie had watched him open the big, leaded window and scramble out with the enthusiasm of a child and the agility of a monkey. But the treacherous conditions outside and the height of their room on the third storey seemed to have somewhat quelled the Doctor's appetite for escape.

'Why don't you let me try?' asked Jamie helpfully.

The Doctor shook his head and moved his feet a fraction. 'Don't argue. I'll be able to accomplish far more when I'm on the other side of the door.'

His right foot slid across the ledge and he dug his fingers into the wall, feeling his nails scrape against the powdery mortar.

Some four feet away was another window, identical in design but slightly ajar. The Doctor had taken careful note of the layout of the third storey on their way back from their audience with Cromwell. He was confident that the open window would lead him into the corridor and, from there, he could organise Jamie's escape and find Richard Cromwell's room.

As the darkness stole over the scene, the Doctor breathed a sigh of relief that he was not only practically invisible to an onlooker but that he could see less and less of the ground below.

He reached out his hand and began to slide further. Jamie looked on helplessly, his hands describing anxious little circles as he leaned out of the window.

The Doctor took a deep breath and made three or four quick steps. His boots rang off the frozen stone but his grip on the wall didn't falter. He looked back to wink at Jamie but the boy's image was disappearing in the dusk.

Turning back to face straight out, the Doctor steadied his breathing and shuffled his feet again. He could see the casement of the next window only a few feet away.

Emboldened by this, he began to move more rapidly, hoping to get the whole process over and done with. Reaching for the elaborately carved exterior of the window, he shifted his left foot and suddenly slipped.

A great, lurching, sickening rush raced through him as his foot met empty air and he struggled to right himself. His fingers scrabbled at the brickwork, desperate to find purchase, but there was nothing bulky or strong enough to take his weight.

In a second he had fallen.

The Doctor's breath was knocked out of him as his chest connected with the stone ledge. He hung in silence for a moment, wondering how on earth he had been saved.

Jamie's voice came sailing through the dusk. 'Are you all right, Doctor?'

The Doctor felt the cold wind streaming over his back and realised that his cloak had caught on the windowsill as he fell. It was ripped from the bottom almost to his shoulder and it was the only thing keeping him from falling.

'Doctor?'

He dug his fingers in and pulled at the ledge, trying to hoist himself back up. There was a dreadful tearing sound and the cloak split further. The Doctor felt it flapping about him like a damaged wing.

'Jamie!' he gasped at last. 'I'm in a bit of bother!'

He heard scrabbling nearby. 'Hang on! I'm coming!'

The Doctor shook his head, for the benefit of no one in particular. 'No. It's too dangerous. Wait a minute.'

He glanced upward and saw that the cold breeze was stirring the heavy brocade curtains of the room he wanted to enter. Biting his lip, he made a huge effort and managed to heave his elbow onto the ledge. His legs swung below him, kicking at the air.

The Doctor had timed it well, and, as the curtain billowed outwards, he grabbed hold of it for dear life just as his cloak tore completely in two and floated to the darkened ground.

Smiling to himself, the Doctor grasped the curtain with both hands and began to haul himself up, his feet clashing against the wall.

'It's all right, Jamie. I've got it now—' he began.

The curtain began to tear, just as the cloak before it, and the Doctor could see the wooden rings that attached it to its rail splinter and crack under his weight.

With a worried bellow of fear, he dragged himself up onto the ledge and did a neat forward roll into the corridor, casting the curtain out as he did so.

He stood in the darkness for a moment, catching his breath, and then poked his head out of the window.

'Jamie!' he hissed. 'I'm in. Just wait there and I'll have you out in a tick.'

He didn't wait for Jamie's assent but raced down the dark, deeply carpeted passageway, slowing only as he approached the outside of their room.

The guard stood there, looking bored and tired, his

helmeted head drooping onto his chest.

The Doctor watched him in silence for a while, sucking on his finger and gazing at the long rug which stretched the length of the corridor. He frowned deeply and, reaching a decision, pressed himself flat against the wall so that the shadows cloaked him completely.

Then, without warning, he began to sing in a quiet, gentle voice.

"'Her husband was a soldier, and to the wars did go, And she would be his comrade, the truth of all is so…'"

The guard looked up, dragged from his reverie by the unexpected voice. He peered into the darkness and thrust his pike out before him. 'Who's there?'

There was silence in the corridor and then the Doctor's voice sprang up again.

"'She put on man's apparel, and bore him company, As many in the army for truth can testify.'"

The guard slid the visor of his helmet upward and began to advance, slowly and carefully, along the corridor. 'Who's there, I say?' he barked, steadying the pike in his hands.

Again there was silence and then the Doctor stepped out from his hiding place, holding his hands above his head.

The guard was puzzled. 'What the devil…?'

The Doctor smiled sheepishly. 'No. Not the devil. The Doctor.'

He threw himself down onto the floor and, grasping the trailing end of the rug in both hands, pulled with all his strength. Wrong-footed, the guard was sent sprawling against the corridor wall. His head slammed against the plaster, and with a groan he slumped unconscious to the floor.

Losing no time, the Doctor rifled through the keys that hung at the guard's waist, found the one that gave access to

181

the room, and then, slipping his hands under the guard's armpits, dragged the unfortunate man into a darkened recess.

The keys rattling in his hand, he stole across the corridor and slipped a heavy black one into the lock.

'Hang on, Jamie,' he whispered. 'Almost there.'

As the door opened, the Doctor's head jerked round. Footsteps echoed dully on the floor. Footsteps coming his way

Jamie's grinning head appeared around the door and the Doctor immediately pushed him back inside.

He slipped inside himself and closed the door. They stood in silence, listening, as the footsteps came closer and finally paused outside.

The door began to open and the Doctor gestured frantically to Jamie to get to the other side of the room and close the window.

The young Scot had just managed this as the Doctor threw himself down on to the bed and affected an air of the utmost nonchalance.

The door opened fully, revealing Thurloe with a puzzled expression stamped on his wily features.

The Doctor looked up and smiled. 'Come to tuck us in, Mr Thurloe?'

Thurloe looked down at the keyhole. 'This door has been left unlocked,' he stated flatly.

The Doctor swung his legs off the bed. 'Oh dear. You mean we could've escaped any time we liked?'

Thurloe frowned and then shrugged. 'Escape? Why would you want to escape? You're the general's guests. Now, come along, he wants to see you.'

The Doctor threw an exasperated look at Jamie as Thurloe ushered them out. 'Well,' he whispered out of the corner of his mouth. 'Worth a try.'

*

With the addition of a lacy white cap and apron, Polly looked every inch the serving girl.

As Whyte and Copper had promised, a tiny door at the back of the castle had been left unguarded and she stood outside it in the darkness, shivering.

She knocked twice and then left a pause before the third knock, as instructed. There was no response from beyond the solid black door. Polly pulled her cloak tightly around her slim body and cast a worried glance back towards the shore where she knew Whyte and Copper to be waiting.

She was about to knock again when she heard movement and a series of latches and bolts being drawn back. The door opened and a strange, wizened old face appeared, framed in a halo of thinning white hair. The old man looked Polly up and down and grunted to himself, then gestured impatiently for her to follow him.

With one last look behind her, Polly dashed inside and the old man slid the door gently shut behind her.

She found herself in a roomy kitchen, lined with pots and cutlery. Baskets of firewood were stacked in each corner and there were freshly killed grouse and even a couple of swans laying across marble tables, their throats cut and congealed with blood.

Polly shuddered and looked away. 'Thank you for your help, Mr…?'

The old man held up his liver-spotted hands. 'No names, girl. It's better that way. I seek to serve His Majesty and that is all. Now we must get you upstairs.'

Polly nodded her understanding and slipped out of her cloak. The old man walked past the huge, crackling fire and began to quietly ascend a rickety staircase which occupied the centre of the room.

He put his finger to his lips and beckoned for Polly to follow.

Hitching up her skirts, she did so, keeping closely behind him all the way up.

'Are you the one who has seen my friend?' she whispered.

The old man shushed her again with the same gesture and Polly lapsed into silence. Eventually they reached a trap door inset in the ceiling and the old man paused before opening it.

'Up there you will find a tray of food and drink. You must take it up the second flight of steps on your left. Do you understand me?'

Polly nodded vigorously. 'Second on the left, yes.'

The old man clasped his hands together. 'You will come out next to a room with two doors. There are guards posted there and they will be expecting another girl. You must say that she is ailing and that you are to replace her tonight.'

'And who am I supposed to be?'

The old man shook his head testily. 'What matters that?'

Polly shrugged. 'Quite a lot if they're suspicious.'

The old man seemed to see the wisdom in her words. 'Yes, very well then. You are to say you are Spufford's niece.'

Polly looked up at the trap door. 'And that's you, is it? Spufford?'

The old man grunted. 'I see that it is no use playing the cloak and dagger with you, mistress.'

Polly pushed at the trap door and it opened easily. 'No. It isn't,' she muttered, and slid through onto the next level.

She found herself in a long passageway, panelled in some dark wood and lit only by a single candle which stood on a tray close to the trap door.

As quickly as she could, Polly picked up the tray and moved left. In the gloom she could scarcely make out the entrance to the first stairway but she kept her shoulder pressed to the wall and soon found herself at the relevant place.

This second stairway seemed narrower than the first and

perceptibly older. What she could see of the steps in the candlelight showed them to be of splintered, spiralled wood, rising up into the darkness.

Polly took a deep a breath and moved swiftly up them, grimacing as the pressure of her feet made the ancient wood groan.

The landing onto which she emerged was far better lit and much more cheerfully furnished than what she had so far seen of the castle. Huge and elaborate tapestries of crimson and gold hung from the walls, depicting scenes of bygone hunting days, picked out in delicate thread.

Spluttering lanterns were bracketed to the walls on either side of an impressive set of double doors and standing stiffly before them were two Roundhead guards, pikes in hand, their faces set into hard, unyielding frowns.

Polly took in all this in an instant as she poked her head around the top of the stairway. She jerked back into the shadows and took stock of the situation, trying to keep the tray steady in her shaking hands.

Whyte had told her very clearly what was to happen. His agents within the castle had drugged most of the Parliamentarian guard but it would be impossible to get near the two actually guarding the King's quarters. This was where Polly would come in.

She set the tray down on the top step and felt around in the candlelight until her fingers came upon a small glass phial. Inside was a glutinous, honey-coloured substance and, with the greatest care, Polly poured it into the jug of wine.

Stirring it rapidly with the candle taper, she watched as the red liquid swirled in a little vortex within the jug. At last she was satisfied and, picking up the tray once more, stole quietly into the passageway.

The Roundhead guards responded immediately.

The closer one, indistinguishable from his companion because of his helmet, swung round and jabbed his pike within inches of Polly's abdomen.

'Halt!' he barked hoarsely. 'What do you want?'

Polly put on her sweetest smile. 'It's only the King's food,' she said simply. 'We can't have him starving, now, can we?'

The guard kept his pike in place. 'Where's Margaret?'

Polly was prepared. 'Oh, she's taken on bad, she has.'

The other guard stepped forward. 'Oh, no,' he said with genuine concern. 'Poor Peg? What ails her?'

Polly let out a fearful moan. 'An ague, it is. Shivering like all the snows of the north had settled on her bed.' She smiled inwardly, rather pleased with the simile.

The guard's pike drooped in response. 'I'd not heard,' he said in a low whisper.

His companion let out a cruel little laugh. 'Why, Sam. And you meant to be engaged to the girl!'

Polly felt a little lurch in her stomach, immediately regretting the elaborate nature of Margaret's feigned illness. 'Oh, no. Don't take on so. She'll be fine, I'm sure. She's gone to her bed and will see no one. I shouldn't take it personally.'

The guard called Sam lifted up his visor and his face was full of anxious concern. 'Do you really think so?'

Polly nodded confidently. 'You know what's she's like. She wouldn't want the man she loves to see her in such a state.'

The other guard laughed raucously. 'Aye, that's true enough, Sam. Your Peg'll not be seen without a dollop of rouge and powder all over her pretty face.'

They seemed satisfied and Polly made to move towards the door, but the first guard didn't move. He lowered his pike but shifted his armoured bulk a few inches to block her path.

'So, no Margaret but a new young lass instead, eh?'

Polly nodded demurely.

'And who might you be?' asked the guard, lifting his own visor. His gaze travelled rapidly and appreciatively over Polly's figure.

'I'm Master Spufford's niece. Polly.'

The guard grinned. 'Why, who'd've thought the dry old sticks in Spufford's brood would have juice in their loins enough to sire a kiddie? Never mind such a bonny one as this.' He reached out with his gloved hand and gently caressed Polly's cheek.

She stopped herself from brushing him away and fluttered her eyelashes instead. Lord, the things she did for the Doctor!

'What's your name?' she asked flirtatiously.

The guard shot a quick look at his friend Sam and smiled. 'Daniel, lady. Daniel Ancrom.'

Polly cocked her head. 'Well, Daniel Ancrom, you just let me take this lot to His High and Mightiness in there and then, mayhaps, I'll come out and see you again.'

Ancrom licked his heavy lips and grinned boyishly. Polly moved past him but Sam flattened his hand against the door.

'You're sure my Peg is all right?'

Polly felt bad about deceiving him but she knew she had to get on with this if she was to rescue the Doctor and get away.

'It's nothing, Sam. Honestly. Now let me take this in before the King dies of thirst.'

Daniel Ancrom grimaced sourly. 'Let him, I say. 'Twould save us the trouble of a trial.'

He and his colleague laughed heartlessly. Then, as Polly had hoped, he grabbed the jug of wine and raised it to his mouth. 'I'll have some of this before he does.'

He gave a throaty chuckle and narrowed his eyes as he looked at Polly. ''Twill be something to tell our children, eh, Polly? That their father supped the late King's wine?'

Sam found this very amusing and slapped his armoured

side. Ancrom took a hefty swig from the jug and offered it to his friend. To Polly's chagrin, Sam refused. 'Better to spit in it, I say.'

Ancrom shook his head. 'Nay, Sam. Better to drink it and then spit in it.'

They broke into a renewed gale of laughter. Polly sighed. She couldn't take much more of this bonhomie.

Sam drank deeply of the wine and then spat back into it. He handed the jug back to Ancrom, who added his own gobbet of saliva before plonking the jug back onto the tray.

He bowed to Polly and opened one of the doors. 'Now, Mistress Polly, just you hurry up in there with Master Charles ruddy Stuart and get your sweet little rump back out here, double quick.'

As Polly swept past him, he patted her on the backside. She dashed quickly through the doors, which at once closed behind her.

The chamber beyond was plunged in a warm, chocolate darkness, the orange glow of the fire which dominated the room throwing shimmering abstract shapes over the heavily tapestried walls.

Polly caught glimpses of familiar faces sewn into the threads. One showed King Henry the Eighth astride a horse that seemed almost as massive as himself. Another, the delicate features of Henry's only son, the boy king, Edward the Sixth. Yet another, the chalky, imperious features of Queen Elizabeth.

These were all figures familiar to Polly from countless school lessons, their lives and loves documented in dry detail on far-off dusty afternoons.

Another figure from those days suddenly stepped into the glow emanating from the fire. He was small and slight, his grave face and neat beard almost lost in shadow.

King Charles moved towards Polly and spoke in his stammering Scots burr. 'Is it t-time?'

Thurloe chose his own chambers for the appointment. It was important that he feel at ease and in control and there was nowhere that produced such an effect better than his own rooms.

He had always liked the place – the cool tiled floor, the grandiose fireplace, the high ceilings and richly patterned drapes. In the summer it was quite the most temperate and equable place in Parliament and many an important measure had been agreed within its four walls by some sweating member or other.

Thurloe sat by the fire, gazing up at the huge painting that hung above the mantel. It depicted a scene from classical times: the murder of Julius Caesar. Thurloe's gaze flickered over the two-dimensional forms of the conspirators, daggers raised. In the foreground stood Brutus, his blade coated with his Emperor's blood. Next to him was Caesar himself, in his death throes, a look of astonishment on his face.

It wasn't a terribly good picture. But Thurloe had always liked it. It seemed curiously appropriate for the business he was in.

There was a sharp rap at the door.

Thurloe immediately contrived to look busy, setting his hand to a sheaf of documents which littered his broad desk. 'Come!' he called.

The door opened and Thomas Culpeper strode inside. Striking and handsome in his Roundhead uniform, he carried his helmet under one arm and bowed to Thurloe as he crossed the threshold.

'Ah,' said Thurloe, 'Captain Culpeper. Please come in, come in.'

Culpeper did as he was bidden, taking up a position by the fireplace.

'You may sit if you wish,' offered Thurloe, extending a hand.

Culpeper looked straight ahead. 'I prefer to stand, sir.'

Thurloe nodded and sat back in his chair, crossing his hands over his chest. 'I won't delay, Culpeper,' he said suddenly. 'I do not like you and you, I know, have little but contempt for me.'

'Sir—' began Culpeper.

Thurloe held up a gloved hand. 'Please, do not insult my intelligence by protesting. You regard me as an interfering old fool who gives General Cromwell all manner of bad advice. Is it not so?'

Culpeper looked straight ahead. 'I have my opinions, sir, and am entitled to them.'

Thurloe nodded and smiled smoothly. 'Quite so, quite so.' He picked up a piece of paper from his desk and tapped it. 'Do you know what this is?'

'Sir?'

'It is a draft copy of John Lilburne's new pamphlet.'

Culpeper laughed shortly. 'That hot-head. His Levellers are a spent force—'

'Don't interrupt me!' barked Thurloe with sudden ferocity. He rubbed his hand over his brow. 'You underestimate them, sir. These Levellers are a strong force. Their crazed ambitions for manhood suffrage and republicanism are but a heartbeat away.'

Culpeper frowned. 'What has all this to do with me?'

Thurloe leaned forward urgently 'Do you not see, man, that the Levellers are claiming Cromwell wants the crown? That the whole conflict was engineered that he might snatch the bauble from Charles's head?'

Culpeper shook his head. 'That is a silly falsehood.'

'Naturally!' cried Thurloe with a sigh. 'But these things have a habit of gaining ground, do they not? We all know that Charles must die, yet if popular opinion be persuaded that we are simply exchanging one king for another, what might the consequences be?'

Culpeper looked at Thurloe for the first time. 'We must have strong leadership. A figurehead.'

Thurloe jumped to his feet and stalked towards the soldier, shaking his fist angrily. 'And does not the general provide such leadership? Have you cause to complain?'

'No, but—'

'Then, sir,' spat Thurloe, his voice almost choked off with fury, 'cease your prattling counsel. We shall have a council of state in place of the King. And that is the end of the matter. Good day.'

Culpeper put out his hand. 'Thurloe, I never meant—'

'Good day!' snapped Thurloe.

With a frustrated sigh, Culpeper turned on his heel and strode to the door. As he opened it, Thurloe spoke again.

'You are an ambitious man, Thomas Culpeper. I have watched you as I watch everything that comes within the general's circle. Take care that I do not crush you.'

Culpeper hovered impotently in the doorway for a second and then stalked out, slamming the door behind him.

Thurloe smiled, pleased with his performance.

He walked back to the desk and picked up the piece of paper he had brandished earlier. The stuff about Lilburne's pamphlet had done the trick admirably, although the document in his hand was nothing of the sort. It was a death warrant for Thomas Culpeper which Thurloe had had the foresight to draw up some months before.

He opened a drawer in his desk and carefully placed the

warrant inside. You never knew when these things might come in handy.

Tearing like a greyhound across the deck of the *Teazer*, Ben didn't pause for breath.

He and Winter had managed to lash together tarry ropes from the ship's rigging which they fixed to the metal capstans which studded the outer hull of the vessel. Then, half-wriggling, half-crawling, they had dragged themselves across to the *Teazer*, splitting up as soon as they crashed onto her deck. Ben's task was to ascertain whether Stanislaus was aboard or had joined the attack on Winter's ship, while the lady captain headed straight for the Pole's cabin.

'If I know him, he'll be as far from the fight as possible,' she'd said. 'And now they've set sail, he must have this blessed package with him!'

Reluctantly, Ben had agreed with the plan but tried to cover the length and breadth of the ship as quickly as he could in order to rejoin his friend. After all, she had lost an arm, a leg, and her nose, so she probably needed all the luck she could get.

Ben was conscious of the sound of his own breathing as he ran across the deck, crouching low as he moved, his shoes slapping against the wet planks.

He cried out and jerked backwards as a slew of men suddenly charged right past him, arms flailing as they fought, shirts and sashes creating a blur of colour. There was sharp tang in the air as steel rang against steel, and Ben threw himself down to avoid getting caught up in the fighting. He encountered a dozen or more of the *Demeter*'s crew who had taken the fight to the enemy ship, their swords clashing as they took on the *Teazer*'s band of pirates.

Sorely tempted though he was to come to the aid of Sal

Winter's crew, he knew he wouldn't help the captain by getting himself pointlessly killed. So he pulled himself snugly into the shadows as booted feet raced by and the air was filled with rallying yells. He carefully avoided them all and, though he saw many he recognised, there was no sign of Captain Stanislaus.

Ben crouched down low and scurried towards the cabin, confident that he and Winter could ransack the place unmolested, at least for the time being. He raced forward and then pulled up sharply as he collided with a heavy weight which was swinging in the air directly before him.

A cry of horror left him involuntarily as he realised the weight was a man's body, swinging from the yardarm. Worse than that, it was the body of Isaac Ashdown, his face bloated and black, his purple tongue protruding sickeningly from his open mouth. A viciously tight noose was wrapped around his broken neck.

So, Stanislaus had rumbled them, he thought, and tortured the truth out of the only decent man in his crew, just as O'Kane had said.

Filled with bitter anger, Ben ran towards the captain's cabin. A light was blazing within and Ben positioned himself as close to the little window as he dared.

Inside, he saw a sight that made his heavy heart sink further still. Winter stood behind the desk, her hands raised above her head, being covered with a pistol by Godley. Another man, all in black, whom Ben did not recognise, stood by the cabin wall, a thin smile on his skeletal features.

'Quite a prize!' Godley was saying. 'Wait until the captain returns. It seems he had no need to board your ship. You were in too much of a hurry to come here!'

Winter scrutinised him closely. 'Mind your tongue, lad, lest you lose it.'

193

Godley cocked the pistol and levelled it coolly at Winter's face. 'You don't scare me, you she-ape. I've faced down far more dreadful apparitions than you.'

Again Winter looked at the young man and this time her weathered, powder-pocked face assumed a puzzled frown. 'Do I not know you, sir?'

Godley smiled, almost, thought Ben, like some actor stopped for his autograph. But then the handsome fellow shook his rich curls. 'I think not, Captain. Unless you have seen me in your nightmares!'

Winter shook her massive head. 'No. I think it would have been somewhere altogether more corporeal.'

Godley seemed a little unnerved by her attention and glanced quickly at the other man. 'Where is that idiot Pole?' he hissed. 'We must get him word that the *Demeter*'s mistress is our prisoner.'

The stranger nodded but made no move to help.

'Well?' thundered Godley. 'Away, man! 'Sblood! Must I do everything myself?'

For the first time, the curious man spoke and Ben found himself physically recoiling, even with the window between them.

'I am not concerned with this pettiness. I have work elsewhere.' The voice was dry as dust and Dutch in accent.

Ben suddenly realised that this must be the man Stanislaus and Godley had visited in Amsterdam.

Godley raised his pistol as though to strike the man and Ben took his chance. He hurled himself through the window, which exploded inward, and landed flat on his face on a carpet of shattered glass.

Winter reacted at once, sliding her bulk over the desk and smashing Godley's wrist against the woodwork. Again and again she moved until the pistol fell from the young man's grip.

Ben jumped to his feet and stood there, breathing heavily as Winter pointed the weapon at Godley and the Dutchman.

'Well, my boys, seems the boot's on the other foot, now, eh?' cackled Winter.

Godley sighed. 'If you think you can get off this ship, peg leg, then you're a bigger fool than you look.' He smiled nastily. 'And you look pretty foolish.'

Winter's face darkened. 'I give you one minute to tell me who you be. Then I'll plaster these four walls with your brains.'

Godley seemed entirely unfazed. 'My name is Robert Godley. I have some business with the captain. If I realised how he supplemented his commissions I should certainly have gone elsewhere.'

Winter waved her hand. 'Never mind that. What is this package you were to bring back?'

A flicker of fear fluttered over Godley's face. He licked his lips and couldn't help but glance at his companion.

Ben turned to him. 'Perhaps you know, Dutch? Eh?'

Winter grunted her agreement. 'Yes, surely this fellow knows. Did they not pick up the package from you?' Suddenly the captain's eyebrows lifted and a gleam of excitement came into her good eye. 'Or... or are you the package yourself?'

Ben looked at her. 'What?'

Suddenly there were shouts outside, and the sound of feet tramping closer.

'Stanislaus!' cried Ben. 'It must be Stanislaus coming back!'

Winter looked rapidly round the cabin. 'Well, well. No time for answers. This treachery ends here.'

She pointed the pistol towards a coil of rope which was swinging from the wall. 'Ben. Tie them up.'

Ben dashed to the wall and, within seconds, had secured Godley and the Dutchman together by their wrists.

Winter hustled Ben to the door and then kicked Godley in

the small of the back, sending him and the strange Dutchman sprawling into the corner.

She bowed low and raised the pistol.

'Farewell, gentlemen,' she said with a flashy smile.

Godley screwed up his face in expectation of the shot but, instead, Winter pulled a small, round object, which looked to Ben like a cricket ball, from her coat. It was like a hard leather sack and had a long, tapering cord trailing from it.

With a throaty laugh, she struck a flint and set light to the cord, which immediately began to burn.

Then she placed the bomb carefully on Stanislaus's desk and dashed out of the cabin.

Despite her clumsy gait, the captain moved quickly and she and Ben were soon on to the ropes and back aboard the *Demeter*, where, from a safe distance, they watched Stanislaus and a dozen of his men marching back towards the cabin.

The *Demeter* began to pull away and Winter stood on her deck in the pitch dark, waving her hat above her head. 'They've been beat!' she screeched. 'My brave lads have fought 'em off.'

Ben looked quickly around. He could see much devastation, but most of the crew seemed to be intact and had lined up alongside their captain, grinning and sweating with exertion, their swords hanging slackly at their sides.

'Now, Pole!' cried Winter. 'Let's see how you like that!'

There was a long pause and Ben wondered what the strange woman was going on about.

Then there came a tremendous, shocking roar and the darkness exploded into fiery light. Flames raced up the rigging of the *Teazer* and Ben let out an involuntary whoop of delight.

The crew of the *Demeter* threw themselves onto the deck as flames licked over the remains of Stanislaus's cabin. They had put a good hundred feet between themselves and the Pole now and the ship sailed steadily on into the night.

Winter watched the destruction with satisfaction and then turned to Ben. 'Now, my buck,' she grumbled. 'Let us see what the cur has left of me ship.'

CHAPTER
8

The King regarded Polly with an interested air, rubbing his bearded chin and watching as she crossed the room, swept back the curtain, and looked out into the night.

'You are very industrious, lady. Would you not rest a w-while?'

Polly shook her head but did not look round. 'There's no time.'

She began to search the room for a lamp but then, settling on the candle she had brought into the room, sat down on the window seat.

The King seemed baffled but amused by Polly's behaviour. He smiled slightly to himself and looked up at the darkened ceiling.

'I've received intelligence that I am to be r-rescued, is this not so?'

'It is.'

'And are you to be my rescuer?'

Polly turned at last. 'No. I'm just the first part of the plan. Once those two guards are out of the way, I'm to signal and the others will arrive.'

The King raised the glass of wine to his lips and Polly raced to his side. 'I wouldn't. It's drugged.'

'Ah,' said Charles. 'Of course.'

He settled back in his chair and folded his hands over his knee. 'Tell me, madam. Is it not customary to curtsy in the presence of one's monarch?'

Polly stopped in her tracks, becoming suddenly aware of the bizarreness of the situation. Eventually, she genuflected slightly and gave a little bow just to make sure.

'You'll forgive me, Your Majesty. But you are not my monarch.'

Charles frowned. 'But are ye n-not an Englishwoman?'

Polly laughed and was about to sit down on a chair before her when her sense of protocol intervened. 'Do you mind if I…?'

The King waved airily. 'It is the common lot, my dear. I can scarcely insist on formalities when the army plan to c-cut off my head.'

Polly sat down heavily. She was filled with a strange kind of remorse, as though she felt personally responsible for what would happen to this sad, quiet little man.

She looked at him, imagining how soon his head would be detached from his narrow shoulders, how soon those glossy curls of hair would be congealed with royal blood.

Shuddering, she looked away. 'I'm English by birth, sir,' she said at last. 'But I have been away for a long time.'

Charles nodded. 'Then perhaps you know little of the terrible pass to which I have brought my land.' He glanced down and a look of infinite sadness swept over his face. 'The land I l-love.'

'I know enough,' said Polly flatly.

Charles looked at her again. 'And that is why you would help me?'

Polly didn't answer at first. Then, reluctantly and without meeting the King's gaze, she said, 'I'm here to find my friends.'

Charles cocked an eyebrow. 'Do you count me one of them?'

Polly smiled kindly. 'I'm doing what I can to help.'

Charles bowed his head. 'Then I am grateful to you. What is your n-name?'

Polly was on the move again, rising to her feet and resting her ear against the door.

Charles made an impatient clucking in his throat. 'Will you not rest a moment, madam? You vex us severely.'

Polly turned, looking slightly wounded. 'I have to listen for the guards. As soon as the drug takes effect—'

Charles waved his hand. 'Yes, yes. But we shall not miss those great 1-louts crashing to the floor, shall we?'

Polly moved back to the chair and sat down. 'No, I suppose not.' She sniffed and looked the King straight in the eye. 'My name is Polly.'

Charles nodded. 'P-Polly,' he stated.

'I must say you're taking this all very calmly,' she said, intrigued.

Charles sighed. ''Tis what I was trained to do, Mistress Polly.'

'Don't you get sick of it, though? All that regal-bearing stuff?'

Charles gave a rare chuckle. 'Sicken of it? It is my life. What else am I fit for if not to rule?'

Polly thought with sadness that the question was about to be answered with some finality. 'And what will you do now?'

'If I am rescued? Well, I fear we must know each other a little better before I impart all my secrets. But I shall not forget you, my dear. Nor the ray of hope you have afforded me.'

There was a heavy, distinctive thump against the doors.

Charles extended a thin finger. 'You see, our friends the guards have d-dropped off.'

Polly jumped from her chair and carefully opened the double doors. Ancrom and Sam were slumped inside, mouths open slackly as they slept.

'Right,' cried Polly to herself and dashed back to the window. She raised the candle and passed it three times across her face, then set the candlestick down and turned back to Charles.

He had risen from his chair and seemed to be betraying some signs of excitement at last. His thin legs in their black stockings and breeches were trembling slightly.

'These friends of yours,' he said. 'They are in the castle, too?'

Polly nodded slowly, a trace of her former suspicion returning. 'Yes. They're to be released once I've got you out. That was the bargain.'

Charles tugged at his tunic and then ran a nervous hand over his beard. 'I wish you well, madam. And your friends. When all this unhappy business is c-concluded...'

'I know,' said Polly. 'I'll come and ask for the Order of the Garter.'

Charles's reply was lost in the sudden tumult that erupted from the corridor beyond. In a moment, the double doors were thrown wide and Copper, Whyte, Moor, and three other men raced into the room. Copper looked quickly about, located Charles, and gave a low bow. 'Your Majesty. Come! Come! We must hurry.'

The King nodded and dashed across the room. Moor threw a heavy cloak around his shoulders, which all but swamped the little man, and then hurried him out without a backward glance.

'Now, Chris, we must away,' said Copper. 'They'll discover us in a shot.'

Whyte nodded and turned to Polly with a grateful smile. 'Thank you, Polly. We could not have done this without—'

'Never mind that,' said Polly. 'Where's the Doctor and the others?'

Copper made an apologetic tutting sound and walked slowly towards her. 'Of course, my dear. Your friends! Quickly, this way.' He held out his hand to usher her out after the King.

Polly gave Whyte a quick grin and hopped over the sleeping Roundhead guards.

At once, Copper raised his dagger and prepared to plunge it down into her neck.

'No!' gasped Whyte, appalled. He thrust out his arm and knocked the weapon away. Copper glared at him furiously but, before Polly could turn, he had cracked her across the head with his gloved fist.

She crashed to the floor like a felled tree.

'You fool!' hissed Copper. 'We cannot let her live! She knows us!'

Before Whyte could reply, they heard shouts and the angry clang of a bell.

Both men exchanged fearful looks. 'We're discovered!' cried Whyte.

Copper dashed across the room but Whyte hung back, gazing anxiously down at the prostrate Polly.

'Chris! Come! We must fly!' shouted Copper.

He fled from the room.

Whyte lingered a moment longer, his face a picture of regret. 'Farewell, dear Polly,' he murmured. 'I am sorry.' Then he turned and hared from the room.

Oblivious to the clamour, Polly lay sprawled in a heap, a livid bruise developing on her skull.

Half running, half stumbling, Frances Kemp made her way through the dirty, snow-covered lanes towards the baker's shop she knew so well.

Her lovely face was pinched with the cold but had an altogether more haunted expression, which the severity of the weather could not explain.

Despite the gloom of the encroaching night, several friends of her family stopped and tipped their hats as they recognised her, but Frances ignored them all, keeping her head low and bustling forward, oblivious to the icy water splashing at her skirts.

This time, the door to the bakery was already slightly ajar but Frances paused some feet away, listening to the sound of her own breathing, the hammering of her heart in her ribs.

She knew Thomas would be inside there now, waiting patiently, listening out for her soft tread upon the doorstep. But how could she face him now? How could she when her heart was filled with the poison of treachery?

Frances put her hand to her head, as though trying to stop it from spinning. She hardly knew where she was. First, her new friend Polly, who had been such a comfort to her, had been spirited away, and then she had been forced to wheedle the secrets of the King's confinement from her beloved.

She walked on, her little feet crunching through the snow, and pushed gently against the woodwork of the door.

Thomas was revealed at once. He was standing in profile and Frances's heart seemed to leap into her mouth as she saw him. How handsome and noble he looked.

He turned as she entered and his face was suddenly wreathed in smiles. He dashed across the room and swept her into his arms, holding her so tightly she thought he might crush her.

She ran her hands through his long hair and smiled simply. 'Put me down, put me down,' she cooed gently.

Thomas shook his head. 'Nay, Frances. What say I carry you like this throughout all our lives?' He chuckled at the thought.

Frances tapped him lightly on the shoulder. 'But I should hate to make my husband into a crook-back, Tom!'

Thomas set her down and cupped her face in his hands. 'Why, you're no weight, my pet.' He frowned and brushed a lock of hair from her eyes. 'But you look pale, Frances. Are you ill?'

She shook her head and sat down, deliberately avoiding his attempted embrace. 'Nay, Tom. I'm tired, that's all. Father has been very bad again.'

Thomas sighed angrily. 'That man. He storms around that inn like a loosened bear.'

Frances rested her weary head on one hand. 'Nevertheless, he is my father, Tom. And we are stuck with him.' She turned suddenly and clutched his hands in hers. 'But tell me, my love, what have you been about today?'

Thomas shot her look of mock indignation. 'What's this? Taking an interest in my affairs again?'

She laughed lightly. ''Tis true I've always regarded your politicking with… indifference…'

'Disdain!' cried Thomas.

She inclined her head slightly, in agreement. 'But if we are to be married then I will want to take a far more active part in your work than has heretofore been possible, Tom.'

Thomas dragged a chair to her side and sat down. 'If we are to be married? Where does this indecision come from?'

Frances tapped him lightly across the chin. 'You know what I mean, you scoundrel.'

They both smiled and gazed deeply into each other's eyes. Then Thomas looked down and shrugged.

'Well, Franny. If you really want to know, my day was taken up with nothing more exciting than trying to find the funds to pay our troopers' back salary. I'm afraid that the reality of power is far less glorious than you might imagine.'

Frances looked up into his earnest face. 'And did you find the money?'

'Enough for now, I think,' he murmured with a frown. 'And enough to appease Sir Thomas Fairfax. But we'll only really be able to release funds when the King is dead.'

A chill gripped Frances's heart like the fingers of a ghost. 'Must it come to that?'

Thomas nodded gravely. 'I can see no other outcome.'

They sat in silence for a minute. Then Frances cleared her throat. 'But how is the trial to be administered? Surely these things will take much organisation?'

Thomas nodded quickly. 'Oh, indeed. And that is to be my task in the coming weeks. The general is soon to address a meeting of the rump of this Parliament to decide who is to sit on the trial, who is to judge and all other matters.'

'Oh?' said Frances lightly. 'And when is this to be?'

She listened in respectful silence as her lover explained, and played directly into the hands of her father and Sir John Copper.

'Wait, wait!' cried Oliver Cromwell, sucking his fingers and almost bouncing in his seat with excitement. 'The right! No, no. The left! The left!'

The Doctor stood before him, his hands held out in fists and a broad grin on his face.

'Are you sure, General?' asked the Doctor slyly.

'Oh, don't make me doubt myself again, Doctor. I can't bear the suspense. No. It is in your left hand, I know it.'

Slowly and deliberately, the Doctor opened his left hand, revealing it to be quite empty. Cromwell groaned disappointedly but then let out a small gasp of astonishment as the Doctor opened his right hand, also empty.

Cromwell smote his forehead. 'But…?'

At once, the Doctor leaned forward, reached behind the general's ear and produced the little spiral seashell he had spent most of the morning apparently making disappear.

Cromwell clapped his hands together. "Tis wonderful! I've seen tricks before, Doctor, but nothing like yours.'

The Doctor kept smiling but was sighing inwardly. His repertoire wasn't too large and Cromwell's appetite for distraction was eating up every trick he knew. But anything was better than revealing more of the future, the Doctor had decided. It was simply too dangerous. And when Jamie had gone into one of his 'trances' and started talking about flying machines and mechanical men, the Doctor had stepped on his toe to shut him up and launched into his series of party tricks.

Cromwell sat forward eagerly and looked over at Jamie. 'What say you, McCrimmon? Is not this Doctor of yours quite an extraordinary fellow?'

Jamie glanced ruefully at his companion. 'Aye. He is that. Ask him to do the one where he makes the two visitors vanish, will ye?'

Fortunately, Cromwell didn't hear this as Thurloe came gliding into the room.

Ah, John,' cried Cromwell happily. 'Come see what this Doctor can do. 'Tis a fine distraction from...'

He tailed off as he saw how ghastly pale Thurloe appeared. He clapped his aid on the shoulder. 'What is it?'

Thurloe shot a quick glance at the Doctor and Jamie, then bent to whisper in Cromwell's ear.

Quietly, the Doctor put away his seashell and stepped away from the chair, keeping his gaze fixed on Cromwell the whole time.

Jamie swivelled round to face him. 'What's happened, Doctor?'

The Doctor shook his head and crossed his hands over his chest. 'I don't know, Jamie. But I don't like the look of this one bit.'

Cromwell's hard, flushed countenance suddenly drained as though transfused with milk. He shifted away from Thurloe and sank back into his chair.

'What?' he muttered to himself. Then, again, increasingly louder: 'What? What?'

Blood surged back into his cheeks until he turned almost purple with rage, his bulbous nose wobbling like a great red beacon.

Thurloe bowed his head. 'I'm afraid 'tis true, General.'

Cromwell seemed almost physically afflicted. He pulled himself forward by the arms of the chair but seemed not to have the strength to rise. His eyes stared blankly at the floor for several long moments before fixing themselves on Jamie.

At first he seemed to stare right through the boy, but then he focused more clearly on him. Jamie's hair stood on end.

The general's lip began to curl upward and his breath came in short, stabbing, furious bursts. 'You did not predict this, my Scotch Cassandra!' he screamed across the room.

The Doctor cleared his throat. 'Predict what, General?' he inquired mildly.

Cromwell seemed about to speak but sank back into his chair, chewing feverishly at his knuckles.

Thurloe turned to the Doctor. 'The King has escaped,' he said simply.

'I beg your pardon?' said the Doctor, genuinely astonished.

Cromwell found his voice and shook his fist at his guests. 'Aye! Escaped! Spirited out of Hurst Castle this very evening as though the walls were made of butter!' He staggered to his feet and advanced menacingly on the little man. 'You fill my head with talk of flying engines but fail to warn me of this great

208

peril at my very door!'

The Doctor recoiled from the general's wrath and his dreadful breath. 'I explained that the McCrimmon's powers of prediction are not... er, predictable. He sees all possible eventualities. It is up to others to interpret what he sees.'

'Very convenient,' muttered Thurloe, glaring at them with renewed suspicion.

Cromwell swung back to Thurloe and stood with his arms behind his back, his head sunk upon his breast. 'What are we to do, John?'

'I have search parties scouring the city, sir—'

Cromwell held up his hand. 'But it must be kept secret. It must! If Charles escapes abroad there will be another war!'

Thurloe nodded. 'Indeed, General. Only a few commanders know what has occurred. Their men are instructed to seek out an impostor who resembles Charles Stuart and is attempting to stir insurrection among the people.'

Cromwell nodded and allowed himself a little smile. 'You've done well, John. But we cannot waste more time. Bring Thomas Culpeper to me. I would seek his counsel too. We must find the King!'

He was about to stomp out of the room when he noticed the Doctor and Jamie again. He growled like a beast at the sight of them.

'And get these two out of my sight. I have had enough of trickery for one day.'

The sound of booted feet approaching made them all look up and the doors to the room were flung wide. A knot of soldiers marched inside, Thomas Culpeper at their head. The men carried something between them, a figure, its head covered in a cloth sack, kicking and struggling for all it was worth.

'Tom?' said Cromwell. 'What's this?'

Thomas Culpeper saluted Cromwell and then stepped aside.

The figure was flung to the floor where it made renewed efforts to free itself from the ropes that bound it.

'Forgive me, General' said Culpeper, 'but this person was found in the King's quarters at Hurst Castle. She had substituted herself for the serving girl employed there and had given drugged wine to the King's guards.'

Cromwell shook his massive head. 'What bloody treachery is this? She must have had accomplices. What of the other guards?'

'All drugged,' said Culpeper. 'The two she bamboozled say she claimed to be the niece of the old castle retainer, Spufford. But he has flown and must be regarded as the chief suspect.'

Cromwell sighed and slammed his fist into his palm. Then he bent down and ripped the sack from the figure's head.

The Doctor tried to push Jamie back as Polly was revealed but she saw them almost at once, blinking like a newborn lamb.

'Oh, Doctor! Jamie! Thank goodness. I thought—'

She glanced quickly round and took in the scene in an instant.

Cromwell's eyes flashed dangerously. 'Well, well. Known to you, eh, Doctor?' He shook his head disappointedly and then swung his arm over his head wildly. 'Take them all to the Tower!' he screeched hoarsely.

Culpeper's men immediately grabbed the Doctor and Jamie. Polly found herself back on her feet and once more in custody.

'You're making a terrible mistake, General,' said the Doctor sadly.

Cromwell didn't reply but turned instead to Thurloe. 'John, you will get the truth out of these people, even if you have to break them in two. Understand me?'

Thurloe nodded.

Cromwell swept from the room, his cloak fluttering behind him. 'Captain Culpeper!' he called over his shoulder.

Nathaniel Scrope counted out the last of the coins onto the counter of the merchant's shop and nodded.

'How long's it been, Jabez?' he asked in his cracked voice.

He was standing a dark, low-ceilinged room that bristled with seafaring goods. The walls were thick with coiled rope. Barrels of salt and tar crowded for space with ship's biscuits and pewter pots.

The old man across the counter, who looked just as ancient and weathered as Scrope, leaned back on his stool and scratched his sunburnt head.

'Well, now, Nat, that's a good question. You come and did the scrapings last when our Betty was having her little 'un. And that must be all of three year back.' He grinned broadly. 'Aye. Three year come Christmas.'

Scrope chuckled. 'Plenty for me to get my trowels into then, eh, Jabez?'

The other man let out a high-pitched laugh like a whistling kettle and slapped his knee.

'I can't say I'm not glad you've come, Nat. The smell was disturbing my sleep of a night!'

Scrope pulled a strange little spade from his belt and held it up high like a sword. ''Tis the Lord's work I do!' he announced, and he and his friend dissolved into further laughter.

The merchant led the way through the back of the shop and out into the frost-rimed yard. This dingy patch of land was so close to the Thames that it regularly flooded and there was a wide, smooth, frozen pool occupying the bottom half of the yard.

Scrope's attention, however, was fixed on a ramshackle wooden structure which had been erected against the far wall. Its woodwork was peeled and blistered with age and there were all kinds of unmentionable stains blemishing its surface.

'There she is, Nat,' said Jabez happily. 'As proud a privy as there's to be seen in all London!'

Scrope tapped his hat and scuttled bandily across the yard. 'I'll not be two shakes, Jabez.'

The other man nodded and began to walk back towards his shop. 'I'll prepare us something nice and warm to frighten off this chill.'

Scrope advanced on the toilet with his trowel in one hand and a small leather bucket in the other.

'Now then,' he muttered to himself. 'Where are you?'

Anyone might have thought he was addressing the saltpetre that he came in search of but Scrope seemed more concerned with the back wall of the yard than the stinking structure before him.

He opened the privy door and set his tools down on the hard frozen ground. Inside was a crude wooden shelf with a large hole in it, and beneath that, visible through a muddy hole, was the grey water of the river.

Scrope should have been interested in the deposits that surrounded the hole but he turned and stood by the wall, waiting until a long, low whistle sounded close by.

He placed his filthy fingers in his mouth and returned the signal. Nothing happened for a moment and then, with extraordinary speed, a young boy scrambled over the wall and landed with skill on the hard, frozen ground.

Scrope nodded quickly. 'Good day, Petie. What news?'

The boy was dressed in little more than rags and his cherubic face was smeared with grime. He looked quickly about as though in fear of discovery.

'I've heard tell a woman was seen in Kemp's inn these past couple of nights.'

'A woman like the one I described?' queried Scrope.

The boy nodded. His quick eyes were restless as he continued. 'And she had a man with her – but he got coshed on the 'ead. I know someone who saw 'im taken down the docks and put aboard the *Teazer*.'

Scrope frowned. 'The *Teazer*? She's that Polish captain's ship, ain't she?'

The boy shrugged.

Scrope stood in thought for a moment. 'And where was the *Teazer* bound?'

'Amsterdam. But not for long. Due back any time, I hear.'

Scrope nodded. 'And the woman?'

Petie shrugged. 'She was seen with Kemp's daughter but no one has clapped eyes on her in a while.'

Scrope felt inside his purse and slipped the boy a dull metal coin.

'Thank 'ee, Nat,' said the boy with a grin. 'I'll find you again if I hear more.'

Scrope tipped his hat at the boy and watched as he scrambled back over the merchant's wall. He stood in silence for a moment, lost in thought.

The sound of Jabez the merchant whistling tunelessly woke Scrope from his reverie.

Hastily he went back to the privy and, sinking to his knees, began to dig.

The *Demeter* seemed to have taken on a life of her own as she ploughed her way majestically through the surging grey waters of the North Sea.

Captain Winter was already on deck as the bleary dawn bled across the horizon. Scanning her ship, she noted with

213

dismay how much damage Stanislaus had inflicted.

Some of her best and most loyal men had lost their lives in the battle with the *Demeter*, but now, at least, they had put paid to whatever treachery had been at work. They could get back to London with happy hearts, knowing they had done their best for General Cromwell.

Winter plunged her hand into the pocket of her great green coat and pulled out the bundle of letters she had retrieved from the Pole's cabin. She gazed down at the elegant, florid writing and a small smile formed on her battered face.

Then, swiftly, she put them away again and pulled out her stubby telescope.

She unfolded it and clamped her good eye over the lens, then began to move it back and forth with great deliberation. Something was niggling at her, a vague uneasiness that she found difficult to ignore.

A big, blurred shape loomed into sight and she jumped in spite of herself, her wooden leg thudding against the deck.

She pulled away the telescope and realised that the shape was Ben emerging from below decks.

'Ah, good day to thee, Ben,' called Winter.

Ben waved over at her. He looked pale and rather unsteady. Winter laughed and aimed a mock punch at Ben's stomach as he approached. 'Too much rum last night, my fine lad, eh? Well, 'tis not every day we beat off a pirate ship, is it now?'

Ben smiled wanly. 'No. Suppose not.'

He glanced out over the sea and felt, with a brief flush of shame, suddenly sick. He clamped his eyes tightly shut and tried to focus his mind on something else.

'How long till we reach London?' he said at last.

Winter shrugged and began to look through the telescope once again. 'We're making good speed. But there's no hurry now, is there?'

214

Ben shook his head. 'You mean because we got rid of Stanislaus's mob? Well, I know. But I'm still concerned about Pol and the others, even if England's all right.'

Winter suddenly stopped dead, the telescope tight against her eye like an arrow.

Ben noticed the change at once. 'What is it?'

'By Christ. I knew it!' whispered Winter. 'I've felt it in me bowels since I rolled out of that pit of a bed of mine this morning. There, Ben, do you see her?'

She tossed the telescope to Ben, who immediately jumped up to Winter's level and swung round to face the direction in which the captain was pointing.

At first he saw nothing in the glass but a circle of grey sea. Then the image cleared and a small, dark shape was revealed bobbing on the horizon some miles behind them.

'Is it…?' began Ben.

'It is,' hissed Winter, shaking her broad head in disbelief. 'The *Teazer*. By God, the Pole has the devil on his side and no mistake.'

Ben dropped the telescope to his knee. 'But the gunpowder… the explosion…'

Winter nodded. 'We must only have damaged her. And, whether we destroyed their precious cargo or not, Stanislaus will be out for revenge!'

Ben put the telescope back to his eye. The *Teazer* was moving steadily closer.

The Thames lapped sluggishly at the little jetty, its ice-thickened water sloshing around the structure's rotting, weed-covered posts.

Looming over the jetty like a great blackened skull was a warehouse, nominally used to store salted meat and wine but, for now at least, the hiding place of King Charles.

215

Several rooms on the upper floors of the building were occupied by Sir John Copper's men and, while the King slept, they kept a constant vigil, aware that Roundhead troopers were combing the city in search of him.

Copper sat alone in the largest of these rooms, staring into space and constantly fiddling with his beard in agitation. His eyes flickered from side to side as though he were weighing up some great decision.

At last, his solitude was disturbed by the arrival of Christopher Whyte, who came quietly into the room and sat down.

Copper looked up. 'Well?'

'Still sleeping,' murmured Whyte, avoiding Copper's eyes.

Copper shook his head and sighed. 'Does he not understand the urgency of the situation?'

Whyte did not reply and Copper changed tack. 'Chris, I had no choice.'

Whyte turned sharply round, his face flushed with rage. 'No choice? No choice but condemn an innocent girl to the headsman's axe?'

Copper held up both his hands, palm outward. 'We both deceived her, did we not?'

Whyte let his breath hiss from between his teeth. 'Aye! Deceived her so that we could rescue the King, but you would have killed her!'

Copper nodded firmly. 'And because you prevented me, she will now give us away to Cromwell.'

Whyte shook his head. 'She will not. I know it.'

Copper gave a cynical smile. 'You know her so well, do you, Christopher? Under torture she'll say anything.'

Whyte dragged his chair closer. 'But what matters it if we are discovered? Surely now the King is free we can raise another army and settle this civil war once and for all?'

Copper rubbed both his thumbs over his weary eyes. 'Aye, if His Majesty would only see sense! He cannot remain in London, and the longer he does so the more difficult it will be to get him out!'

Whyte hunched forward, his clasped hands between his knees. 'What can we do?'

'We must prevail upon him to go. There can be—'

Copper stopped and looked around as he heard footsteps approaching. The door was opened by Moor, who immediately stepped aside, ushering in the little figure of the King, who stepped through into the dank, unpleasant room.

Copper and Whyte bowed low and Charles acknowledged them with a slight inclination of his head. He looked about, as though expecting a chair to be there for him, and Copper hurriedly gave up his own. Charles seated himself and placed his hands in his lap.

'We th-thank you, gentlemen for your most efficacious rescue of our person from Hurst Castle.' He glanced about with his sad brown eyes. 'And, though our present circumstances are not the most pleasant we have ever encountered, the air of freedom is no less sweet.'

Copper and Whyte bowed again and then the older man moved forward. 'If I may make so bold, Your Majesty?'

Charles inclined his head once more. 'Speak, Sir John.'

Copper shot a quick look at Whyte and then pressed on. 'I must urge Your Majesty to fly from the city at once. It can only be a matter of time before we are discovered.'

Charles nodded. 'Do you not think, though, that it would be far more risky for me to attempt to l-leave when the exits from London will all be guarded?'

Copper shrugged. 'Nevertheless, sir, it is a chance we must take.'

Charles did not respond and Whyte stepped forward. 'May

I remind His Majesty that we did not rescue him from his confinement only for the Roundheads to recapture him and cut off his head!'

Charles looked Whyte up and down. 'You are very bold, sir,' he said at last.

Whyte bowed. 'Forgive me, sir, but I feel I must be. The situation is critical. We are confident that we can get you away to France and from there to a place where your security will be assured. Then we can set about invigorating the Royalist movement here. If they know their King is safe, they will surely rally once more to our cause.'

Charles looked down at his shoes. 'Your sentiments are very noble, sir. But would you have it said that the King fled his own c-country just to save his skin?'

Whyte flung up his hands in exasperation. 'Sir, if you die then our cause dies with you. Parliament will rule unchecked and never more will a king sit upon the throne of England.'

Charles held up his neat little hands. 'You must not concern yourself so over our welfare. There are… other plans afoot.'

Copper and Whyte exchanged glances. Charles opened his tunic and produced a piece of crisp, folded paper which he handed to Copper.

'S-Sir John, I desire you to meet a certain ship upon her arrival in the East India Docks tonight. The rest of my instructions are contained within that document.'

Copper glanced at the paper, which bore the royal seal. 'Your Majesty, I do not understand.'

Charles looked his saviours up and down and gave a small, tight smile. 'It is not always necessary to understand in order to obey. Is that not so?'

Copper hesitated for a moment before giving a small, unwilling bow. 'Your Majesty,' he intoned through clenched teeth.

'Now, gentlemen,' said Charles, rising, 'I shall keep my own counsel for the remainder of the morning. You must not worry yourselves. We shall forever keep your good works in f-fond remembrance. But you must be content to let us lie low for a while. Then we shall see what we shall see.'

He turned on his heel and walked to the door. To his surprise, it was not opened at once by a courtier and he stood expectantly for a second before Copper raced forward and opened it for him.

Without another word, Charles went out.

Whyte thumped his fist on the table. 'Perhaps his imprisonment has addled his brain,' he said bitterly.

Copper shook his head, 'No, no. He has something at work here. Something few others know about.'

Whyte pointed to the document and raised his eyebrows.

Copper pulled up a chair and reverently broke the seal, which disintegrated into fine red dust. He smoothed out the square of paper and rapidly scanned its contents. Then he looked up at Whyte, a look of shock and repressed astonishment on his face.

'Sir John?' said Whyte concernedly.

Copper licked his lips and looked back at the paper to confirm what he had read. There was no mistake.

'The King,' he breathed. 'The King is planning to assassinate Cromwell!'

CHAPTER
9

Narrow strips of light fell across the Doctor's face as he gazed out solemnly over the frozen Thames.

Hands gripping the bars of the window, he looked like some old illustration of a desperate prisoner. Although he wasn't feeling particularly desperate, he, Jamie, and Polly were most definitely on the wrong side of a locked door.

The discovery of the knocked-out guard had done little to aid their cause.

They had been taken with indecent haste to the Tower of London, dragged up its endless, winding stairs, and finally deposited in the small, bleak room in which they now resided, its massive stone walls chilly to the touch, rivulets of brackish water streaming incessantly from the ceiling to the floor.

Jamie was struggling to sleep, while Polly sat cross-legged on the floor, feeling very sorry for herself, her long blonde hair hanging over her face.

The Doctor stepped back from the window and, noticing his companion, gave a small, encouraging smile. 'Cheer up, Polly,' he cooed. 'Might never happen.'

Polly didn't look up but continued to stare at the bolted door. 'But it did happen, didn't it, Doctor? I've messed everything up.'

The Doctor sat down beside her, heedless of the damp patch which immediately spread across the seat of his checked trousers. 'Well… not quite everything,' he said.

Polly looked up. 'I think so. I lost Ben, I got myself kidnapped, then I fell for those Cavaliers' tricks, end up freeing the King and incriminating you two so we all end up in the Tower!'

The Doctor frowned with mock seriousness. 'Well, now you put it like that…'

Polly grinned and poked him in the ribs. 'I know you're trying to make me feel better, Doctor, but it's pretty serious, isn't it?'

The Doctor cleared his throat. 'Oh, Ben'll be all right. I'm sure he'll turn up sooner or later and they won't keep us in here for long once they think about it. Cromwell's too intelligent to take us for Royalist spies.'

Polly shrugged. 'That's as may be, but what about King Charles?'

The Doctor began to chew his fingernails distractedly. 'Ah, now that is a problem. He's due to stand trial on January the twentieth. There's no record of this escape, so we've got to get history back on its proper course.'

'Or else?' It was Jamie's voice. He was sitting up on the grim straw mattress and had been listening to their conversation for some little while.

'Oh, I've been through all this before, haven't I? You know what the consequences could be.'

Polly let her tongue trace over her lips thoughtfully 'Doctor, have you ever seen any of these… possible futures?'

The Doctor frowned, almost pulling back from her. 'Eh? What possible futures?'

Jamie warmed to Polly's theme. 'These ones you always warn us about.'

The Doctor shook his head and got quickly to his feet. He

turned his back on his companions and resumed his vigil at the window.

'You know what will happen,' he said gravely. 'We know how history turned out, but we have to make sure of it.'

Polly inclined her head. 'You're avoiding the question.'

The Doctor didn't reply for a moment, and then his voice came rumbling through the air towards Jamie and Polly, as though from a very long way away.

'Have I seen them? Yes, I've seen them. Or heard of them. Englands with a third, fourth, or fifth Civil War. A resurgent monarch who ruthlessly oppresses all democracy. Or a triumphalist, hereditary Puritan Protectorate that rules the country until the twentieth century. Or an invading Catholic army which takes advantage of England's crisis to take over most of the known world. Oh yes, they're all out there. All kinds of futures. Some great, some truly terrible.'

The little man swung round and his face seemed suddenly ancient, like a stone gargoyle on a cathedral. 'We have to pay the price for travelling as we do. It's up to us now.'

The black-and-white-tiled floor of Cromwell's chamber rang with the sound of his pacing feet. Wearing an impressive buff jerkin with great hooped sleeves and a fresh linen collar, the general cut a magnificent figure.

It was a day for putting the fear of God into his men and he knew it. It had to be impressed upon every single friend of their cause that the King's escape could bring ruin upon them all. Charles Stuart had to be found, tried, and put to death with all possible speed.

There was a tap at the door and Cromwell took up position by the fireplace, legs akimbo and arms behind his back.

'Come!' he barked.

To his surprise and annoyance, it was Richard who came

223

inside, oscillating from one foot to the other like some weedy metronome.

'Oh, Richard,' wailed Cromwell. 'What do you want?'

Richard came forward, almost tripping over his feet. 'I bring news, Father.'

'Hmm?' muttered Cromwell. 'News? What news?'

Richard smiled triumphantly. 'News of the future.'

Surely, he had concluded, this was the way to win his father's respect. He would show him the book and its incredible information about the years to come. All the mistakes they would make would be set out in detail and, therefore, strenuously avoided. It would be the making of him and of the new English republic.

Cromwell shifted uneasily, his boil troubling him again. 'The future? What are you talking about, lad?'

Richard sidled up to his father and leaned back confidently against the globe that stood next to him. 'What would you say, Father, if I told you that I know when the King will die and exactly what will happen next?'

Cromwell scowled. 'I'd say you'd been at your mother's sherry again.'

Richard frowned and waved his hand in irritation. 'No, no. I am in earnest.'

Cromwell advanced on his son threateningly. 'Have you been speaking to that Doctor and the Scot?'

Richard smiled happily. 'Yes! They have shown me the most wondrous things! The future, all mapped out for us, Father.'

Cromwell sighed and smote himself across the forehead. 'Clot! Do you not know that I have thrown them in the Tower? They are Royalist spies who seek to baffle us all with their fakery.'

Richard felt his legs begin to shake. 'But, Father, the book—'

'Book?' snapped Cromwell. 'What book?' He swung around

and turned his back on Richard. 'Enough, lad. I am too busy to play out your idle fancies. Leave me.'

'But, Father—'

'Leave me!' bellowed the general.

With a little sob, Richard turned and slunk from the room.

He was replaced at once by Thomas Culpeper, who came swiftly inside, glancing after Richard's retreating back and shutting the door behind him. He saluted to his superior and immediately produced a scroll of paper from inside his tunic.

'Tom,' said Cromwell with a little bow. 'What news?'

Culpeper sighed and waved his hand helplessly. 'A multitude of sightings, General,' he said. 'But nothing substantial, I fear.'

Cromwell stamped his booted foot on the floor. 'He cannot be out of the city, else we would have heard of it by now And yet, if he remains, what can be the point of it?'

He stared into space for a long moment and chewed his bottom lip thoughtfully. 'There is something afoot, Tom, or I do not know that dissembling man.'

Culpeper nodded slowly. 'If I may suggest, General, Thurloe's agents—'

Cromwell swung round. 'Do not get above yourself, Captain. John Thurloe's agents are doing the best they can. I have every confidence in 'em.'

He turned an interested eye on his aide. An ambitious lad, of course, but capable and loyal. It would be better for all if his energies were given direction.

Cromwell lifted the back of his coat and warmed himself before the crackling fire. 'However…'

Culpeper's face lit up excitedly. 'General?'

'Mayhap Master Thurloe is too preoccupied to properly prosecute his investigation of this rescue. I am convinced that we have been betrayed. There is a rotten man among our number, Tom.'

Culpeper looked at him eagerly.

Cromwell nodded to himself. 'I'd like you to look into it, Tom.'

Culpeper bowed low and Cromwell gave him a light-hearted slap across the shoulder. 'Away with you, I'm not the King.'

Culpeper looked up and caught the general's eye. He smiled.

Cromwell laughed. 'Nor ever shall be! Despite what you might think, my lad!'

He waved Culpeper away but the young man hesitated.

'A question, sir?'

Cromwell's eyebrows lifted a fraction. 'Hmm?'

Culpeper chose his words carefully. 'Should not the business of the trial continue as though naught had occurred? If there is one sure way to make tongues wag it is for you to stay and brood in here.'

There was a long and dangerous, pause like the atmosphere before a thunderstorm. Then Cromwell nodded.

'Y'are right, Tom. As ever. I am not some widower to be stopped in his house with grief! We must prepare the death of Charles Stuart so that, when he is recaptured, none shall ever know he managed to fly.' He crossed to his chair and picked up his gloves and hat. 'Away with you now. I have business in Parliament, do I not?'

Culpeper bowed, smiled, and marched off happily and unknowingly to investigate himself.

Captain Winter swivelled around on her false leg and cast a beady glance at the darkening sky. Then she hobbled across the deck and gripped the rail as she leaned out over the edge.

Grunting to herself, she beckoned to Ben. The young sailor trotted quickly towards her and Winter pulled him close to her massive chest.

'I don't like the look of that sky, Ben,' she confided. 'And the *Teazer*'s coming damnably close.'

Ben looked up at the sky, which was indeed becoming increasingly threatening. 'Can we outrun her?' he asked.

Winter looked around at her men, all hard at work. It was important not to lower morale with defeatist talk but she knew they were in trouble. The *Demeter* was a clumsier ship than her enemy's and, with the cannon damage sustained in the battle, she was no match for the ship speeding so rapidly towards her.

A drop of heavy, warm rain splashed against Winter's cheek and she wiped it thoughtfully away.

'Nay, Ben. We can't outrun her. But we might turn this weather to our advantage. The *Teazer*'s a big bugger and not so manoeuvrable as her cursed captain likes to think.'

She gazed out over the sea, which was already starting to roughen up, choppy grey waves crashing against the hull.

Ben followed her gaze. 'We can't be far off port now.'

Winter shook her head. 'Nay, we're close. But we can't have the Pole taking us just as we have old London in sight. Come.'

She began to totter towards her cabin.

'What have you got in mind now, you old rascal?' asked Ben with a grin.

Winter flashed him a black smile. 'I know many a route back to port, my lad. What say we give Stanislaus a game of it? Eh?'

She threw open the door to her cabin and writhed till her bulk worked itself through into the cramped space.

With urgent strides she made her way to the desk and began pulling maps and charts from the drawers. With a cry of satisfaction, she found what she was looking for and cleared everything else from the desk with a broad sweep of her arm.

'Here, Ben! Here!' she cried, stabbing at the chart with a fat finger.

Ben looked closer. He recognised the coast of Kent and the approach to London through the Thames Valley. But the whole charted area was outlined in fine dashes, as though defining a phantom country just next to the land he knew.

'Do you know what they are?' cackled Winter.

Ben shook his head. 'No. What?'

Winter rolled up the chart and tapped it against her head. 'Marshes, my buck!'

Ben frowned and then smiled broadly.

Winter began to hobble towards the door. 'I can get the *Demeter* up a crack as narrow as the top of a Scotchman's purse. Let's see if the Pole has the same skill!'

She threw open the door. 'Hugh!' she bellowed. 'Where are you, lad? Make haste. We're changing course!'

William Kemp was in his accustomed place behind the long bar of the tavern when the door opened and Sir John Copper slipped inside.

He seemed nervous and distracted, not at all the graceful, confident figure Kemp knew. Glancing quickly around, he caught Kemp's eye and indicated with a jerk of his head that they should talk upstairs.

Sarah Kemp was also behind the bar, struggling with a tray of ale.

As Copper moved through the crowded room towards the stairs, Kemp pulled off his leather apron and slung it down over a barrel.

'Look after things here a moment, Sarah,' he muttered.

Sarah Kemp let out a sigh. 'What? Now, Will? 'Tis our busiest time—'

Kemp raised his massive fist and held it perilously close to

228

her face. 'Do not vex me, woman. I have business.'

Despite the threat, his wife did not back down. 'I recall a time when your business was your business,' she murmured sourly.

For a moment it appeared that Kemp would strike her. Then, face flushed, he strode across the room, knocking into his drunken patrons, who called a series of good-humoured oaths after him.

Sarah Kemp looked sadly at her husband's retreating back until a shout broke her reverie.

"Sfoot, Sarah! Where's the ale?'

She turned and gave her broadest, warmest smile to the drunken youth sprawled over the wooden bar.

Kemp was glad to be out of the steaming, heaving room. The stench of tobacco smoke, to which he was normally inured, seemed to be clinging to his lungs tonight and he gave a great hacking cough as he made his way swiftly up the stairs.

In truth, he was greatly preoccupied The revelation of his daughter's treachery had shaken him dreadfully and somewhat taken the shine off the news of the King's escape. But still, it was true! His beloved monarch was free and the pressure to keep silent was almost tearing Kemp apart.

He approached the door to the little room and knocked gently. Copper's voice from beyond bade him enter.

'I am sorry for the delay, My Lord. My wife—'

Copper waved away his excuses. He did not look in the mood for trivia. 'Sit down, Will,' he said, pulling out a rickety chair from beneath the table.

Kemp sat down, feeling like a schoolboy about to get in serious trouble. He began to lick his dry lips. 'What ails you, Sir John?'

Copper looked at him, his white brows drawn tightly. 'The King ails me, Will. He refuses point blank to leave London.'

Kemp nodded. 'Aye. On the grounds 'twould look like cowardice. God, the man is a saint, I shouldn't wonder if—'

'Shut up,' hissed Copper. 'If you knew half of the situation you would not make light of it so. The King is a fool, God save me for saying it. And I fear for him every hour he remains in this stinking city. But he is ahead of us.'

Kemp leaned forward, his hands clasped between his knees. 'What do you mean?'

'His Majesty has plans to disrupt the Roundheads' cause. Disrupt it in a terminal fashion.'

'How?'

'By removing its figurehead,' said Copper evenly.

Kemp stroked his chin. 'Cromwell, you mean? Remove him?' He peered closely at Copper. 'Kill him?'

Copper nodded. 'Plans have already been laid. It is a risky venture and I would never have done things this way myself, but we have come this far in order to serve our King and we must not fail him now.'

Kemp sniffed. 'What must we do?'

Copper began to drum his fingers on the table. 'Fate has placed a happy coincidence in our laps, Will. A spy on the enemy side who we thought might only provide useful intelligence.'

'Spy? Who do you—' Kemp sat suddenly upright. 'You cannot mean my Frances?'

Copper nodded. 'I do.'

Kemp shook his head violently. 'But she is little more than a child. To involve her in a conspiracy of this order…'

Copper snorted. 'Oh, come now, Kemp. Was it not you calling her strumpet and whore only t'other night? If she has years enough to take a Roundhead as her lover she is surely of an age to help us.'

Kemp's head sank to his breast. 'But if it should come out…'

Copper turned away dismissively. 'You should have considered such things before you became involved. You do not think your wife and child would in any case be spared if your part in all this should be revealed?'

Kemp shook his head. He had heard the accounts of Roundhead atrocities, of unborn infants ripped from their mothers' wombs and troopers washing their hands in the resultant blood.

'What do you want of her?' he asked sadly.

Copper took out a square of paper, which was covered with his neat writing.

'We need to know Cromwell's movements between today and the end of the week. In detail. I don't fret over how she gets them – she can sleep with half of Parliament for all I care – but she must find out. You will receive further instructions then. Is that understood?'

Kemp did not reply, thinking, for the first time, that he would gladly strike the aristocratic gentleman who sat at his side.

'Is that understood?'

Kemp looked up and nodded.

Copper got his feet. 'Good. I shall await your signal. She must hurry. Time is of the essence.'

He turned and strode out of the room.

Kemp sat stock still, his breathing hot and fast, then tears sprang like pearls to his eyes. Great God, he thought miserably, what would become of him?

From his vantage point by the dockside, Nathaniel Scrope could see all of the bustling river traffic. A raw, freezing wind was howling over the spindly black rigging of the moored ships, flapping at tethered sails and making the windowpanes of the adjacent offices rattle like loose teeth.

From time to time, a few small rowing boats would plough their way through the half-frozen water, their passengers bundled up like wool-swathed dummies against the cold.

Scrope sat on an upturned barrel, puffing away at a clay pipe, looking like a disreputable elf on a rum-stained toadstool.

His rheumy eyes scanned the water and then flicked round as his friend Petie came scrambling over the jetties towards him.

"Swounds, if I ain't froze half dead!' cried the lad as he took his place by Scrope's side and hopped from one foot to the other, struggling to keep his skinny frame warm.

'I thank 'ee for coming, Petie. In such weather as this an' all.'

Petie shook his head mournfully. 'I'd a doxy lined up tonight, Nat, that would fair turn your toes up. I'd sooner be in her warm arms than out here by the blasted river.'

Scrope gave a little chuckle. 'The Lord will remember your forbearance, my lad, and no mistake. Now, come, what news of the *Teazer*?'

Petie wrapped his arms tightly about his skinny chest. 'Sighted by a sloop as she passed Canvey Island, Nat. She's hugging the coast like a babe at its ma's breast.'

'But heading for London?'

Petie shrugged. 'Hard to tell. My mate says she could be making for the Gravesend marshes.'

Scrope's weathered old face contracted in surprise. 'The marshes? Whatever for?'

Petie stamped his feet on the rotten duckboards. 'There's a brig close in front that she seems to be a following.'

'Name?'

Petie shrugged. 'My mate couldn't be sure. He's stuck out on a lightship and the weather's closing in fast. But he said she looked like the *Demeter*.'

Scrope roared with unexpected laughter. 'What? Old Sal Winter's ship?'

He laughed again and slid down from the barrel. 'I tell you, Petie,' he said, using his glowing pipe to gesture, 'if Stanislaus is on Winter's tail then this storm'll prove as nothing compared to the tempest they'll blow in.'

Petie rubbed his hands together feverishly. 'And how do you reckon this lad, this Ben Jackson, is tied to 'em?'

Scrope shrugged and began to move back towards the street. A curtain of wet sleet was already descending on them. 'I know not as yet. But we must get over to the marshes to see the outcome of this battle royal, Petie. Then we'll find out how the Doctor's friend fits into this merry picture.'

They shambled through the growing gale and back into the winding streets of old London.

'Now think, Polly,' said the Doctor earnestly. 'These men who rescued the King. Who were they and where would they go? The information might just save our lives.'

Polly shrugged. 'The only one who told me his name was Christopher. Christopher Whyte.'

'He could've been making that up,' offered Jamie.

'Yes,' muttered the Doctor. 'And they were based at the inn? Close to where the TARDIS landed?'

'That's right. But I hardly think they'd go back there. They must've assumed I'd be forced to tell everything I knew.'

The Doctor's brows knitted together. 'No, no. You're right. They'd try to get the King out of the country. Then they could raise an army and invade.'

Jamie gave a small, despairing sigh. 'That's it, then, isn't it? If the King's out of England then we must've put time out of joint.'

Polly's mouth turned down anxiously. 'One of your nightmare scenarios is unfolding as we speak.'

The Doctor wagged his finger. 'Not necessarily. History says that Charles was imprisoned right up to his trial. That's still some time away.'

'Aye,' lamented Jamie. 'But we've not much chance of putting things rights banged up in here!'

There was some activity outside the room and then bolts were drawn back. The door swung open and Thurloe stepped inside. He nodded to the jailer, who slammed and locked the door after him.

'Aren't you afraid we might try to eat you, Mr Thurloe?'

Thurloe permitted himself a tiny smile. 'You do not seem the type, Doctor. Besides, I have come here to help you.'

'If it's in return for us trying to persuade the general against the kingship, I'm afraid we didn't have much chance...'

Thurloe waved his hand. 'Nay. I know you did what you could. Besides, we cannot have a new king until we have found the old one, eh?'

The Doctor smiled. 'Quite.'

Thurloe moved across the room and let his hand trail over the damp, rotten stonework. 'Not the most salubrious of places, Doctor?'

The Doctor looked about. 'Oh, don't you like it? Of course, when to buy is always such a difficult decision, but we were sick of renting, weren't we?' He turned to Jamie and Polly as if expecting an answer.

Thurloe ignored the Doctor's comments. 'I could arrange for somewhere rather more pleasant. In fact, I could arrange for the charges of treason against you all to be dropped altogether.'

'That's very good of you,' said the Doctor blandly.

'On certain conditions.'

Polly threw up her hands. 'Why did I know he was going to say that?'

Thurloe put his hands behind his back and regarded the three of them steadily. 'Tell me all you know about the plot to rescue the King.'

Polly groaned. 'Look, I told that Captain Culpeper. We don't—'

The Doctor held up his hand to silence her and Polly immediately stopped talking.

'All we know about the plot? And then you'll let us go?'

Thurloe nodded. 'I'll see you safely back to Parliament and you can make your way out of the city from there.' He loomed closer, drawing his face right up to the Doctor's. 'I must find Charles, Doctor. You understand that? All we have laboured for will come to naught if he escapes us. Now, will you help me?'

The Doctor nodded. 'I'll tell you all I know.'

Thurloe smiled and sighed with relief. 'Excellent! I shall see to the arrangements at once. You shan't regret this, I promise you.'

He turned and marched to the door. A sharp rap brought the jailer inside and then Thurloe disappeared in a swirl of black cloak.

Jamie jumped off the bed, shaking his head. 'But Doctor, we don't know anything!'

The Doctor gave a mischievous smile. 'Exactly. And that's what I've agreed to tell them.'

A full gale was blowing now and the sky was as black as an old coffin as the *Demeter* and the *Teazer* struggled through the foaming sea.

Winter's ship just had the edge, rounding the coast at a brisk pace, with the damaged and bulky enemy lurching behind.

Ben stood on the fo'c'sle, soaked to the skin as he peered

through the spray towards the *Demeter*. He gripped the sodden rigging with both hands to stop himself from falling as the ship lurched and groaned in the storm.

Winter was at the wheel. Illuminated occasionally by a stab of brilliant lightning, she looked like a child's nightmare come to life. Her ham-like hands were fast on the wheel, feeling her ship rock beneath her like a twisting dragon.

'She's gaining!' shouted Ben above the roar of the wind.

Winter did not respond but kept her eye on the approaching coastline. Ben could see a vista of black mud stretching from the water's edge to the glorious safety of the land. If they continued on their present course, they were bound to run aground.

'You'll kill us all, you mad woman. We're heading for the marshes!'

Winter pushed Ben away. 'I know our course, sir, and I know that we will shortly strike the marshes. But so will the *Teazer* and then the Pole will have to face me!'

Ben shook his head. 'There's more to this than your ruddy vendetta, you know. I thought we were trying to trap them in the marshes, not us!'

'So we are!' cackled Winter. 'So we are! I shall see the whole of Stanislaus's miserable crew marooned on those flats.'

Ben looked about desperately. The channel they were sailing up was growing narrower and narrower and the sails of the *Teazer* loomed so close behind that they appeared to be reaching over Ben's head.

There was a loud crack and a musket ball whistled past Ben's ear. He turned back to Winter but was astonished to see that the captain had vanished.

She had lashed the wheel onto the ship's course with rope.

Cursing to himself, Ben scrambled up the rigging and threw himself down onto the wheel platform. Sleety rain and sea spray coursed down his face as he tried to untie the bulky knots that the captain had tied into the rope.

His hands slid over the saturated surface and he dug his nails desperately into the wet twine.

Then he felt the great weight of Winter's hands descend onto his.

'Nay, belay there, Ben!' screamed the sailor, her black eye flashing.

Ben threw up his hands. 'All right! You get on with it, Sal. Just let me get off this ship and back to London.'

Winter looked wounded. 'I shall not abandon you, friend.'

'I know that,' shouted Ben, glancing feverishly about, convinced that another bullet would shortly find its way into his skull.

'I'm not trying to force a confrontation,' cried Winter, gazing ahead at the encroaching mud.

'Looks very like it to me.'

Winter shook her massive head. 'Nay, Ben. We could never outrun the *Teazer*, damaged as she is. The Pole would keelhaul us and sail straight up Old Father Thames with that Dutch package of his.'

Ben's strained face betrayed his exasperation. 'But he'll do that anyway if we finish up in the mud!'

Winter looked Ben in the eye but seemed to be staring right through him. "Tis your task now, Ben. Alone. The Pole will get no further. This is where our conflict ends.'

As though for dramatic emphasis, the *Demeter* suddenly lurched and there was a deep, percussive boom as she slammed into the mud banks.

Ben and Winter were thrown down and the captain slid across the wet deck like a coin across a wooden board.

The prow of the ship rose up in the air and Ben found himself tumbling towards the rail.

Just as suddenly, the ship seemed to settle and there was a moment of strange calm with only the lashing of the elements audible.

Then the *Teazer*'s cannon roared out, hitting the *Demeter* at point-blank range. The fo'c'sle erupted in flame, deadly shards of ancient wood streaking through the air like fiery darts.

Ben threw himself down and covered his head. 'Sal?' he bellowed.

But the captain had disappeared again.

The cannons spoke again, missing this time, and a ball slapped into the black mud that now embraced the ship, sending a choking, filthy plume high into the air.

Ben struggled to his feet and tottered across the deck, then he fell to his knees again as the vessel was struck amidships by the *Teazer*, which had now run aground herself.

There was a tremendous splintering groan as the prow of Stanislaus's ship ripped through the heart of her, scraping through the woodwork like a chisel.

What remained of the *Demeter*'s crew were swarming all over the grounded vessel. Ben watched as they took on Stanislaus's men in yet more fierce hand-to-hand fighting.

Determined to find Winter, Ben clattered through the debris until he found himself peering over onto the deck of the *Teazer*.

He swallowed nervously at the sight that met his eyes.

Young Hugh the cabin boy stood at Stanislaus's side, his eyes wide open in desperate appeal. They stood near the shattered remains of Stanislaus's cabin which looked like a massive, blackened flower, charred beyond recognition by Winter's bomb. There were signs of the explosion all over the ship. Shards had streaked into her fine woodwork and powder had darkened the deck for yards around. The bomb had done its job, thought Ben with a sigh, but its intended victims had obviously been well clear.

Some of Stanislaus's crew were grouped around them with Godley and the Dutchman close by.

Stanislaus held his cutlass to Hugh's throat.

'Captain Winter,' he called. 'Sal? Are you there? Surrender yourself.'

He looked around, the gale blowing his long black hair off his face.

'Surrender yourself or this boy will gain a new mouth. Just here.'

He jerked the cutlass and nicked the side of Hugh's throat. The boy gasped and a little bead of blood glistened down his skin.

There was movement close to Ben and he looked up as Winter appeared, her arms above her head, still brandishing her cutlass.

Stanislaus smiled delightedly. 'Tell your men to surrender their arms.'

Winter scowled at him.

'Tell them!' hissed Stanislaus.

With a heavy sigh, Winter bellowed orders for her men to cease fighting.

Reluctantly, the men dropped their swords and were instantly rounded up by Stanislaus's cackling crew.

'Now,' cried the Pole, 'Down here, Sal. Come along. I'm a busy man.'

Reluctantly, Winter made her way across on to the deck of the *Teazer*, where she was instantly grabbed and tied up, then placed back to back against Hugh.

Stanislaus began to strut up and down like a peacock.

Winter spat with contempt. 'Would you use a boy to win your battles, Pole?'

The crew laughed but were silenced at once by Stanislaus's reptilian sneer.

239

He strode up to her, his face only inches from hers. 'By Christ, I have tolerated you all these long years, dogging my every bloody step. But no longer. This is too big for such fry as you.' He drew his cutlass.

Winter laughed scornfully. 'And now would you end it like this? After all these years? You took my comeliest feature, remember. And now you would end our association by stabbing me through the gullet in cold blood.'

Stanislaus shook his head. 'Nay. Nothing to do with you has ever been in cold blood.' He raised his cutlass high above his head and prepared to bring it down into Winter's throat.

Without thinking of the consequences, Ben jumped like a spring-heeled gazelle from one ship to the other.

'Sal!' he cried, hurling his own sword, which the captain neatly caught. She jumped clear of Stanislaus's blade and looked swiftly in Ben's direction.

'Away now, Ben! And thank 'ee!'

As the crew surged towards him, Ben threw himself over the side of the *Demeter*, landing with a soft splash in the shallow, muddy water.

'After him!' roared Stanislaus, turning with surprising agility as Winter's sword crashed against his own.

Ben knew that his only chance was to hide for a while. He would present too easy a target struggling over the mud flats. Silently, he waded through the water, his breath coming in great whooping draughts. He pulled himself close to the beached hull of the *Demeter* and crouched down in its shadow, curling himself into a ball.

He could hear shouts above him and the clash of sword on sword as Winter and Stanislaus settled their conflict once and for all. But he was currently more concerned with the sound of the approaching crewmen, splashing through the water in search of him. He was bound to be discovered sooner or later and he uncurled himself, looking about desperately in the black night for some means of escape.

The wind was howling over the marshes and he felt his face numbing as sleet slapped against his skin.

Dimly, he could see torches blazing in the darkness and he reached out to pull himself out of the water. Instead of the expected hull, his fingers found an empty space and he realised, with a thrill, that he was close to one of the ship's ruined cannon ports. She had crashed into the mud at such an angle that he could easily clamber back inside.

Swiftly, he scrambled up the sodden planks, his hands and feet slipping over the weed-covered surface until he was able to swing himself through into the dark interior of the ship.

'Any sign?' he heard someone call through the gale. There was no answer for a while and Ben sat in silence, hugging his knees to his chin, ears pricked.

'He'll be away across the flats,' came another voice at last.

Scarcely daring to believe his luck, Ben stayed as he was, listening to the sound of his own breathing.

'God help him, then,' came a third voice. 'The mud will have him soon enough.'

He heard them splashing back through the shallows.

Around him, the old ship creaked and groaned like a discontented grandmother. Ben got to his feet as quietly as he could and stood in the darkness, his mind racing. What could he do?

If he abandoned Sal and Hugh they would be at Stanislaus's mercy, yet his imperative was to get back to London as soon as possible and warn them that some danger loomed.

He would wait until he was certain the crew had called off their search and then make his way across the marshes to safety. How he would make the journey to London was a bridge he would cross when he came to it.

Ben poked his head out of the cannon port and looked out onto the mud flats that stretched before him. It was so dark and stormy now that he could see virtually nothing, but there were lights blazing what appeared to be a short distance away and that could only be the shore.

He could still hear the steely rattles of the two captains' swords and the roar of the crew as they cheered the fighters on.

Seizing his chance, Ben vaulted out of the safety of the *Demeter* and landed with a satisfyingly quiet splash in the murky water. He rose to his feet at once and tried to get his bearings. The two grounded ships were right behind him, the shore some five hundred yards away across the black mud. The water seemed to sluice around his legs like treacle as he waded forward, keeping his head low, aware that he might be spotted as soon as he left the shadow of the wrecked ships.

Gritting his teeth, Ben sloshed out of the shallows and suddenly found himself on the mud. He looked back over his shoulder and got a vague impression of the action on the *Teazer*. Then, seizing the opportunity, he began to pelt across the mud, his feet sinking inches into the glutinous stuff.

He ran like a man possessed, his lungs and muscles bursting, slipping and stumbling over the treacherous mud, feeling it spume over his trousers and up his shirt.

He pitched forward suddenly and put out both hands. The mud was chilly to the touch and swamped his outstretched fingers like inky glue.

Righting himself, Ben lifted his foot and made a long stride forward. He could see the firm shoreline only a few feet away.

Suddenly, with a lurch that made his stomach flip, he felt his leg sink right up to the thigh.

Thrown off balance, he fell forward again, this time managing to stay upright and throw himself backward.

Desperately, he tried to pull his leg out of the powerful suction but it seemed only to sink deeper and he felt the clammy mud close around his backside as he stumbled forward once more.

His bent knee began to sink now and a sudden panic stole over him like a blast of cold air. Instinctively, his arms shot out and scrabbled at empty air. He was sinking.

The mud pooled around him like a living thing and he felt its gurgling grip as his body vanished up to the waist.

Coughing and whining with panic, Ben let his arms splash against the mud and tried to pull himself out.

With a jolt of horror, he felt those sinking too. There was nothing he could do. He was slipping inexorably into the black mud.

CHAPTER
10

Stanislaus whirled about on his heel and brought his cutlass crashing down onto the side of the ship. The blade sheared off a great slice of wood and, as he struggled to drag it back out, Sal Winter struck, kicking the Pole viciously in the gut.

Stanislaus doubled up in pain and fell down, his knees connecting with the deck with a report like pistol shots.

As the crew whooped and cheered, Winter spun around on her peg leg and thumped Stanislaus under the chin, sending him sprawling backward.

'You see, my friend. I am more than a match for you, imperfect as I am!'

Stanislaus glowered at her from where he lay sprawled. 'You? You're a cripple! What have I to fear from a cripple?'

Winter's face contorted with rage and she swung her cutlass round in a wide arc, missing Stanislaus by only a fraction as he rolled out of the way.

In seconds, the Pole was on his feet. He dashed to the side of the ship and, grasping the hilt of his cutlass with both hands, tugged for all he was worth.

The blade came free in a shower of white wood and he swung round, sweat coursing down his handsome face.

Stanislaus straightened to his full height and put one hand

on his hip. Then, his lip curling into a sneer, he began to advance towards Winter, his cutlass flashing back and forth like a pendulum.

Winter parried every blow with expert skill, her own weapon scraping and clashing against the shining silver blade of her opponent.

'Ha! Who's the cripple now, Stanislaus!' cried Winter, pressing forward.

Stanislaus redoubled his efforts, attempting to deflect Winter's blows long enough to undercut her and sink his cutlass into the captain's ample stomach.

But Winter was quite the Pole's match. She seemed to positively radiate confidence as she smashed repeatedly into Stanislaus's attack.

'You are nothing!' spat the Pole, breathing hard. 'A booby! A peg-legged, one-eyed, tin-nosed bitch not fit to command a barge!'

Godley, who had muscled his way to the front of the baying crowd, seemed amused. He dabbed his mouth with his handkerchief and raised an eyebrow. ''Sblood, if the cripple ain't got you beat, Captain Stanislaus!'

Stanislaus fell back on his haunches as the massive woman bore down on him. He shot Godley a vicious look and rammed his cutlass against Winter's, striking again and again and again, his teeth sinking into his lip until it bled.

'God damn you, Winter!' he screeched. 'What do you want of me?'

'I want your soul, you filthy cur!' hissed Winter. 'All these years I've followed you, hounded you, waiting for the right moment to take my revenge.'

Stanislaus slid across the deck, fighting a desperate rearguard action against the onslaught of Winter's cutlass. 'Revenge? Revenge for what? For breaking your heart? Christ almighty, 'twas half a lifetime ago!'

Winter stamped her peg leg against the deck with savage fury. 'Nay, you scum. I was a mere slip of a thing. And girls get over such trifles. It is for this that I hate you!'

She placed her thumb and forefinger on the tip of her silver nose and flicked it. The strange metal shape clanged like a miniature bell.

'It is for this that I despise you. And for this that I have sworn to eviscerate your filthy Polish hide!'

Stanislaus was tiring, his arm falling further and further back as he fought off Winter's blows.

Exhausted, he glanced up and saw the shadow of the great ship's block and tackle hanging above him. His face brightened as a possible avenue of victory opened up. His gaze darted rapidly from the block and tackle to Winter and to the side of the *Teazer*. He leapt to his feet and blew air out of his cheeks as though infusing himself with renewed vigour.

'That bauble?' he replied acidly. 'What have I to do with that? For, God strike me down if I lie, I have no recollection of cutting the blessed thing off.'

The crew laughed loudly, cheered by their captain's recovery.

Winter glanced quickly round and neatly sidestepped the resurgent Pole's attack. 'You did not have to cut off my nose, Stanislaus. But I nevertheless lay its loss at your door.'

Stanislaus grinned and threw another quick glance at the block and tackle. If he could only manoeuvre Winter around and then make a dash for the poop deck…

'I'faith, I can remember our liaison,' he cried. 'She wrote me such letters! And I kept them, just as I promised. You cannot imagine it now, gentlemen, but she was once a pretty thing!'

Again the crowd laughed and Winter swung her sword down, catching Stanislaus on the shoulder. The blade bit into the thick cloth of his coat but the Pole ignored it, pressing on and attempting to force Winter into the position he wanted.

'I was!' shouted Winter. 'Indeed I was most comely. Until the Captain here afflicted me with Cupid's love.'

Stanislaus almost stopped in his tracks, genuinely surprised. Then he began to laugh and used this as his means to break off the fighting and jump onto the poop deck, the block and tackle just a foot or so in front of him.

'The pox?' he said, laughing through his teeth. 'I gave you the pox? It was that which claimed your nose?'

Winter dropped her sword to her side, breathing hard. 'Aye, you hog! Rotted off half my face afore it was done, and you never bearing so much as a scab!'

Stanislaus threw back his head and laughed, and his crew laughed, too.

'Well!' he said. 'I suppose I'm just lucky.'

With that, he leapt from the poop deck and landed on the block and tackle, swinging out across the deck with tremendous force. He stretched out his long legs and caught Winter square in the chest, knocking her off balance so that she tottered backwards, crashed into the rail and, with a startled cry, fell head over heels into the mud.

The crew gave a great cheer and Stanislaus leapt back to the main deck, sword high above his head.

Godley and the Dutchman were applauding and he nodded to them as he made his way swiftly to the side of the *Teazer*.

He looked down into the darkness and saw Winter attempting to right herself, her wooden leg stuck fast in the slimy black mud.

Turning to his men, Stanislaus barked his orders.

'I want preparation made at once to refloat the ship. I shall finish off this business myself.'

With that, he placed one hand on the rail and jumped off, landing on the mud flats with the grace of an athlete.

Reluctantly, the crew resumed their work, but Godley and the Dutchman strode to the side.

Godley peered out. He could see Stanislaus making his way towards the stationary figure of Winter, who was flailing about in the mud.

'I fancy this will be a sight worth seeing,' he said with a smile.

The flat of Ben's hand slapped against the mud as he made another effort to pull himself free. Yet again, his fingers sank deep into the wet slop, and he had to haul his hand out with a supreme effort.

He had sunk as far as his midriff now and his initial panic had given way to a strange calm. He knew that if he didn't manage to escape soon he would be sucked into the mud and drown. It was as simple as that and the sudden clarity of his mind was a great comfort to him.

There were no tree roots projecting through the mud on which he could get a grip, no patches of mysteriously solid ground. So his one hope was outside intervention.

Yet if he raised his voice, Stanislaus and his crew were sure to hear and he might be spared the indignity of suffocation only to find a musket ball in the back of his brain.

He strained and gasped as he tried to lift himself up. There was a tremendous, crushing pressure on his legs and stomach and a crazy image flashed into his mind of a cartoon character stuck in quick-drying concrete.

Conscious of the need to stay alert and moving, he was nevertheless aware that, every time he shifted in his muddy prison, he sank a little further.

Perhaps he could remain there till morning, then, if the

tide had not claimed him, the *Teazer* might have gone on to London and he could scream himself hoarse.

The mud gave a vile belching sound and Ben cried out as he felt himself slide further in, the black mire forming a slick around his ribs.

In his heart of hearts he knew he couldn't last that long.

He turned his head at a sudden and unexpected clamour some distance behind. Of course he could not turn around but he could just make out two figures splashing about in the shallows by the beached *Demeter*.

They must have spotted him. They were coming for him. He was sure of it.

Seized with the desire to escape, he scrabbled at the mud, his hands burrowing deep into the sloppy sediment, but it was no use. He was left gasping for breath and sank still deeper.

'Oh, Doctor,' he wailed. 'How did I ever get into this?'

He started as a loud, bright whistle like the cry of a sea bird shattered the calm.

His head jerked from side to side as he tried to locate its source. Was it coming from the figures behind him or from the shore?

The whistle sounded again and then a hoarse, whispered call.

'Can you move?'

Ben knew now that someone had seen him from the shore, only twenty feet or so away.

'No,' he called back as quietly as he could. 'Stuck fast. Please, help me. Quickly!'

Almost as if it knew what was planned, the mud gave a great sucking burp and Ben slid further into its grasp. He yelled with sudden fear as he sank up to his armpits, feeling the cold, clammy stuff pressing against his flesh.

'Quick!' he gasped.

There was some activity on the shore and then a kind of whiplash sound. Ben saw something fall in front of his eyes and recognised it suddenly as the end of a rope. He gave a great sigh of relief and grabbed at it with both hands, wrapping it repeatedly around his wrists for better purchase.

'Pull! Pull!' he squawked, feeling the pressure of the mud against his bones.

His rescuer gave a great heave and Ben waited for his body to pop from the mud. Nothing happened.

'Again!' he insisted. The rope stretched taut and he gripped it even tighter till his knuckles whitened.

'I must have help!' came the voice again. 'Wait a moment.'

Ben rolled his eyes. To come so close to rescue…

'I'm not going anywhere,' he whispered ruefully. The rope went slack and Ben swallowed anxiously. If only he could keep still now he might be all right.

There was a loud splash behind him and Ben remembered the figures he had seen.

'Not now!' he lamented.

He tried to swivel himself round but immediately felt the mud tighten its grip. Instead he stared ahead and waited for the figures to reach him.

To his immense surprise, it was Sal Winter who toppled down into the mud before him.

Despite her size and the great weight of her mud-filled green coat, the captain did not sink as Ben had. Clearly he'd had the misfortune to stumble into a pocket of quicksand.

But Winter was still in trouble. Her wooden leg had sunk deep into the mud, she was exhausted, and then Captain Stanislaus appeared like a devil from the darkness, his cutlass flashing in the moonlight.

'Sal!' cried Ben. The captain swung round, her leg sunk in the mud.

'Ben, my lad,' she gasped. 'You made it.'

Ben was about to say that he hadn't made it very far but it didn't seem the most appropriate time. He felt Stanislaus's looming presence behind his back.

Stanislaus managed to find a semi-firm spot and stood there, both hands on hips, looking down at his enfeebled enemies.

'Well, well. Two pretty birds for my table it seems. How sad that they are to be so easily taken.'

He lifted his cutlass above Ben's head and Ben braced himself for the killing blow, which he knew would decapitate him.

With a roar of fury, Winter launched herself at the Pole.

Ben realised with a start that she had unbuckled her wooden leg and it stood there now, stranded in the mud, the leather straps that had held it in place sliding down into the murk.

The big woman crashed into Stanislaus and they fell together into the marsh.

Stanislaus let out a muffled roar as he splashed down, but then one of Winter's hands was round his throat while the other pummelled his head. His long hair billowed over his face like weed as his head was forced backwards into the mud.

'Do you think I would let ye win after all these years?' spat Winter, her face a mask of righteous wrath. 'I shall pursue you to perdition. My shade will haunt yours. I will never rest!'

Ben wanted desperately to help Winter, to make certain that Stanislaus went to his watery grave. But he could only watch helplessly as the Pole slipped out from Winter's grasp, pulled himself between her legs, and jumped on her back, grappling her like a bear.

Winter roared with frustration and punched repeatedly at Stanislaus's face but, unbalanced by the loss of her false leg, she toppled forward and Stanislaus had only to step aside to watch her fell flat on her face into the mud.

The Pole stood up straight, his face twisted into a grimace of hatred, his chest heaving with exertion.

'Now it comes, Winter. Feel my blade open your throat. Ye shall haunt me no more.'

Ben saw the cutlass flash down and, with the reactions of a tiger, reached forward and looped the trailing end of the rope around Stanislaus's foot.

As the blade sang past, he hauled on the rope and Stanislaus came crashing back to the ground, landing on his back and smacking the wind out of himself.

Winter recovered at once and struggled to her knees.

'Thank 'ee Ben!' she gasped, lifting her own sword and steadying it over Stanislaus's throat.

The Pole let out a long, miserable groan. Ben saw the rope whip across the mud flat like a sidewinder and grabbed desperately at it.

It tautened at once and he heard the voice of his rescuer again.

'There's three of us, lad. Hold on!'

Ben wound the rope around his hands once more but he was unable to take his eyes off the scene before him.

Winter paused before delivering the final blow to her hated enemy.

'Goodbye, then,' she said with a smile, the moonlight glinting off her silver nose.

Stanislaus gritted his teeth and stared up at Winter. 'I curse you, Winter. With my dying breath I curse you.'

Winter laughed. 'You'd not be the first.'

There was a short, loud crack and Ben looked round. He was just beginning to slide from the mud and thought for a moment that the rope had snapped.

But it was still firm in his hands and, as he shifted and writhed, he began to be pulled free of the dreadful mud.

He looked quickly round. Sal Winter was no longer kneeling above the prostrate form of Stanislaus. She was lying on her back, blood pumping from a huge hole in her neck.

Ben realised at once that the sound had been a shot. He could already see figures from the beached ships racing across the mud towards them.

He began to scrabble at the great, filthy mass around him as his rescuers pulled from the shore. Then, in one swift movement, he was free and lying flat out on the mud.

Stanislaus was lying there too, bewildered and not quite sure what had happened.

He looked over at Ben and then, with shocking speed, jumped to his feet, almost delirious with joy. He kicked Winter's body and swung round to face the exhausted Ben.

Ben didn't wait for the Polish captain's latest smart retort. With a snarl he leapt to his feet and, with a rapid one-two, smashed him full in the face.

Stanislaus hovered for a second and then toppled backward.

Ben was tempted to grind his face into the mud, to drown the bastard there and then, but he could see the figures approaching and was, in any case, far more concerned with his friend Sal Winter.

Swiftly, he knelt down and lifted the woman's head from the mud. She was already ghastly pale but managed a flicker of a smile as she focused on Ben's face.

'Sal—'

Winter shook her head and wagged a fat finger in Ben's face. 'It's over, my lad,' she whispered. 'The sea shall claim me at last.'

Ben stroked the blood-matted hair from Winter's eyes and shook his head sadly.

'You must promise me… you must promise me that you will avenge me, Ben,' gasped the old sailor. 'Avenge me… with style.'

She smiled and then the smile froze on her face. Her one rheumy eye rolled upward.

Ben sat for a long moment before the voice from the shore broke his reverie.

'Come! Come! They are almost upon you!'

Gently, he let Winter's head fall to the wet ground. Then, with a final look at the unconscious Stanislaus, he raced across the mud towards the land, little caring whether he hit another pocket of quicksand.

As he reached the firm shore, another musket ball whistled by him. He had escaped just in time.

Three men were waiting for him as he scrambled across the shingle. Two were little more than boys, dressed in ragged, disreputable clothing. The third was an old man with a leathery face and the most appalling body odour Ben had ever encountered.

Even in his desire to thank them for saving his life, Ben couldn't help but avert his nose from the fearful stink.

'Ben Jackson?' said Nathaniel Scrope, extending a hand.

Ben was too astonished to shake it. 'How do you know my name?'

Utterly dejected, Frances Kemp ascended the stairs that led to the room above the inn and made her way sluggishly down the corridor. Her heart was leaden in her breast, and her every movement spoke of her misery.

In her hand she carried a rolled parchment in which she had written down in great detail all that her dear Thomas had told her about General Cromwell's movements.

She carried the paper lightly, unwillingly, secretly hoping

255

that some strange breeze would blow it away and she would be free of her treachery. But she reached the door unscathed and knocked lightly upon its panels.

Sir John Copper opened the door himself and ushered her inside. Without a word, he snatched the parchment from her and took it to the lamp on the table. He angled it to the yellow glow and rapidly scanned its contents. Then, with a smile of triumph, he turned to Frances.

'You've done well, my dear. Very well. The nation owes you a great debt.'

Frances looked him in the face. Her eyes were lifeless and rimmed with tears. 'May I go now?' she said, her voice broken with emotion.

Copper examined her amusedly. 'So soon? Come. Sit with me a while.'

He kicked at a chair, sending it scraping across the floor. Reluctantly, Frances sat down in it, her head sinking onto her chest.

Copper sat down next to her and, to Frances's surprise, took her hand.

'You must not take on so, Frances. What you have done is only right and proper. You owe your allegiance to His Majesty.'

Frances raised her other hand to her face and wiped a heavy, salty tear from her eye. 'Even if it means betraying the one I love?'

Copper gave a good-humoured chuckle, like a kindly uncle dismissing a child's bad dream. 'Oh, lass. Y'are scarcely out of the cradle yourself. What you feel for this... Roundhead is no more than a schoolgirl's fancy.'

Angered, Frances pulled her hand from Copper's grip but he immediately took hold of it again, his strong fingers pressing hard against her knuckles.

'You're hurting me,' she protested.

Copper suddenly pulled hard on her hand, swinging her off the chair and onto his knee.

Frances immediately tried to get off but his arm was snaking around her waist, hugging her closer. 'Leave me be!' she cried. 'I shall… I shall…'

'You'll what, girl?' snarled Copper. 'Cry out? For whom? That spineless father of yours? Why, he'd as soon see you burnt on a pyre than refuse me anything!'

He planted his other hand onto Frances's pretty face and pulled her round to kiss him, his fingers pinching her soft cheeks.

Disgusted, Frances tried to drag her face away but Copper persisted, his aged, bristly face scraping over her lips.

Fighting back the only way she could, Frances found Copper's lips and savagely bit into them. She felt the soft flesh yield beneath her incisors and Copper yelled in anguish.

He tried to push her off but she held on as long as she could. Finally, he smacked her on the side of the face and she fell to the floor, her head ringing.

Copper shot to his feet, blood streaming from his mouth. His hand rose automatically to the wound and he examined his bloodied fingers.

'Slut! Harlot!' he raged. 'I shall make you pay dearly for this!'

There were heavy steps on the stairs and the door was flung open to reveal William Kemp.

He looked down at Frances and then at Copper, taking in the scene in an instant.

'What perfidy is this?' he bellowed.

Copper looked round, holding a lacy handkerchief to his torn and bleeding lip.

'This animal you call daughter tried to force herself upon me, Kemp. I'faith, she is even more the whore than we took her for.'

Frances groaned and shook her head violently. 'It's not true, Father. He… he tried to…'

She tailed off miserably. What was the point? Her father never took any notice of her.

Copper laughed through his handkerchief. 'See? She cannot even gather her wits sufficient to lie! If I were you, Kemp, I should—'

Copper was suddenly silenced by Kemp's fist, which lashed out and caught him directly on the point of his bearded chin. He staggered backward and fell against the window casement, dragging the curtain down from its rail with a great rending tear.

There was a stunned silence and then Kemp advanced on him, his shoulders down like a fist-fighter's and his face red with fury.

'You scoundrel! Get out of my house! Out, I say. And never return!'

Copper got to his feet with as much dignity as he could muster. Then he snatched the scroll from the table and moved to the door. He turned as he departed.

'You are a fool, Kemp. I could have helped you and your wretched family. Now you have nothing. And I warn you, if you attempt to disrupt our plans I will bring down ruin and destruction upon your head.'

His face, already swollen from Frances's attack, contorted into a snarl and he stormed from the room, slamming the door behind him.

For a long moment, Frances remained sprawled on the floor. Then she picked herself up and sat down at the table.

She avoided her father's look, not sure how to take this new development. Hands shaking, she began to rearrange her hair beneath her cap.

Kemp walked slowly to the table and sat down opposite

her. He looked at her delicate face, flushed with emotion.

'Frances…'

She glanced quickly upward and held out her hands across the table. Kemp took them gratefully in his own and then swung himself around so that he was able to embrace her.

'Oh, my child,' he sobbed. 'My little child.'

The Doctor, Jamie, and Polly were patiently awaiting the arrival of Thurloe's promised transportation when the door to their Tower cell was opened again and Richard Cromwell was ushered inside.

He nodded at the jailer just as Thurloe had done before him but with such fumbling indecision that the jailer wasn't at all sure what Richard wanted him to do.

'That's all,' explained Richard. 'I'll call when I need you.'

The door was slammed shut and Richard jumped a little at the crash it made. He advanced meekly into the room.

Polly frowned. 'Who are you?'

The Doctor intervened. 'This is Richard Cromwell, Polly. Son of Oliver and one day to be Lord Protector of England.'

Richard heaved a huge sigh. 'Don't try to humour me, Doctor. It really doesn't matter what becomes of me.'

The Doctor rushed forward and took him by the arm. 'Matter? Of course it matters. Whatever gave you that idea?'

Richard shook his head. 'I cannot please my father, no matter what I do. He won't even look at the book.'

Sniffing to himself, he took *Every Boy's Book of the English Civil Wars* from his cloak and handed it to the Doctor.

'Here,' he said feebly, 'have it back. It is no earthly use to me.'

The Doctor took the book and pressed it to his chest like an old friend. He grinned from one ear to the other and patted Richard on the shoulder.

'Now you just listen to me, Richard Cromwell.'

Richard looked up, defeated. 'Hmm?'

The Doctor tapped the book and frowned seriously. 'It isn't given to all of us to be great men. Sometimes it's more important to play your part in the whole great tide of history. You'll be important in all sorts of ways that haven't even occurred to you yet.'

Richard wasn't convinced. 'Like what?'

The Doctor looked at Jamie and Polly, momentarily flummoxed.

'Well,' he said at last. 'The Protectorate will end with you. Your side will realise too late that they should not have used the hereditary principle and Charles the Second will be invited to take the throne.'

Richard snorted. 'And I should be happy to be remembered as that? 'Sblood, I'd rather die in obscurity.'

The Doctor stuffed the book into his pocket and walked towards Richard. 'Sit down, please,' he said calmly.

Richard sat down on the end of the straw mattress and folded his arms.

'Now then,' murmured the Doctor. 'You must understand that it's always hard for the children of great men and women. So much to live up to. Such expectations.' His voice was soothing and regular, like a steady pulse.

'Yes,' said Richard. 'Such expectations.'

The Doctor came closer and looked deep into Richard's eyes. 'And you're doing very well, you know. Very well. I don't see how you manage. Such a burden on your shoulders. I don't know when you find time to sleep.'

'Sleep,' muttered Richard, his eyelids drooping.

'Sleep,' repeated the Doctor. 'Time to sleep.'

'Time to... sleep,' said Richard in a drawl.

His head fell forward onto his chest.

Polly got up and crossed to Richard. 'Doctor!' she exclaimed. 'How did you do that?'

The Doctor chuckled. 'You don't think a little elementary hypnosis is beyond me, do you? I knew someone ages ago who taught me. Of course, he was an absolute master…'

Jamie peered at Richard. 'He's sound as a top.'

'Good,' said the Doctor softly. 'Then I'll begin.'

He bent down in front of Richard. 'Richard, I want you to listen very carefully to me. Everything I have told you, everything you read in that strange little book, was all untrue. A dream. You must forget it. Forget it for ever…'

Bruised and in a foul temper, Captain Stanislaus stood by the wheel of the *Teazer* as his ship finally slunk into London.

The night was fine and clear now, the rich black sky sparkling with stars, but Stanislaus did not waver from his contemplation of the port and scarcely moved as his ship manoeuvred through the ranks of silent vessels already moored there. He did not look over his shoulder but could sense the blackened ruin of his cabin lurking behind him like the bones of stranded whale. The air was still acrid from the smoke and tiny fragments of his precious documents crumbled beneath his boots as he stood in silence. It was a miracle he had managed to get Godley and the Dutchman out of the cabin in time, but then he had not survived this long by being a half-wit.

And now Sal Winter had paid dearly for the damage she had inflicted upon his beloved *Teazer*. Soon, all those who defied him would meet a similar fate.

Footsteps echoed below and Godley emerged on to the deck. He grinned at Stanislaus's sullen features and looked out over the water.

'Come, come, Captain,' he said. 'Not mourning over the fair Winter, are we?'

Stanislaus's mouth tightened into a thin line. 'She was mine. You should not have acted as you did.'

Godley's smile vanished. 'Had I not, then you would be face down in the mud now, sir, or have you forgotten that?'

Stanislaus whirled round. 'I could have bettered her. I know it. 'Twas but a matter of time.'

Godley shook his handsome head. 'Time was what you did not have, Stanislaus. My musket ball saved your skin. That is what you cannot bear to admit.'

Stanislaus folded his arms and stood in sullen silence. At last he sighed and, without turning to Godley, said, 'Is all prepared?'

Godley nodded. 'As soon as we disembark I shall make contact with my men. They will furnish me with the latest intelligence and we will proceed from there.'

'And van Leeuwenhoek?'

'Is below,' replied Godley. 'Readying himself.'

Stanislaus nodded. Then he started as he saw something approaching through the black water. He extended one long arm and pointed. 'What's that?'

Godley moved to the rail.

A small rowing boat was slicing through the water towards them. Godley frowned and then, in the flaring light of the ship's torches, he recognised the passenger.

''Tis Arkwright,' he said to Stanislaus, swinging round. 'The man I spoke of. If he is coming to greet us, there must be something afoot.'

The little boat moved rapidly to the side of the *Teazer* and the rower, Arkwright, a thin, nervy creature with sparse yellow hair, hastily tied it up before hauling himself up the rope ladder and onto the deck. He ran to Godley's side and bowed deeply. 'Sir, I bring great news.'

'Well?' asked Godley impatiently.

'The King, My Lord, has escaped!'

Stanislaus's eyes widened. 'What?'

'Escaped? How?' cried Godley.

Arkwright was wringing his hands in excited agitation. 'It seems there were others at work for His Majesty's welfare. They sprung him from Hurst Castle on the Solent. He awaits your presence now.'

Godley gripped Arkwright by the arm and whooped with joy. 'But this is marvellous! Marvellous! How much easier will our task be with His Majesty free! As a focus for resistance he will be matchless.'

Stanislaus moved swiftly across the deck and called for the bosun. 'Come, man! Get us into port and anchored. There is not a moment to be lost!'

Ben and Scrope were concealed behind a line of barrels just by the jetty where the latter had spent his long, freezing vigil.

They had used the speedy journey from Gravesend to London to compare notes. Ben told the smelly newcomer of what he and the late Captain Winter had discovered. Scrope, in turn, told Ben of his encounters with the Doctor and Jamie. Added to that was the news that the girl called Polly had now joined them and, though they were prisoners in the Tower, they would be quite safe for the moment.

Their priority now had to be the identity of the mysterious Dutchman and what exactly Stanislaus and Godley's package meant for them all.

Ben sank low behind a barrel, his hand pressed tightly over his mouth against the smell of his companion. Taking the bull by the horns, he turned and whispered to Scrope. 'No offence, mate, but don't you ever take a bath?'

Scrope cackled merrily. 'Oh, no, lad. Nasty things, baths. Injurious to the health, don't you know?'

His face turned suddenly grave and he held up his hand for silence. 'There!' He pointed through the gap in the barrels and Ben could see the high masts and rigging of the *Teazer* silhouetted against the moon.

'So,' smiled Scrope. 'We are one step ahead of them after all.'

They watched in silence as the ship lowered her anchor into the water and several dim figures descended the rope ladder into the rowing boat.

It took only a few moments for the party to make it to the jetty and Stanislaus, Godley, Arkwright and van Leeuwenhoek stood for a moment, deep in conversation.

'I recognise the Pole,' hissed Scrope to Ben. 'Who are the others?'

'I don't know the little one. But the one in the hat is Godley. The other is the Dutchman.'

Scrope nodded, his old eyes narrowing as he peered through the darkness. Then he pulled himself and Ben back against the wall as the party began to walk towards them.

Arkwright clambered back into the boat but the others moved swiftly along the jetty. Godley carried a lantern and he set it down on top of the barrels, only inches from Ben's face.

'Very well. I shall be only a moment.'

For a few seconds, his face was fully illuminated in the glow of the lamp and Ben heard Scrope emit a little gasp.

He turned, thinking the old man might be ill, but Scrope was simply staring ahead, his mouth opening and closing in wonder.

Godley returned and, picking up the lamp, led the way through the narrow buildings towards the street.

Ben jumped to his feet but Scrope grabbed his arm.

'Come on, mate. We've got to get after them,' said Ben urgently.

'Wait, wait!' cried Scrope. 'Yon fellow. What did you say his name was?'

Ben shrugged. 'Godley, he said. Richard Godley.'

Scrope shook his head in wonder. 'You have been travelling in far more illustrious company than you knew, Ben. That man is not Richard Godley. He is Prince Rupert!'

CHAPTER
11

John Thurloe let a long sigh hiss through his clenched teeth as he strode towards the Doctor.

The little man stood with Jamie and Polly, all three grouped in a tight cluster in the centre of Cromwell's room. Guards had been posted at the door in case any of the three time travellers tried to make a break for it. The general himself was absent, busying himself with the preparations for the King's trial.

'Doctor, you are being evasive,' said Thurloe angrily.

'Am I?' murmured the Doctor. 'I'm so sorry. Force of habit.'

Thurloe loomed over him, his long face clouded with suspicion. 'I know that you and the Scot are not what you claim. You are no more in touch with the other side than I am.'

'What other side?' queried Polly. 'The King, you mean?'

Jamie shook his head. 'No. He means the spirit world.'

Polly burst out laughing. 'Oh. I see.'

Thurloe swung round to face her. ''Tis no laughing matter, lady. These accomplices of yours claimed to see into the future.'

Polly shrugged. 'Well, there's a lot of truth in that.'

Thurloe frowned and returned to his scrutiny of the Doctor. 'Listen well. I am not taken in by your wizardry, Doctor. But, equally, I do not believe you to be a man of wicked designs.'

'Oh,' said the Doctor. 'I'm so glad.'

He could see the network of ruddy, broken veins that crazed Thurloe's skin.

'Tell me the truth, Doctor. How did you come to be here and what connection do you have with this Royalist spy?'

The Doctor sighed and held out his hands in a gesture of supplication. 'She's not a spy. She's our travelling companion. The one I told you about. There's another one, too. We simply… arrived here in London and got caught up in this mess.'

Thurloe tapped his finger against his chin. 'And you did not seek to release the King?'

'Of course not,' snapped Polly. 'I was duped into it by the men I told you about.'

Thurloe nodded. 'This… Christopher Whyte. My men can find no record of him.'

Polly pulled a helpless face. 'What about the other one? The older man?'

Thurloe shook his head. 'You furnished us with a description, but no name. I cannot act upon such flimsy evidence. Though I do have my suspicions.'

'Well, regardless of that,' concluded the Doctor, 'you must see that we are innocent of any crime. I mean, if it hadn't been for the saltpetre man we'd never even have been arrested.'

Thurloe's ears pricked up. 'Saltpetre man? What are you talking about?'

Jamie gave a short laugh. 'Och, you dinnae want to bother about that, Mr Thurloe. Just a smelly old fool with ideas above his station.'

Thurloe advanced on Jamie, his eyes full of interest. 'What was this fellow's name?'

'Scrope,' said the Doctor. 'Nathaniel Scrope.'

Thurloe clapped his gloved hands together. 'You know

Scrope? Why did you not say so before?' He gave a huge and unexpected grin. 'How come you to know him?'

'Actually,' said the Doctor humbly, 'we saved his life.'

Thurloe began to pace up and down. 'Then he will vouch for you. This changes everything, Doctor.'

The Doctor was astonished. 'It does?'

Thurloe nodded vigorously. 'Scrope is my best agent.'

The man known as Richard Godley sank down into a chair and threw off his hat with a contented sigh. How nice it would be throw off his alias with such ease. But in these mad, topsy-turvy times it was imperative that he remain incognito. Godley. Rupert. Sometimes he forgot himself, just as he forgot why he had set out on this insane expedition. Why did he have to place his fate in the hands of barbarians like Stanislaus?

Rupert shuddered as he remembered their experience in Amsterdam. First, the visit to the odious, skeletal van Leeuwenhoek and then, after Rupert had suggested they forget their cares for a few hours, where had the Pole taken them? To the vile House of Correction!

There, for a price, visitors could watch the poor, imprisoned wretches undergoing all manner of unthinkable tortures.

For a man of Rupert's healthy, athletic sensibilities, such base sadism was sickening. He had watched in horror as two boys had been thrown into a flooded cellar, the water rising so rapidly that it was around their waists in minutes. Furiously, they had laboured at two pumps. Rupert had asked the point of this and Stanislaus had smiled his evil smile. 'They must pump it out or drown,' he had said simply, turning to lay a bet on the outcome.

With a shake of his handsome head, Rupert attempted to wipe the memory away. He looked around the dank room and drummed his fingers on the table.

He did not think much of the surroundings in which he found himself – how different from his old life in the glorious city of Prague – but it was a relief at least to be back on dry land, even in such a grim hole as this Thames-side warehouse.

There was food and wine on the table and Rupert ate ravenously, tossing morsels to his pet monkey, which the little creature chomped and chewed with vigour, its bright eyes darting from side to side.

There was a knock at the door.

'Come!' called Rupert.

Christopher Whyte came quickly inside, closing the door behind him. He looked Rupert up and down before bowing.

'Your Highness,' he said.

Rupert smiled. 'It's Whyte, isn't it? I have had a full report of your excellent conduct in this matter, sir. Believe me, when this business is settled you will be handsomely rewarded.'

Whyte gave another modest bow. 'Was there anything else, sir?'

Rupert ran a hand through his tousled black hair. 'Yes, Whyte. 'Tis a little more delicate, I fear. I need a man I can rely on.'

Whyte frowned, intrigued. 'Your Highness can, of course, rely upon me for anything.'

'Of course,' repeated Rupert. 'But I would rather this was done as an act of friendship, not duty. Please be seated.'

Whyte did so, a little uneasy at not standing before the Prince. The monkey looked at him, as if it sensed his discomfort.

Rupert steepled his fingers and glanced up at the ceiling. 'I have not yet seen the King.'

Whyte nodded. 'Aye, I was informed as such.'

'There are reasons for this,' continued Rupert without

pausing. 'As you may know, my uncle and I did not part on the best of terms.'

This was putting it mildly. The Prince, having commanded Charles's army, had fallen out of favour after giving up the crucial port of Bristol to the Parliamentarians.

'In fact,' said Rupert with a soft sigh, 'His Majesty sent me into exile.'

Whyte gave a little grunt. 'Then the King is not aware of your part in this scheme?'

Rupert shook his head. 'He believes it to have originated with the Queen. In point of fact, the whole thing was my idea from first to last. My dear aunt took some persuading but finally she saw the merit of it.'

Whyte puffed air out of his cheeks. 'For myself, sir, I would wish the King were safely abroad before this… assassination is attempted.'

Rupert nodded. 'Alas, if the King were not such an obstinate fellow we would never have found ourselves in this plight.'

Whyte shifted his weight on the rickety chair. 'What would you like me to do, sir?'

Rupert scratched his head. 'I do not want my presence here to be a surprise. I should like you to inform His Majesty that I am here and that the scheme is mine also. That I carry the full blessing of Queen Henrietta Maria and that myself, Captain Stanislaus, and the er… package from Holland all await his pleasure.'

Whyte raised his eyebrows and sighed. It was no small request. But this was no time to stand on ceremony. The King's life and the future of the monarchy itself were in the hands of the small group gathered in that dank warehouse.

'As you wish, Your Highness.'

'Capital!' cried Rupert.

He called to his monkey and it skittered across the room

and jumped onto his shoulder. He plucked a grape from the bunch on the table and fed it to his pet, making little clucking noises with his mouth.

Sensing that Whyte had made no move to leave, Rupert looked up. 'Was there something else?'

Whyte leaned forward. 'May I ask what plans His Majesty has once Cromwell is dead?'

Rupert opened his hands wide and shrugged. 'An army has been raised, of course. In the chaos caused by old Ironsides' death, they will invade.'

Whyte looked uneasy. 'An invading army? From where, sir?'

Rupert sat back in his chair. 'Oh, all over. But mainly Poland.'

Whyte was aghast. 'A Catholic army? On English soil?'

Rupert looked away. 'Needs must when the devil drives, Master Whyte.'

Whyte stood up, the chair scraping behind him. 'Sir, this is unconscionable!'

Rupert shook his head. 'No, sir, it is pragmatic. We must restore His Majesty to the throne, by any means we can.' He waved dismissively. 'Now, you may go.'

Whyte stood his ground for a moment, his mind full of questions, then he turned and stalked from the room.

Ben and Scrope had tailed their quarries for some distance before the men disappeared into a large covered wagon which had obviously been sent for them.

As the vehicle rattled away over the cobbles, Scrope announced that they must make for Parliament with the utmost haste.

After an exhausting journey spent weaving through the narrow, choked London lanes, they approached the broad square which faced the Commons.

Ben could hardly believe how recently he had stood before it with Polly, wondering what was occurring before its great black doors.

Scrope had belied his years and set an amazing pace throughout their journey. Sometimes he moved so swiftly that Ben could scarcely keep up, and several times he had to stop and look about to see which particular warren-like alley the old man had darted through.

Ben caught his breath and turned to face Scrope.

'Now,' he said patiently, 'this is going to be difficult. But just let me do the talking and maybe we can get to see someone in authority.'

Scrope laughed his high, cackling laugh and held his sides, like a filthy leprechaun. 'Lord save you, lad!' he chortled. 'There's no need for diplomacy Just come with me.'

To Ben's amazement he marched straight to the great double doors. Two Roundhead sentries were posted there and, at the sight of Scrope, both nodded and stepped aside.

Scrope beckoned to Ben, who, not quite believing what was happening, was ushered through into the draughty stone interior.

He had visited the Commons, the other Commons, as a child but this was a much smaller and more intimate place. The beamed roof was quite low and there was not the same kind of ornamentation as the more familiar Parliament possessed. The overall effect was like a great tithe barn.

While Ben was gazing about, Scrope walked boldly past further sentries, exchanging chitchat all the way.

Ben followed close behind, noticing that all the soldiers held their noses as Scrope passed. Some looked at him almost with pity, as if to say 'Rather you than me, mate'.

They reached a further set of doors, this time guarded by a single sentry. He barred Scrope's way with his pikestaff.

'I wish to see John Thurloe,' said Scrope imperiously.

The sentry nodded. 'Yes, sir. One moment, sir.'

Ben tapped the old man on the shoulder. 'Who are you?'

Scrope grinned at him but didn't reply. A second later, the door opened and they were ushered into a large and rather sumptuous chamber.

The guard went out again, leaving Ben and Scrope alone in the room.

''Ere,' said Ben worriedly. 'Is this all right? I mean... are you sure we should be 'ere?'

Scrope shrugged. 'Is it not our right? This is our Parliament after all. And Parliament is for the people.'

Rapid footsteps sounded outside and two figures entered in a great hurry. One was a neat, black-clothed man with a long, bony face. The other, imposing, red of face and looking very angry, was very familiar to Ben.

'Blimey,' said Ben swallowing. 'Cromwell!'

Thurloe and Cromwell turned to him, then back to Scrope.

'Nat?' said Thurloe impatiently. 'What is it? What do you have for me?'

Scrope bowed to both men and then indicated Ben. 'This is Ben Jackson, sir. A most loyal fellow, recently returned from Amsterdam.'

Cromwell peered at Ben. 'I trust you had a pleasant trip, sir?'

Ben shook his head. 'No, I didn't. You see...'

He trailed off, not quite sure how to begin. Scrope patted him on the shoulder.

'You are the Doctor's friend?' said Thurloe.

Ben's expression betrayed his relief. 'He's here?'

'Aye,' said Cromwell. 'And facing grievous charges.'

Thurloe held up a gloved hand. 'Nay, General. Those cannot stand. I do believe this Doctor to be a man of honour.'

Cromwell harrumphed. 'And what of this girl? She who abetted the King's escape?'

Thurloe grimaced impatiently. 'Please, General. Let us hear Master Scrope's story.'

'Oh,' said Cromwell sulkily. 'Very well.' He stepped back a little and placed his hands behind his back in his familiar pose.

Rapidly, Scrope outlined what Ben had told him: the mysterious voyage to Amsterdam, the Dutchman and the strange reference to a 'package', Stanislaus's known enmity to the Parliamentarians, and finally the revelation that the man Godley was none other than Prince Rupert.

'Rupert?' spat Cromwell. 'I thought we'd seen the last of that arrogant puppy.'

Thurloe clasped his hands together and frowned. 'What is it that they can be planning? If Rupert has dared to return it must be a grand matter. No petty plot would bring him back to England.' He began to pace up and down. 'I must speak to the woman Polly. She is our one contact with these conspirators.'

Cromwell spun on his heel and to face the guard. 'Fetch the Doctor!'

Stanislaus, Rupert, and van Leeuwenhoek stood in a line, awaiting the arrival of the King.

The Pole was so tall that his head almost brushed the rafters of the cramped room and he sighed periodically, impatient and anxious simultaneously. Rupert, deprived of his pet monkey for reasons of protocol, was incessantly twiddling his thumbs.

Only the Dutchman remained aloof. He stood stock still, his blanched white face perfectly motionless.

Rupert shot a glance at him and shuddered. The man had made him uneasy ever since their first meeting. Perhaps it was because his trade was death. It was hardly surprising that the atmosphere of the tomb seemed to cling to him. It was tangible in the hollows below his cheekbones, in the deep lines on his face and the musty black cloth of his garments.

The door opened and Rupert looked away, glad of the distraction.

Sir John Copper and Christopher Whyte came inside, immediately followed by the diminutive figure of King Charles.

The atmosphere in the room changed at once.

Charles deliberately avoided Prince Rupert's gaze and chose to concentrate on making his way to his chair. He sat down with his usual grace and looked steadily ahead.

Rupert was shocked by the change in his uncle. The Civil Wars had taken their toll, of course, but he seemed far older than his years. His hair was streaked with grey and there was a dead-white pallor to his skin not helped by the added dimension of this unnatural hiding. His cheeks were roughly shaved and his clothes, obviously borrowed, were of a coarse and ordinary kind.

Tears sprang to Rupert's eyes to see such a thing and he leapt forward involuntarily, seizing Charles's hand and kissing it. 'Oh, Uncle…' he said, his voice breaking.

To his relief, the King did not snatch his hand away. Instead, he raised his other hand and gently patted Rupert on the head. 'Nephew,' he said kindly, 'come. It is t-time to put away our past conflicts and look to the f-future.'

Rupert sat back on his haunches, his eyes wet with tears. 'I am glad to hear you say it, Your Majesty.' He got to his feet and stepped back, glancing over at Whyte and giving him a quick, grateful smile. 'May I present Captain Stanislaus, a most loyal servant of the crown, who ferried us here to England…'

Stanislaus stepped forward and kissed Charles's hand.

'And how is our friend the King of Poland?' asked Charles with infinite politeness.

'Most well, Your Majesty,' murmured Stanislaus. 'I bring his greetings and best wishes for your speedy return to the throne.'

'And,' continued Rupert, 'it was the captain who furnished us with our... er, Dutch "package", Master Gustavus van Leeuwenhoek.'

The Dutchman stepped forward, bowed swiftly, and set his thin lips to Charles's knuckles.

'We are very g-grateful for your energies on our behalf, gentlemen,' stammered Charles. 'And hope that our freedom has not come as too great a shock to you.'

The men laughed politely, leading Rupert to reflect that it was strangely like the fawning atmosphere of Charles's old court.

Charles indicated Copper and Whyte. 'I have these f-fine fellows to thank for my no longer being incarcerated. But they, like me, would like to be fully apprised of this plan of yours.'

Rupert squared his shoulders. 'May it please Your Majesty, we have already consulted with Sir John and Master Whyte here. Thanks to the information they have been able to... procure, we know that General Cromwell plans to attend the Commons tomorrow in order to speed up the process of your trial.'

Charles looked amused. 'I f-fail to see how it can go ahead, unless he means to try me in *absentia*.'

He smiled benevolently and again the company laughed – all except Whyte, Rupert noticed.

'Nevertheless,' he continued, 'in the Commons he will be. It is there that we intend to take him. Or, rather, that Mr van Leeuwenhoek will see to it that old Ironsides finally goes to rust.'

'You are much skilled in these matters, sir,' said Charles evenly. 'May we know how you intend to d-do it?'

The Dutchman splayed his bony fingers wide like a conjuror with a fan of cards, his deep-set eyes blazing. 'It's a surprise!' he cried.

The King looked momentarily discomforted and Rupert leapt quickly into the breach.

'All is prepared. By ten tomorrow the Roundheads will have lost their best man and will descend into chaos. It will be child's play to take control.'

'With a foreign army?' interrupted Whyte. 'A Catholic army?'

Rupert stepped forward to reprimand him but Charles held up his hand. 'What ails you, sir?'

Whyte sighed and began to tug at his gloves. 'I mean no offence, Your Majesty. But surely we have fought these wars to preserve the lifeblood of the Church of England, not to taint it with Popish mercenaries.'

Charles gazed levelly at him. It was a fair point, of course, and one put to him many times these past few, bitter years. He had lost many loyalists because of it and his intractable defence of his beloved wife's religion.

'Mr Whyte,' he said at last, in a low, grave whisper, 'rather than lose my throne to these r-rebels I would come to terms with the devil himself!'

Polly ran at full pelt across the room, and Ben caught her in his arms. She tried to swing him round but was too exhausted.

'Duchess!' he cried joyfully. 'Oh, love. Are you OK? What's been happening?'

Polly practically crushed the young sailor in her embrace. 'Too much to tell you,' she said happily.

The Doctor and Jamie greeted Ben too and then the Doctor turned to face Scrope, Thurloe, and Cromwell.

'I appear to have done you an injustice, Doctor,' said the general with a smile.

'Not half the injustice I have done Master Scrope,' said the Doctor, reaching out to shake the saltpetre man's hand. 'It seems you really are engaged on state business.'

'Of the highest order,' said Thurloe. 'Even if his… er, *modus operandi* is a little eccentric.'

Scrope patted his filthy hair. 'No one bothers a man who reeks like me!' he said merrily. 'But let us to the matter at hand. We know that Prince Rupert is in London and has brought a Dutchman here.'

'For what purpose?' asked the Doctor.

Thurloe shrugged. 'That is what we must ascertain and you, Mistress Polly, must furnish us with an answer.'

Polly freed herself from Ben's embrace. 'Me?'

'Aye,' said Cromwell. 'Were not you in the thick of these conspirators, albeit against your will?'

Polly shook her head. 'But I don't know anything about their plans or their organisation, only…' She trailed away.

Thurloe leaned forward eagerly. 'Only?'

'Only that they met at the inn where Ben and I went that first morning. They may only have hired the room but it's the one place of theirs I know.'

Thurloe clapped his hands. 'Excellent! We must not lose a moment.'

The Doctor nodded. 'I'll come with you, Polly.'

She smiled and squeezed his hand. 'Thank you.'

'And I,' said Scrope. 'If you'll give me a few moments.'

The strange old man dashed from the room, leaving them all somewhat bewildered.

The night had turned bitterly cold, an arctic wind blasting the old city like some primal force let loose on the world.

There was no new snow yet, but everyone could sense it in the air, ready to cover the frosty cobbles, making them even more treacherous to the few souls who dared to venture out. Those who did huddled themselves up, clutching their tall hats tightly to their heads and swathing themselves in layers of extra clothing.

The wind picked up and whistled down the alley where stood Kemp's inn, the place seeming like the only house occupied and merry, its patrons determined to forget their troubles and the weather in a pint of foaming ale.

The sign above the World Turn'd Upside Down swung wildly as the Doctor, Polly, and Scrope stole inside.

All three stood on the threshold for a moment, shivering and stamping as they became used to the blaze from the fire and the sudden fug of human warmth. The Doctor blew into his hands and turned to Scrope.

To everyone's astonishment, the old man had returned transformed. Quick ablutions had taken away the cake of dirt that had covered his skin, revealing a face that now seemed far more wise and noble. His hair was brushed back from his high forehead and he was dressed in neat black livery from head to toe. Altogether he looked quite the gentleman.

The Doctor smiled as the scent of lemons came to him from Scrope's newly washed body. 'Shall we take a seat?'

He ushered Scrope and Polly forward into the rowdy tavern.

Polly was looking out immediately for Frances but it was Sarah Kemp who stood behind the bar, dealing gamely with a gang of rough young lads who had come in from the cold.

'Anything?' said the Doctor, sitting down and peering at the rough, packed crowd.

Polly shook her head. 'I know the girl who works here. She might have some idea of who—'

The door clattered and swung open, banging against the wall with a loud crash.

Polly stopped talking and whirled round, thinking the wind had blown open the door. Instead, she saw Christopher Whyte framed there, his clothes stiff with frost, his face fixed into a murderous glower.

Polly looked away as he marched in and made straight for the bar.

Sarah Kemp caught his eye. She pointed upstairs but Whyte shook his head. They exchanged words and Sarah poured him a large glass of some ruby-coloured spirit which he swiftly drained. He pushed the glass back across the bar and Sarah refilled it.

'Looks like a man in need of company,' muttered the Doctor.

'That's him,' whispered Polly. 'Christopher Whyte.'

The Doctor leaned closer and nodded. 'See what you can do.'

Polly got up and threaded her way around the tables and stools, struggling to avoid the maze of outstretched legs and backsides.

A big, burly lad stepped straight in front of her, grinned stupidly, and was about to mutter something cheeky when Christopher Whyte glanced round.

He saw Polly at once, took in the situation and pushed the youth roughly out of the way. The boy crashed to the floor and didn't get up, already the worse for drink.

'Polly!' cried Whyte delightedly, making room for her to stand by him. 'I am so pleased to see you. I had thought…'

Polly looked him up and down. 'You thought the Roundheads would have tortured and killed me.'

'At the very least!'

Polly's face remained impassive. 'Yes, well, fortunately they're a lot saner than some people seem to think.'

Whyte put out his hand as if to touch her face but then let

it fall to his side. 'I confess that I thought you dead. After what happened at the castle...'

Polly nodded. 'You left me for dead, Christopher.'

Whyte shook his head. 'I prevented your death!' he cried. 'I must tell you that Sir John's behaviour left me much vexed.'

'It left me with a bump on the head,' said Polly sourly. 'But never mind that. You also lied to me.'

Whyte looked down and bit his lip.

'You lied to me about Frances Kemp. You lied to me about the Doctor being in that castle. And you lied about your desire to help me.'

'No,' insisted Whyte. 'I did... I do want to help you, Polly.'

Polly nodded. 'Then will you join my friends?'

Whyte looked over. He could just make out the Doctor and Scrope deep in conversation. 'Is this the Doctor of whom you spoke?'

Polly nodded. 'Yes. He wants to talk to you.'

Whyte drained his glass and followed Polly to the table. Both ignored the constant, ribald mutterings that accompanied them. After introductions, Whyte took a seat next to Polly.

The Doctor looked at him with interest. 'I gather you seek to put the King back on his throne, Mr Whyte,' he said.

Whyte snorted and rubbed his eyes. 'Aye. I did. And have risked much in that cause.'

'Did?' queried the Doctor.

Whyte stared into space, his face betraying his troubled mind. 'I cannot speak of it,' he mumbled at last.

Polly looked him directly in his bright blue eyes. 'Please. If you do want to help me.'

Whyte looked from one to the other of the three seated next to him, then sighed. 'I... I no longer believe this King to be a man of honour. Nor worthy of his great office.'

'Then will you tell us where to find him?' urged Scrope quickly.

Whyte shook his head. 'No. I cannot. I have fought for Charles these past seven years. I cannot betray him now.'

The Doctor said nothing and it was left to Polly to continue. She grasped Whyte's hand tenderly.

'Listen, Christopher. We know about Prince Rupert and the Dutchman. We know that some plot is being hatched.'

Whyte was surprised and shook his head. 'You are indeed a most formidable lady, Polly.'

'But we don't know what they intend,' she continued. 'And we shall never escape from here if we don't find out.'

Whyte looked at her tenderly for a moment, as though they were alone in the room and talking of matters a million miles from the King and Parliament.

'And where,' he murmured, 'where do you wish to escape to?'

Polly felt a rush of affection surge through her. Flustered, she shook her head and looked down at the table.

The Doctor intervened. 'Polly's telling the truth, Mr Whyte. Our friends are still with Cromwell and Thurloe. They'll be asking all kinds of awkward questions if we come back empty-handed.'

Whyte's head drooped defeatedly. Then he looked up and smiled grimly. 'They intend to bring in an invasion force,' he said quietly. 'A Catholic invasion force.'

Scrope scowled. 'And that is their plan?'

'Aye,' nodded Whyte. 'But only after the first stage is complete.'

The Doctor crossed his hands on the table. 'And what is that?'

Whyte looked at him and then at Polly. 'Tomorrow morning at ten, General Cromwell will arrive to address the

House on the matter of the King's trial.'

Scrope was astonished. 'How do you know this? The general's movements are known to only a very few.'

Whyte smiled grimly. 'The King has contacts.' He cleared his throat before continuing. 'As Cromwell rises to address the Commons, the Dutchman, van Leeuwenhoek, will cut him down where he stands. He is an expert assassin from Holland.'

'Great God,' said Scrope, gulping. 'Bloody Dutch. A plot to murder the general.'

'And what do you… do they hope to gain by this?' asked the Doctor.

Whyte looked down at the table. 'Anarchy. A chance to allow their foreign army to sweep in and take control.'

The Doctor sat back and folded his arms. 'Where is the King?'

Whyte shook his head defiantly. 'I cannot tell you.'

Scrope leaned forward earnestly. 'Come, come, sir. You have told us of the plot against Cromwell.'

'Aye,' spat Whyte, 'I have. And that is all I will tell you. You may save his miserable Puritan hide but I will not give up my King, no matter what he has become.'

Polly gave him a reassuring smile, impressed despite herself.

Whyte looked long and deeply into her eyes, then got to his feet. 'Now, if you'll excuse me, I wish to get drunk.' With a final glance at Polly, he stepped back into the bar and was instantly swallowed in the crowd.

For a long while, the three remaining sat in silence, brooding. Then the Doctor looked up.

'Polly. May I speak with you? In private?'

She frowned. 'Of course, Doctor.'

Scrope glanced at them both. 'Oh, don't worry. I know when to make myself scarce. People tell me to do it every day.'

The old man rose and elbowed his way towards the bar. Perhaps he could persuade Christopher Whyte to tell them the King's whereabouts after all. Thurloe would provide ample reward for such information and there were few men who did not have a price, in Scrope's experience. He looked back over his shoulder and saw that the Doctor and Polly were already in animated conversation.

Scrope found Whyte propping up the bar, constantly jostled by the same gang of lads. Leaning over, he ordered ale from Sarah Kemp but, as he moved to tap Whyte on the shoulder, the young man got groggily to his feet and slammed his mug down on to the wooden bar.

With surprising swiftness, he forced his way through the crowd towards the door. Scrope tried to follow him but the weight of the inn's customers forced him back like a rolling tide. At last, after much pushing, shoving, and swearing, he returned to where he had left the Doctor and Polly.

The Doctor was alone, staring broodingly into the fire. Of Polly and Whyte there was no sign.

Scrope threw up his hands. 'We have lost him, Doctor!'

But the Doctor didn't reply.

Polly caught up with Whyte only a few yards from the entrance to the inn. She stood for a second in the freezing wind and then called out to him.

He turned at the sound of her voice, his boots crunching on the frozen ground.

'Mistress Polly?'

'You didn't say goodbye,' said Polly, pulling a face.

He gave a small, formal bow. 'God be with you, Polly.'

He made to go but Polly held his arm. 'Must it end like this?'

Whyte's expression melted into a tender smile. 'I wish there could be some other way. But I must flee the country now.

You know of the plot against Cromwell – the King's cause is as dead as he will shortly be. They will surely come for me.'

Polly found tears welling in her eyes. 'I am… grateful for your kindness,' she managed to say.

Whyte lifted her face by the chin and kissed her on the lips. 'Goodbye, fair Polly,' he said.

He was about to turn and go when he seemed struck by a thought. He opened the clasp at the top of his coat and felt about inside under his shirt. His fingers found a silver chain and he lifted out an oval locket which was attached to it. He slipped the chain over his head and dropped the trinket into Polly's palm.

'Here,' he said softly. 'To remember me by.'

Polly felt the weight of the locket in her hand and then clicked the spring. It opened to reveal a beautiful, delicate miniature of Christopher Whyte's handsome face.

'It is a thing of vanity,' he said with a smile. 'Take it.'

Polly was charmed. 'I couldn't possibly…'

Whyte clasped her hand with his and closed her fingers over the locket. 'Take it. I have many of the damned things.'

He held on to her hand for what seemed like minutes, then with a small, sad smile turned and disappeared into the darkness without looking back.

Polly stood in silence, her head bowed.

She clasped the locket in her hand and shot a quick glance back at the inn. Then, with a heavy heart, she began to follow him.

The morning dawned bright and sparkling. The sky was a perfect, cloudless blue, despite the cold, and Jamie felt immensely cheered as he drew back the curtains in his quarters.

Ben, exhausted by his exertions, was still sound asleep.

Even the shaft of sunlight that fell across his face failed to wake him. Neither the Doctor nor Polly was anywhere to be seen and so Jamie made his way swiftly downstairs, hoping to catch Thurloe or even Cromwell.

He entered into the chamber where he and the Doctor had conducted most of their bogus fortune-telling and came across Thurloe poring over a scrolled document. He looked round as Jamie approached and smiled pleasantly.

'Ah! The McCrimmon of Culloden I presume.'

'Aye,' said Jamie. 'Good morning, Mr Thurloe.'

Thurloe nodded. 'It is indeed if we are to see the King once again in our custody and the general saved from an assassin's blow.'

Jamie looked round. 'Where is everybody?'

'Making the preparations,' said Thurloe darkly. 'If the conspirators are not to suspect anything then we must go on as normal. I have arranged for yourself, the Doctor, and Master Jackson to mingle among the members in the Commons. The Doctor will tell you what we plan to do.'

He turned back to the document and spoke over his shoulder. 'There is a carriage awaiting you. If you would be so good as to awaken your colleague I should be infinitely obliged.'

Jamie went straight back upstairs and shook Ben until he unwillingly woke. Groaning, he stared blearily at the plain Puritan garb that had been laid out for them both to wear.

After a hesitant start, they both found themselves in hysterics as they clambered into the strange, ill-fitting clothes. Jamie's collar made him look like an overgrown choirboy and Ben's hat was far too big for him, but eventually they both made their way into the cold, fresh morning.

They found the Doctor outside in the open carriage, lost in thought. Bells were pealing madly as though the whole city were celebrating, but the Doctor seemed unaffected by it all. He smiled as Ben and Jamie climbed in beside him.

'Where's Pol?' asked Ben.

The Doctor leaned forward and tapped the driver on the shoulder. At once, they began to move off. 'She's joining us later,' he said, sitting back down.

Jamie inhaled deeply of the crisp air and settled back to enjoy the ride. Had it not been so singularly inappropriate, he would have said that he felt a little like royalty. Instead he closed his eyes and let the pale sunshine warm his face as the carriage rattled through the narrow London streets towards Parliament.

'Now then,' said the Doctor. 'Ben, you'll be able to recognise this Dutchman on sight, will you?'

Ben grimaced. 'Blimey, I should hope so. I've seen his ugly mug often enough.'

'Good,' said the Doctor, smiling. 'He'll be there, among the MPs just as we will, so the timing will be crucial. We can't act too swiftly or he might escape. Try again some other day. Ah, here we are.'

They had drawn up outside the massive façade of the Commons and were ushered rapidly inside. Everyone there seemed to be dressed just like them in broad-brimmed black hats and plain tunics. It wasn't difficult to merge into the chattering mass as the members began to take their seats on all sides of the cramped chamber.

To Ben, the panelled room looked remarkably similar to the one he had seen in his own time, although it was noticeably more primitive, with the appearance of a bear pit, its seats five rows deep.

'Can you see him?' whispered the Doctor.

Ben shook his head. 'I don't know if I will with all this lot here. It's like a penguin convention.'

Jamie looked around. 'What if he's not down here, Doctor?' he asked worriedly. 'Maybe he's up there in yon gallery.'

The Doctor shook his head. 'I don't think so, Jamie. These people have no high-powered rifles or anything to assassinate with. Any attack will have to be close up. A dagger or some such. It's the only way to guarantee accuracy.'

'What about a bomb?' said Ben.

Again the Doctor shook his head. 'Why go the trouble of importing this Dutch chap? No, no. He's here. I'm sure of it.'

Jamie tapped the Doctor on the shoulder. 'Look.'

They all turned as the imposing figure of Cromwell entered the chamber. He nodded to some of those present and then strode to his accustomed place on the benches.

Outside, a clock began to strike ten.

The Doctor looked quickly around.

Cromwell got to his feet. And in an alcove above the chamber, the Dutchman raised a strange and slender gun...

CHAPTER
12

Frances Kemp closed the back door and moved quickly towards the kitchen stove. She was humming a little tune, rolling dough on a wide black plate, her pretty face flushed from the heat below her.

There was a slow, tired knock at the door and Frances looked up in surprise. Who on earth could that be?

She wiped her hands on her apron and lifted the latch. A cold wind full of snowflakes blasted inside around the figure of Polly, who was smiling a little wanly.

'Hello,' she said. 'Can I come in?'

Frances pulled her inside, grinning all over her face, and sat Polly straight down at the table. 'My dear. You look half frozen. Here, let me get you something.'

She dashed to the corner and lifted up a little jug of steaming liquid.

Polly sat where she'd been put, shivering. 'I am a bit worse for wear,' she said. 'It's been a long night.'

Frances pressed a tumbler into her hand. 'Here.'

Polly drank the stuff gratefully, feeling its heat invigorate her. Frances immediately fetched some food, which Polly wolfed down with equal enthusiasm.

'Now,' said Frances, sitting down herself, 'where have you

been? My father said you had gone off with those... friends of his on some kind of errand.'

Polly laughed. 'Yes, I suppose you could call it an errand. We went to fetch the King.'

Frances's eyes almost bulged from their sockets. 'The King? He's free?'

Polly closed her eyes a moment and sighed. 'It's a long story, Frances.' She looked at her friend and smiled gently. 'But never mind me. How are you? And how is Thomas?'

Frances grabbed Polly's hands over the table and giggled. 'It is a miracle, Polly! You won't believe it. My father has consented to our marriage!'

'What? How come?'

Frances waved her hand airily. 'He has had a change of heart. I always knew that there was a sweet centre beneath the bear. Mother says he is like he used to be again.'

Polly was pleased. 'That's wonderful.'

Frances looked at her slyly. 'And what of you, mistress? How goes your handsome Cavalier?'

Polly looked away, a surge of emotion rushing through her.

The Doctor was moving with great rapidity through the still-bustling ranks of MPs. Cromwell was on his feet and speaking, seemingly unconcerned that an assassin's hand might shortly be raised against him.

'I move that the King's trial be brought forward with all due expedition,' he thundered. 'A list of commissioners must be named and a chairman found.'

Beneath him moved Ben and Jamie, snaking through the cramped benches in pursuit of the Doctor.

'Can you no' see him?' asked Jamie.

Ben looked about desperately, conscious that he was crucial to the discovery of the assassin. He shook his head.

'He's not here. I'm sure of it. Doctor!' he called out but the little man was already disappearing into the assembly.

'Where's he off to?' said Jamie wonderingly.

Some sixth sense made Ben whirl round, looking past the benches and up into the galleries. It took him only a few seconds to recognise the barrel of a gun projecting through the elaborate trelliswork.

'There!' he hissed, trying to point as discreetly as possible.

Jamie followed his gaze and let out a little gasp. 'That's where the Doctor's going. Come on!'

'No!' Ben grabbed him by the shoulder. 'I'll go. You get to Cromwell and get him off his feet. Quick!'

They split apart and Ben elbowed his way through the crowd towards a narrow spiral staircase which he could see the Doctor already ascending. He looked back to see Jamie having trouble moving in the sea of men. Cromwell was still speaking, listing likely commissioners who would sit in judgement on the King.

Ben pelted on, dragging his weary legs up the hard stone steps. He reached the top of the stairs, gasping for breath, and almost fell over the Doctor, who had stopped dead.

'Shh!' he said abruptly, jamming his finger to his lips.

They were standing at the entrance to a narrow corridor, which was divided in two by a narrow wooden wall. Pale light bled in through the stone lattice of the gallery wall but most of the area was plunged into sepulchral gloom.

Ben looked hard and suddenly made out the black-clad figure of van Leeuwenhoek, his skull-like face pressed close to the lattice, his hand closed around the long iron barrel of a very strange-looking musket.

The Doctor took Ben to one side and whispered urgently in his ear. 'He's waiting for a clear shot. Once everyone is sitting down, Cromwell's a dead man.'

Ben moved at once to rush the Dutchman, but the Doctor held his arm and shook his head violently. Ben made a helpless gesture as if to say 'What?'

The Doctor pulled him down to his height and whispered again. 'If he sees us, he won't think twice about murdering us instead.'

'What can we do, then?' Ben murmured.

The Doctor beckoned to Ben and pointed at the wooden partition. He then prodded his finger into Ben's chest and indicated that he should go around the partition and behind van Leeuwenhoek. Then the Doctor pointed to himself and mimed walking up to the would-be assassin.

'Two-pronged attack, eh?' whispered Ben with a smile. 'OK.'

He crept forward into the corridor and then slipped behind the partition. At once, the Doctor began to move towards the Dutchman, his face fixed in a beatific smile.

At the sound of the Doctor's boots, van Leeuwenhoek whirled around, brandishing the musket, his face filled with surprised anger.

'Ah,' said the Doctor pleasantly. 'It's Mr van Leeuwenhoek, isn't it? I've heard so much about you.'

The Dutchman looked quickly around, confused. Then his sallow face relaxed. 'You are alone, sir? That was a mistake.'

The Doctor nodded. 'Possibly. But you can't kill me and General Cromwell, can you?'

Van Leeuwenhoek sneered. 'Keep back, little fool. I shall kill Cromwell and then take care of you.'

The Doctor held up his hands. 'That's a very interesting weapon. Quite unique I should say. What does it do?'

Van Leeuwenhoek frowned, a little puzzled, and stroked the gun tenderly. 'My life's work. Elegant, efficient… And soon the little dart will fly from the barrel and into the gentleman's neck.'

The Doctor raised an eyebrow. 'Dart?'

The Dutchman smiled, his yellowy teeth showing. 'Yes, a dart. You do not think such a weapon fires a musket ball?'

Frowning, the Doctor looked more closely at the gun. It didn't really resemble a musket – it was more like an airgun. He clicked his fingers. 'I see! And the dart… the dart would be dipped in poison, would it?'

Van Leeuwenhoek shook with silent mirth. 'You think me so crude, little man?'

The Doctor frowned, thinking hard. If he could delay the Dutchman long enough…

Something suddenly flashed in his mind like a signpost. Something about –

'Got it!' cried the Doctor. 'Anton van Leeuwenhoek! The microscope man!'

The Dutchman shook his head. 'My brother. I am Gustavus. But his… samples have come in very useful.'

The Doctor looked at him appalled. 'What have you got on those darts?'

Van Leeuwenhoek shrugged. 'Oh, just a little something. Something from a pustule.'

'Plague?' gasped the Doctor.

Van Leeuwenhoek nodded excitedly and slapped the barrel of the gun. 'I will cut down this Cromwell of yours and he will expire before the week is out. None shall even know he has been hit! The sights here act as a guide.'

The Doctor looked. There was indeed a kind of sight screwed into the long iron barrel. 'Mm,' he said. 'I'm familiar with the principle. However primitive.'

'Primitive!' snorted van Leeuwenhoek. He swung his head round to face the lattice wall. 'We shall see!' Raising the gun, he rested the barrel on the stonework and took aim, his eye squinting, his finger poised to squeeze the trigger.

The Doctor moved forward but stopped as he heard another gun being cocked. To his amazement, the Dutchman had a pistol in his other hand, which was aimed squarely at the Doctor's chest.

'Oh dear,' said the Doctor. 'Do you really think you can shoot him with one hand?'

Van Leeuwenhoek bit his lip in frustration. 'I can. I am the best in the world, sir. And rest assured, you will follow Cromwell into the void.'

He aimed and his long, thin finger squeezed at the trigger of the air-musket.

Ben leapt from behind the partition like an angry tiger and hurled himself onto van Leeuwenhoek's back. The musket fell and clattered to the floor.

Ben and van Leeuwenhoek rolled together and the Doctor stepped neatly over them to retrieve the musket.

Desperately, the Dutchman tried to raise the pistol and press it against Ben's temple. Ben jerked his head out of the way but still the cold barrel bore down on him, van Leeuwenhoek clenching his teeth together in pure, vengeful hatred.

Ben tried to wriggle out of the way but the Dutchman's claw-like hand was fixed around his throat. The other was on the pistol, ready to fire.

'Excuse me,' said the Doctor, stepping in neatly and smashing the pistol from van Leeuwenhoek's hand with the butt of the musket.

It flew across the corridor and crashed against the wall, discharging its deadly ball with a loud crack.

Ben threw himself onto the Dutchman's chest and forced him backwards into a narrow niche in the wall. He punched him twice in the face and, with a sigh, the assassin slid down the wall and collapsed.

The Doctor grimaced and helped Ben to his feet before

gingerly kicking the musket into the corner. 'Better get that thing and its nasty bugs out of the way as soon as possible.'

He glanced down at van Leeuwenhoek, crumpled in the stone niche like a smashed statue.

'Nothing like a handy Parliamentary recess,' he said with a grin.

In the chamber below, all heads turned as the sound of the pistol shot reverberated through the building. Jamie, who was standing at Cromwell's side, ducked instinctively but the general did not flinch.

A murmur began to grow among the assembled MPs but Cromwell held up his hand. 'The crack of doom, gentlemen. It sounds for Charles Stuart.'

Pleased with his *bon mot*, Cromwell sat down and folded his arms, a smile of satisfaction on his warty face.

Some time later, Thurloe and Cromwell were standing in the general's chamber, looking with great interest at the tall blue box that had been deposited there.

The Doctor had asked that it be retrieved from the alley near to Kemp's inn, but as to its function or how it came to be there, they had no idea.

Cromwell walked around it several times, examining the panels and the little frosted windows. Pressing his palm against the double doors, he jumped back in shock. The box seemed to be humming. Almost as though it were alive…

He looked over at Thurloe, who bent down to examine the thing more closely. There was some kind of notice fixed to it.

'Free… for the use of the public,' he read, bemused. 'Officers and… cars… respond to urgent calls.'

He straightened up just as the Doctor, Jamie, and Polly came marching in.

'Ah, there she is,' cried the Doctor, rubbing his hands together. 'How thoughtful of you to fetch her.'

Cromwell walked up to him. 'What is this cabinet?'

Jamie laughed. 'Och, don't you know? It is the source of the McCrimmon's power!'

Thurloe ignored him and took the Doctor to one side. 'I gather we have much to thank you for, Doctor.'

Cromwell nodded. 'The assassination is foiled and the Dutch fellow in custody.'

Thurloe looked about. 'And your friend Master Jackson?'

'Oh. Well he asked that he might be in on the last act, as it were. I gather he has one or two scores to settle with Captain Stanislaus.'

Cromwell looked agitated. 'But, Doctor. The King is still at large. We have not completed our task.'

The Doctor stepped away from the TARDIS and walked over to Polly, who was sitting disconsolately on a big, cushioned chair. 'Polly?' he said, holding out his hand.

She looked up at him, her big eyes wet with tears. Then she took a small slip of paper from her dress and gave it to him.

'Thank you,' said the Doctor simply. He strode back to Cromwell and gave the general the paper, which he examined quickly.

His expression was immediately transformed into one of unalloyed joy. 'Thank 'ee, Doctor!' he beamed. He began to move off but turned. 'Stay a while, please. We have much to discuss.'

The Doctor shook his head. 'No, no. You must find your own way now.'

Cromwell stopped in his tracks and seemed about to ask the Doctor another question. Instead, he bowed politely and swept from the room.

Thurloe began to fuss agitatedly. 'What is it? What was that note?'

The Doctor was already at the TARDIS doors, slipping the key into the lock. 'I think you'd better follow your general, Mr Thurloe.'

Thurloe nodded then turned. 'What have you got inside there?'

The Doctor smiled and tapped the side of his nose. Then he opened the door just wide enough for Jamie and Polly to slip though.

'You aren't… going anywhere, are you, Doctor?'

The Doctor's head popped around the door. 'I'm waiting for Ben,' he said and disappeared inside.

The warehouse was stormed with minimal fuss, Roundhead troopers streaming through its twisted corridors and dank rooms. Cromwell was at their head with Ben close behind.

They found Sir John Copper and Christopher Whyte in a small room adjacent to the King's chambers.

'Rupert is fled,' said Copper with a smirk of satisfaction as the troopers led him away.

'But I have you,' said Cromwell. 'Take them away.'

Whyte put up no protest, simply staring into space as he was hustled outside.

They found the King alone, sitting by the meagre fire, his sad face looking pale and resigned. He looked up as Cromwell stormed into the room, and gave a small smile. 'Sir, I am glad to see you looking so well. For I believed you dead.'

Cromwell's face twisted into a sneer of satisfaction. 'By your leave, sir, that state will shortly belong to you.'

He jerked his head to one side and the troopers lifted Charles from his chair. He did not look back.

Ben looked around. 'What about Stanislaus?'

Cromwell shook his head. 'He is fled. Gone the way of Rupert, may his bones rot—'

'Sir!' A trooper came darting into the room, his face flushed.

'What is it, soldier?' asked Cromwell.

'We have seen one of them, General. He's away across the rooftops.'

Ben's smiled triumphantly. Perhaps Sal Winter could, after all, be avenged.

'Master Jackson,' said Cromwell, 'we will supply all the aid you require.'

'Thanks, Oliver,' said Ben with a grin. 'But this one's mine.'

He drew his sword and dashed from the room.

Emerging from the warehouse, Ben looked frantically around for some sign of Stanislaus.

The trooper who had brought the news raced to his side and pointed. 'There, sir, there!'

Ben followed his line of sight but could make out only the endless, snow-covered slates of the warehouse roofs.

Then he saw him. A tall, black outline, slipping and stumbling across the treacherous surface, trying desperately to reach the safety of a rickety black staircase.

Ben's head jerked from side to side as he hurriedly examined his options. He could follow the way the Pole had gone, over the back of the warehouse and across the roof. Or he could run as fast as possible to the staircase and cut the villain off.

With a nod to himself and with adrenalin surging through his veins, Ben clattered down to ground level and hared off towards the distant stairs.

He stumbled in the snow and slid across the cobbles, his backside connecting painfully with the stone. Cursing, he leapt to his feet and raced on, his lungs bursting and an iron taste seeping into his mouth.

Rounding the corner of the warehouse, he saw the staircase looming like dark rigging some hundred yards away. Stanislaus had almost reached the top of them and was struggling over the slates, carefully balancing.

Ben tore down the alley that led to the stairs, the muscles of his legs seeming to scream with the effort, and threw himself into a drift.

He looked up at once, breathing heavily, anxious that the Pole had not seen him.

But Stanislaus was too busy trying to manoeuvre himself onto the stairs and didn't see Ben as the young sailor slid silently across the ground and settled himself on the bottom stair.

Stanislaus reached out and grasped hold of the black wooden rails that connected the roof to the staircase. With a quick glance behind him, he took a deep breath and swung himself over, landing agilely on the flat wooden landing.

He gave a smug smile of satisfaction and began to race down the stairs.

Ben was waiting for him only a few steps away.

Stanislaus reeled back in shock and then instantly drew his sword from its sheath.

Ben lashed out with his own sword, forcing the captain back the way he had come.

'Why do you haunt me, sir?' gasped Stanislaus, his blade clashing against Ben's. 'I… I have done nothing to harm you.'

Ben jumped up two steps, slamming his sword down. The Pole neatly parried and then thrust his sword dangerously close to Ben's throat.

Jerking his head away, Ben crouched low and kicked his foot into Stanislaus's stomach.

The captain yelled and recoiled, falling backward onto the black stair.

301

'I'm taking over from someone else,' yelled Ben.

Stanislaus hurled himself backwards, his shoulders scraping against the steps. He raised his arm and drove his sword hard through the air.

Again, Ben dodged the blow but the Pole hit back at once, his fist connecting with Ben's chin and knocking him back the way he had come.

Stanislaus tried to hop over him but Ben reached up at once and grabbed at the captain's ankle, twisting his foot so that he crashed down on top of him with a yell of agony.

'You fool!' hissed Stanislaus. 'You addle-head. Let me be!' He thrust his arms forward and grasped Ben's throat, his thumbs closing on the windpipe.

The pressure made Ben gag and he struggled to sit up. Choking, he lashed out with his hands but met only empty air. Already he could hear a buzzing, crashing sound reverberating in his head.

Stanislaus's strong hands increased their pressure and Ben gasped for air. Then, with a sudden jolt of energy, he brought his knee up and slammed it into Stanislaus's groin.

The pressure on his throat disappeared at once as the Pole fell back, curling into a ball and screeching in pain.

Ben leapt to his feet, swaying woozily, and tried to focus on the recumbent form before him.

He raised his sword above his head.

'This is for Captain Winter,' he cried.

Stanislaus looked up and, in an instant, scooped up a handful of snow and hurled it into Ben's face.

Blinded for a moment, Ben faltered and Stanislaus took his chance, gritting his teeth and stumbling back up the stairs onto the roof.

He had reached the landing when Ben came at him again, roaring with fury and jumping onto the Pole's back. Ben managed to get his hands around the captain's neck and brought him crashing to the landing.

Both winded, they struggled to their feet and tried to raise their swords.

'God damn you, leave me!' screamed Stanislaus. 'Leave me!'

Ben shook his head, his lip and nose bleeding. 'Not while there's breath in my body,' he hissed.

Stanislaus backed away towards the roof, swirling his sword around over his head and snarling. His feet found their way onto the slates and Ben advanced, thrusting his sword forward.

Stanislaus parried the blow and hopped backward onto the roof.

Ben raised his sword. This time. But would he do it?

There was a deep, rumbling roar, like distant thunder.

Stanislaus looked at Ben, his sweating face pale and panicked.

There was a strange pause, as though time had suddenly stood still.

Then the snow on the roof began to move, slowly at first but building into a slide, the tremendous weight of the accumulated drift packing and rolling together with a loud, grumbling roar.

As it slid from the roof, it exposed the glistening black slates in a broad, rectangular trail.

Stanislaus flung out his arms in a frantic effort to keep his balance and avoid the treacherous snow beneath his feet.

He shot a fevered look at Ben and then down at his feet as the rolling snow ploughed into him.

He fell flat against the slates and dug his nails into them, panting and screaming with fear. Then the torrent of snow overwhelmed him and he rattled down the roof, his boots clattering against the tiles.

The snow covered him and thundered to the eaves of the warehouse, then, with a great, satisfying crump, it hurled him from the roof.

Ben looked over from the top of the stairs and watched as Stanislaus hit the ground, his body smashing against the cobbles like a rag doll.

In seconds, the snow around him was stained a vivid scarlet.

Ben sat there for a long moment, feeling his heart rate gradually settle.

Then he sniffed and closed his eyes.

'There you go, Sal,' he whispered. 'With style.'

An hour or so later, Ben walked into the TARDIS, instantly reassured by the hum of power and the familiar white, roundelled walls.

The Doctor was busy at the console, fussing over the controls. He looked up as Ben entered and flicked the switch that closed the outer doors.

'Where's Polly?' asked Ben.

Jamie pointed towards the interior of the craft. 'In her room. She's a wee bit glum. Are you all right?'

Ben waved away Jamie's concern. 'I'm fine. What's up with Pol?'

The Doctor looked up. 'I'm afraid it's my fault. I had to ask her to betray her friend.'

Ben was startled. 'That Cavalier bloke? Is that how they knew where to find the King?'

The Doctor nodded. 'He told us about the plot to kill Cromwell because he could no longer stomach the King's methods. But he wouldn't tell us where to find Charles. I knew there was only one way to ensure history was put back on its proper course and that was for Polly to follow him to their hiding place.' He shrugged apologetically, his lined face crumpling. 'There really was no other way.'

Ben sighed. 'I'll go and see her.' He walked swiftly across the room and disappeared through the inner door.

Jamie walked up to the Doctor and patted his hand. 'We all understand, Doctor,' he said gently.

The Doctor nodded, his black fringe falling into his eyes, then he flicked another switch and the room was filled with the cacophonous sound of the TARDIS engines.

He sighed and stepped back from the console. Then he frowned, noticing a weight in the pocket of his frock coat. He reached inside and pulled out the little book that had been such a problem to them.

Smiling sadly, he placed it on top of the glass column at the centre of the console and watched it rise and fall, rise and fall, as the TARDIS made its way to a new destination.

John Thurloe and Cromwell sat in the former's chambers reflecting on the strange sight they had witnessed that afternoon. They had said farewell to young Ben Jackson and he had entered the tall blue box, just like his three companions earlier.

Then the strange cabinet had vanished from sight with a strangulated, grating whine.

Cromwell sat in silence for a long while, teasing the ends of his sparse grey hair with a finger.

'Are we losing our wits, John?' he said at last.

Thurloe shook his head. 'Mayhap they were sorcerers after all.'

Cromwell sighed and shook his head. 'A trying time.'

'Aye, General,' nodded Thurloe. 'I should not like to go through it again.'

Cromwell fixed him with his beady eyes. 'There must be no

record of our… visitors. Nor of the attempt on my life.'

Thurloe shook his head. 'Naturally not, sir. I shall find a way of being… discreet about these matters.'

Cromwell grunted. 'Well, then. Let us get on with this terrible business.'

Thurloe opened the drawer of his desk and took out the death warrant for Thomas Culpeper.

Cromwell gazed at it as Thurloe smoothed it out over the desk.

'I can still hardly believe it,' he sighed. 'Culpeper! In league with those Royalists!'

Thurloe nodded sadly. 'Sir John Copper has confessed it all, sir. Culpeper passed the information to his lover with the express purpose of leading you to your doom.'

Again Cromwell shook his head, thinking of the force with which young Tom had urged him to carry on with his Parliamentary business as though all were well. And now he knew the reason why.

With a heavy heart, Cromwell took up a quill and dipped it in a pot of ink. Then he scratched his signature on the bottom of the document and got to his feet.

He glanced at Thurloe and then walked slowly and sadly from the room.

Thurloe picked up the warrant and blew on it to make the ink dry.

His attention was caught momentarily by the picture of the assassinated Caesar above his mantel.

He shook his head. Politics was a dirty business indeed.

The morning of January the thirtieth 1649 was a cold one, and Charles Stuart insisted upon wearing an extra shirt so that his enemies would not mistake his shivering for fear.

He stepped out through the windows of Inigo Jones's

Banqueting House onto a specially built platform and faced the huge, expectant crowd.

In a calm, clear, dignified voice he announced that he was going from a 'corruptible to an incorruptible crown'.

Then, after a short prayer, he laid his head upon the block and the axe fell, severing his head neatly from his body.

A tremendous groan went up from the crowd and then there was total silence. It blanketed the old city as effectively as any snowdrift.

Oliver Cromwell, the man who was soon to become Lord Protector of the Kingdom, stared into the bright winter morning as though gazing through time itself.

Also available in the Doctor Who *History Collection:*

THE STONE ROSE
JACQUELINE RAYNER

ISBN 978 1 849 90906 8

A 2,000 year old statue of Rose Tyler is a mystery that the
Doctor and Rose can only solve by travelling back to the time
when it was made. But when they do, they find the mystery is
deeper and more complicated than they ever imagined.

While the Doctor searches for a missing boy, Rose befriends a
girl who it seems can accurately predict the future. But when
the Doctor stumbles on the terrible truth behind the statue,
Rose herself learns that you have to be very careful what you
wish for.

*An adventure set in Roman times, featuring the Tenth Doctor,
as played by David Tennant, and his companion Rose Tyler.*